# DR. ROMY'S *Dance*

To Debbie A.

Thanks for your
support

Yashai B——

10/19/17

# DR. ROMY'S *Dance*

## YASHALINA BLAIR

ARCHWAY
PUBLISHING

Archway Publishing books may be ordered through booksellers or by contacting:

Archway Publishing
1663 Liberty Drive
Bloomington, IN 47403
www.archwaypublishing.com
1 (888) 242-5904

Because of the dynamic nature of the Internet, any web addresses or links contained in this book may have changed since publication and may no longer be valid. The views expressed in this work are solely those of the author and do not necessarily reflect the views of the publisher, and the publisher hereby disclaims any responsibility for them.

Any people depicted in stock imagery provided by Thinkstock are models, and such images are being used for illustrative purposes only. Certain stock imagery © Thinkstock.

ISBN: 978-1-4808-3523-8 (sc)
ISBN: 978-1-4808-3521-4 (hc)
ISBN: 978-1-4808-3522-1 (e)

Library of Congress Control Number: 2016914810

Print information available on the last page.

Archway Publishing rev. date: 2/22/2017

# ACKNOWLEDGEMENTS

For my babies, whom, without knowing, push me to be a better me. I would like to thank my little brother, Aqeel. You're the best little brother in the world. And my husband for helping create a believable criminal element.

Thanks to my very first reader, Megan, my first biggest fan, Michelle. And last but certainly not least, Charlyn, my friend, sounding board, and the giver of advice that made life after a marriage proposal happen for my protagonists.

Thank you Kelly, and Lisa for painstakingly going through the book to find errors. You guys are amazing!

A very special thanks to Mrs. Yvonne Medley, founder of *The Life Journeys Writers Guild*. You are one dynamite lady, and you enrich the lives of everyone you touch.

A special dedication to my angel, and sister, Saba, who believed in me so much that on her death bed she made me promise to publish my book. I did it sweetie.

# CHAPTER 1

*I*t was Friday, and Jerome was late again for class. The night before had been another no-show for his co-worker, Poison. At twelve o'clock, Jerome put in what should have been his final performance of the evening. He was still in his robe as he packed his medical books into his backpack. He looked up when he heard the knock at the door and said, "Come in."

Sin stepped into his dressing room closing the door behind him, and for the second time in the week asked, "Can you cover for Poison? He hasn't shown up again."

Jerome stared at Sin and began to slowly shake his head in a nonverbal tsk, "When are you going to fire him?"

Sin gave a noncommittal shrug that Jerome understood exactly. Sin didn't want to have that conversation with Jerome … again. Poison was a great dancer with a large following—when he showed up for work. But he was unstable, undependable, and unrepentant; and when he didn't show to work, Sin turned to Jerome who always filled in when needed. It was that character trait that made him sought after by club owners in numerous states. Jerome sighed, "How much time do I have?" he asked.

"About twenty minutes," Sin answered.

Jerome nodded, walked to his closet, and opened a door revealing costumes in varying shades, textures, and styles. Sin left

1

the room as Jerome pulled a deep iridescent purple pantsuit from the closet. The suit had black lines with multicolored dots along the seams that reflected and gave the impression of flashing lights with the help of the strobe lights used by the club. The black lines held the suit together magnetically to make it appear as one piece. Jerome slid into a matching thong before closing the skintight suit around his body. He stepped into a pair of soft-sole boots and left his room to walk down the hall to the dancers' lobby. While he waited for his introduction, he picked up a magazine filled with naked women. He needed to be erect.

When his cue came, he was ready. He took a moment, listening as, Johnny, the MC began his announcement. Johnny had a deep, silky voice that was made for communication. With a note of enthusiasm, Johnny proclaimed, "Is there anyone sick in here? Anybody feeling ... feverish? Well, I got what you've been waiting for! The doctor ... is in the house! The doctor of love, Dr. Romy!"

Jerome stepped onto the stage to flashing lights and a packed house. Jerome's pelvis began to thrust to the beat as Usher's voice filled the room, *"Make me wanna say oh oh oh oh oh oh oh oh oh oh oh oh oh my God."* As the music's tempo slowed, Jerome's movements became a vertical facsimile of a horizontal dream, until he slowly peeled away the purple suit. His muscles expanded and contracted as he sought to enrapture every woman in the crowd. A fine sheen of perspiration made his skin glow as his performance reached its finale, and a group of women made their way to the raised stage to toss fistfuls of money and touch whatever parts of him they could reach. His night continued in a very similar fashion until two in the morning. He'd gotten home by three, and was asleep by four.

Jerome picked up speed running down the halls. His polished shoes made a tapping sound along the way. He was three weeks into his last year of med school, slated to graduate in the summer, and until now his academics had gone well. He was slightly out of breath as he approached the closed lecture room door, through which he could hear an authoritative male voice already in lecture mode. Upset with himself, he couldn't believe he was late for class again. *How could I have overslept for the third time this week?* he silently wondered. "Working overtime, that's how," Jerome spoke to himself aloud.

On Tuesday, Jerome had just walked into his condo from working at the hospital when his cell phone began to buzz. He pulled his phone from his pocket to see the photo of his boss, Sin, flash on the screen. He answered, "Hey, Sin, what's up?"

"Romy, I need a favor. Poison just called out. Can you come in?"

"I just walked through the door. Let me freshen up, and I'll be there in forty-five minutes." He worked and stayed to help Sin close until almost three o'clock Wednesday morning and ended up being late for class that morning too.

With his hand fastened around the door handle of the lecture room, he looked at his watch one last time before composing himself and proceeding to open the door—thirty minutes late. A female student sitting toward the back of the class looked up at Jerome appreciatively as he entered the room. Jerome was twenty-six with tawny gold-toned skin and a tall, lean-muscled body brought on by years of physical activity. Jerome was always willing to spend an extra few dollars to have his clothing tailored, but he considered it his only extravagance. Jerome cut quite a figure in his Steve Madden loafers, black slacks, and white collarless shirt with black contrast.

The professor giving his lessons for the morning looked at his watch upon seeing Jerome enter the class. Jerome quietly seated himself in the back of the classroom, painfully aware that his grades had begun slipping as a result of his late nights. This year he would spend the majority of his schooling in the lab, with the exception of two classes. This was one of those classes. Increasing his workload, he'd taken a part-time position as a physician's assistant with the hope of getting acclimated to working in the hospital.

He thought it would get him an up-close and personal look into how the hospital was run, and he needed that since in a year he would be a resident in one. That was why this professor was his favorite. He was highly esteemed in the medical profession and gave a great bit of insight into the world of medicine. He was in good physical condition, and stood just under six feet. His features were almost aristocratic on his well-maintained copper-brown skin. Jerome could definitely say he'd learned a lot from the professor over the last two years, so he always registered for his courses.

At the end of class, Jerome and four of his buddies, all medical students, walked down the hall. Jerome listened quietly while they talked excitedly about a party that "always gets wild," they said almost in unison. All of his friends had been raised with the very best of everything. They were a group of good-looking, fashionable young men: Montgomery, Dillon, Jeffery, and Ronald. Jerome had known them now for four years, but Montgomery was the one he felt closest to, the one he felt he could actually confide in.

Dillon turned to Jerome, "Hey, Jerome, you should come and hang out with us tonight. We told you about the party in Adams Morgan. You really don't want to miss it."

"Nah. Gotta study for next Friday's exams. Maybe next time," Jerome replied.

Jeffery admonished, "Yeah, yeah we know, it's always next time with you, Jerome. And, seriously, how could we be such good friends with someone who is such a bore?"

They exited the college, and Ronald noticed a couple of beautiful girls as they passed. They had eyes for Jerome. Ronald tapped Jeffery on the arm. When Jeffery looked at Ronald, Ronald tilted his head in the direction of the girls.

Jerome was unaware. He'd become so accustomed to the attention of women, that it just didn't affect him anymore.

Ronald said, "I agree with Jeffery. Can you imagine how many girls you could get if you just loosened up a bit?"

"Right, because that's exactly what I need in my life right now, more girls," Jerome replied dryly. *Besides*, he thought to himself, *my heart is set.*

At that statement, the guys all looked at Jerome as though he'd lost his mind, but no one spoke immediately. Finally breaking the silence, Ronald blurted, "You say more girls, but I have yet to see you with one!" The others laughed and nodded in agreement.

Jerome smiled. His signature dimples made an immediate appearance as he looked at his watch, not fazed by his buddy's good natured ribbing. "I really gotta get going, or I'm going to be late. I've got an afternoon shift at the hospital, and I'll be busy for the rest of the weekend. See you guys on Monday." Jerome took off running, well aware of how little time he had to get to the hospital to start his rounds.

Montgomery, Ronald, Jeffery, and Dillon all stood and watched as Jerome sprinted across the lawn. Without taking his eyes off Jerome, Jeffery said, "Is it my imagination, or is he always in a hurry to be someplace?"

"You're not imagining anything. He is always in a hurry, and I wonder how he does it," Montgomery answered, wearing a baffled expression on his boyishly handsome face. He shook his head. His perfectly groomed dark-blond hair glistened as it caught a ray of sun. His gray eyes squinted slightly from the same as he too watched his friend hop on his motorcycle and drive away.

The others turned and looked at Montgomery.

"Does what, Monty?" Dillon asked, wondering not for the first time about the things Jerome didn't tell. Dillon's emerald green eyes glittered brilliantly as he focused them on Monty.

Montgomery glanced at the others, not realizing before now how little Jerome actually talked to any of them. *Hell*, Monty thought, *if it hadn't been for a drunken night about a year ago, I wouldn't even know his secret.* The guys hadn't really witnessed Jerome drunk, except that one time after his father died. Truth be told, he was feeling rather privileged to have those crumbs of knowledge over the other guys. Jerome was so secretive about his world that even his closest friends hardly knew what was going on in it. So Monty decided that if Jerome wanted the others to know, then Jerome would tell them himself. He would, however, tell them this much. "You guys didn't know? Jerome works part time on weekends to pay his tuition."

"Yeah, we know, at the hospital," Dillon added.

"No, I mean he has another job," Monty shared.

With a playful, yet suspicious tone, Ronald asked "Really? Where?"

Without answering the question Monty looked at his watch, and did what he'd seen Jerome do countless times to avoid the questions inquiring minds wanted to know the answers to. If only they were given enough time to ask them. "Hey, I gotta go. What time are we meeting for the party?"

"Eight o'clock, my place," Dillon answered.

Monty left the guys in suspense, but he knew they wouldn't forget.

∾❧

Jerome entered his off-campus apartment. It was almost on the top floor near the penthouse, spacious and well decorated—okay, so maybe he allowed himself more than one concession other than nice clothes, but he felt he'd earned them. Freeing himself from his lab coat, he walked to a washing machine cleverly hidden behind a set of french doors and tossed it in, then continued on to his bedroom. Jerome pulled off his shirt and checked the time. He then turned on the shower and stripped.

Steam filled the bathroom as he stepped inside the shower, sliding the tempered glass door closed behind him. As the hot water ran down his tired muscular shoulders and back, he allowed it to soothe him, and the calm took up residence in his mind and joints. He closed his eyes as the water trailed down his head and face. He smiled as he thought about his buddies' search for the most killer party. They couldn't understand what drove him. Only one of them even knew that he had to work to pay for med school. And that was by design because he was slightly embarrassed by what he did to earn his living. Sure it made a most satisfying income, but it was in his opinion, one of the least respected job positions on a long list of career choices, and definitely something he'd never imagined himself doing.

They were a great group of guys, but they never had to work a day in their entire lives. Being born into families of privilege did that for them. Jerome, however, wasn't so privileged. His father had earned a modest income, at best. He'd sometimes worked two jobs to make ends meet. His mom stayed home to take care of them after quickly learning it was cheaper than working and paying childcare. His dad worked hard to get what was needed for the family, sacrificing so they never had to do without, but all of that changed when his dad passed away four years ago.

Jerome stepped out of the shower and briskly dried himself off before heading into his bedroom. After slipping into a pair of comfortable shorts, he flopped down on his bed as his thoughts drifted to the phone call that completely changed his life.

## F O U R   Y E A R S   E A R L I E R

At twenty-two, Jerome finished pre-med with a degree in Biology, and was enrolled in the medical school of his choice. Jerome had known early in life that becoming a doctor was what he wanted, and he and his family worked hard to get him there. But Jerome was carefree, having just returned to school two weeks earlier to begin his medical studies. He and Montgomery were roommates and had met upon arrival to school. They'd both met Ronald, Jeffery, and Dillon during orientation.

He and the other guys were sitting in the student lounge, already fast friends, sharing a common goal of becoming doctors. The five of them sat in the dorm's lounge trying to best the other with the dirtiest jokes they knew. They were laughing at a joke Ronald told when the dorm counselor walked in and tapped Jerome on the shoulder. She leaned forward and spoke softly to him, "Excuse me, you have an important phone call waiting in my office. Please come with me."

Jerome stood and followed the counselor to her office. After entering, she handed him the phone and quietly left the room with a parting, "I will be here if you need me."

Perplexed, two lines appeared between his brows as he watched the counselor walk away. Jerome put the phone to his ear, not prepared for what he would hear next. His mom had been crying so hard that he could hear the fresh tears in her voice when she said, "Jerome, honey, I need you to come home as soon as possible. Your father had a stroke." Jerome listened in shock while his mom took an audible deep breath before continuing, "It doesn't look good." There was another pause. Jerome, with the phone's receiver plastered to his ear, opened his mouth to speak. He wanted to say something, anything, but nothing came out. His mom finalized, "They say he probably won't make a full recovery."

Jerome dropped the phone, fell to his knees, and cried with his head cradled in his hands. His moans cued the return of the counselor and she hurried to comfort him.

## PRESENT

Jerome turned over in his bed, fighting the renewed feeling of grief that the memory brought with it. He remembered the counselor rushing into the office. He remembered his complete vulnerability, bawling in her arms, like he had, like a helpless boy, which was what he'd felt like. Jerome even remembered some of her comforting words that truly were of no comfort. He'd later vowed never to be that helpless again, but those same feelings had revisited him the moment he entered the hospital to find his family surrounding his father's still form.

FOUR YEARS EARLIER

Five days after the phone call, Jerome found himself standing in a cemetery next to his mom, offering comfort to *her* as best he could. He was numb from the quickness of it all and devastated that though it had only taken him eight hours total to pack, get a flight from Maryland to Connecticut, and get home, he was still too late. His father had passed away without ever again seeing his oldest son. Just like that, standing in the newness of his twenty-two years, Jerome was then the man of the house. He was so confused he didn't know what was to become of them at that point. He looked toward his sister Jessica, standing to the left of him crying silently into a kerchief. She was twenty years old and had just begun her junior year in college. He then looked in the opposite direction, and standing on the right side of their mother trying without success to be emotionless, was seventeen year old, Eric. He was starting his senior year of high school. Standing beside Eric crying on his shoulder was thirteen year old Liana. She'd been crying so hard that her beautiful eyes were almost swollen shut. Jerome looked down as a tear slipped free of his own eye.

The evening wore on and the house finally quietened as their guest slowly departed. Jerome wandered the house unable to sleep, and ended up in his father's study. His mom sat in his father's old comfortable chair. To Jerome, she looked utterly miserable and completely alone, "I thought I might find you here. You okay?"

"I'll manage. I have no choice," she said, and looked at Jerome thoughtfully for a moment. "Come and sit down. There's something we need to discuss." She eyed Jerome as he seated himself, and then looked down at her hands as she began.

"I just wanted to start by saying how sorry I am that you didn't make it here before your dad passed away. I know how hard that was for you."

Jerome struggled to compose himself. A frown of grief marred his features at the thought of his father dying before he could tell him he loved him one last time. He took a deep breath. "I'll be okay. Still can't believe he's gone, though." Changing the subject to get his emotions in check, he said, "So what did you want to talk to me about?"

His mom looked at him sympathetically. Understanding exactly what he was doing, she hesitantly began, "You know your dad did the best he could to support us all. He worked hard to pay for your college and all, but when he died he didn't leave us with a whole lot. The life insurance took care of the funeral expenses, and will allow me to pay for most of the bills, and a chunk of the mortgage payments but ... we can't afford your tuition. And we need help here. We need *you* to come home and help for a while."

Jerome stood up and crossed the room to the window. "But I just started med school! You can't ask me to stop now. Please, Mom, this is what I worked hard in school for. You know that! I can't quit now!"

"Don't you think I know that, Jerome? But there is no money! There *is no money* for your tuition!" She picked up the bank draft that she'd intended to show him and walked to him with it in her hand. She looked up at him imploringly and held the draft for him to see. "One, maybe two semesters more, but that's only stalling the inevitable, and that money's needed here to buy clothes and food for the family, and we aren't even going to mention the hospital bills." She put her hand on his cheek, and turned his face toward hers. "You have a fine education, and with that you could get a really good-paying job. And the fact remains that I still need your help, at least until Liana can take care of herself."

Jerome looked away from his mother, taking a glance at the paper, he frowned. It wasn't enough to pay for one full year of his college, but he wouldn't quit. "Then I'll get a job and pay for my own tuition, and I'll help out. I'm not quitting," he said with finality, "not when I'm this close." And with that the conversation was over—both understanding the desire, and the need. But neither of them could see how Jerome could possibly pull it off.

∽∾

Jerome must have fallen asleep. He jolted awake at the sound of his alarm clock buzzing furiously. It was 9:30 p.m., which meant it was time to get ready for work. He turned off the alarm and turned on the light, still feeling groggy. It wasn't often he allowed himself to think about his dad. He'd loved and looked up to him so much, and missed him more than he could ever have imagined.

Jerome got out of bed and walked into the kitchen. Four years ago, he was forced to rent an apartment off campus when he could no longer afford to stay in the dorm rooms. That apartment had been small and infested with mice, but it was all he could afford. He certainly didn't have that problem now and could afford to live wherever he chose. Actually he preferred to have his own place rather than live in the dorms. Jerome fixed himself a cup of tea, and then padded barefoot back to his room to get himself prepared for the night. The weekends were always the busiest at his job, and he needed to be on his A-game.

# CHAPTER 2

*T*he Sinful Pleasure was busy beyond belief! The lounge overflowed as women, and some men, sat at tables in very comfortable-looking chairs waiting for the night's featured entertainer to be announced. Scantily clad male waiters wended their way through the crowded room with their trays loaded with colorful drinks.

The host ushered a group of several women to the last remaining table close to the stage. Among this group was Sasha. Just as the group was seated, a slight change in the tempo of the music cued the servers that a show would begin shortly. The waiter took their drink orders and quickly moved on.

The MC's voice blasted through the loudspeakers. "Ladies, I must have your full attention!" The entire hall went suddenly quiet with anticipation as Johnny continued with great enthusiasm. "Now, I know you've all been waiting because I can feel your eagerness for this next young man! A man who is sought after on the entire continent, and with good reason. And you get the pleasure to find out why, here, tonight! And so," he continued, his lively intro sounding much like the announcer at a championship boxing match, "without further ado, I introduce to some and present to others, Dr. Romy!"

Jerome, clad in a silver body suit that clung lovingly to his towering form, appeared on stage. His feet moved in a swift succession of heel-toe combinations as his hips drew figure eight motions, followed by hip thrusts and perfect pelvic circles. It was apparent to the trained eye that he'd had some form of professional training; to all others, he was simply a really good dancer. A group of obviously drunk women came to the stage, and each "made it rain" dollar bills in Jerome's direction.

Sasha sat and watched the performance with a feeling of pride. She didn't know why she was so proud of him. It wasn't as though she'd taught him to dance or anything, but it was there anyway. That feeling of pride was accompanied with another feeling. She stared at the man smiling at one of the women "making it rain." He carried himself, tall and erect, and never complained about his circumstances. Confidence and sex appeal seeped from him, and then his eyes found hers in the crowd. She felt pride, yes, but it was accompanied with something else … love. She sat up. *Oh my goodness*, Sasha thought to herself, she was falling in love with this man! When did this happen?

As she watched the performance reach its climax, she thought back, trying to figure out when it happened. It was clear, it happened long ago, the afternoon that the two of them spent together after their four-week split. She thought it may have begun even before that, but that afternoon was definitely when it had taken root. Two months ago, they'd walked in the park, he licking an ice cream cone as he told her about his family. She realized she was far past falling in love, she was head-over-heels.

She was so excited coming to her realization that she decided she would tell him! But wait! She should do something romantic, quiet, sweet, relaxing, and then tell him. When all of that was done, she would *have* to tell her father that she was seeing Jerome again, and that she'd fallen in love with him. Sasha shook her head to herself. Her father would not be pleased she was with Jerome, he would not be pleased she had disregarded his wishes, and he would *definitely* not be pleased that she had gone and fallen in love with him. She would just have to make her dad understand, somehow.

When the night was at its end, Sasha met Jerome in his dressing room. He smiled tiredly when he saw her and walked to her, enveloping her in a warm and gentle hug. "Are you coming home with me tonight? If so, can I just hold you while I sleep? I'm beat, and I have to be at the hospital at eight in the morning. I've got about four hours sleep—maybe." He let her go and walked away, heading to his closet to grab something to wear home.

She watched as he opened the door. His closet always seemed to catch her eye, but she quickly lost interest in the contents of the closet when he slid his robe and G-string off to get dressed. She asked distractedly, "What time will you get off?"

Jerome heard the distraction in her voice and looked up to see her attentively watching. He warned, "Stop that, or we might not get out of here." When her eyes slowly drifted up to meet his, he answered her question, "I get off at about 5:00 p.m. That will leave me about four hours before having to come back here."

"Okay, you go home and get some rest, and I'll call you later this evening, okay?"

"Sounds good to me. I'll walk you to your car." Once they reached Sasha's car, Jerome kissed her long and passionately before he deposited her inside and watched her drive away.

Jerome left the hospital that evening feeling exhausted. It was a day filled with blood and gore, and he needed to turn down the images still lingering in his head. He carried his briefcase in one hand and his lab coat in the other as he headed toward the parking garage for staff members. He looked up and saw Sasha standing in front of his motorcycle, a smile of welcome on her lovely face. She walked to him, wrapped her arms around his waist adoringly, and kissed him with an intimate pleasure meant to convey what her plans were for the evening. Jerome got the message, and suddenly he didn't feel so exhausted. The images of the day were completely forgotten as he participated in the torrid kiss.

With reluctance, Sasha pulled away from the kiss to offer, "Why don't I give you a ride home? My car is just outside the garage." She grabbed his hand and led him toward her car. He allowed her to lead the way. When they reached her car, she unlocked the doors, and Jerome opened the driver door to assist her inside. Instead of immediately getting in the car, Sasha turned and pulled Jerome closer, indulging in a soft and deep kiss. Behind them, a black new-model Mercedes slowly drove by and turned a corner, but the lovers were too consumed in their kiss to even notice.

Jerome finally pulled away from the kiss to say, "You're exactly who I needed to see right now, but what are you doing here?"

"Just thought I'd give you a lift home. I know you must be tired after going practically straight from work to the hospital."

They climbed into the waiting car and drove off.

Twenty-five minutes later, Jerome opened the door to his apartment and headed straight for the shower. While he was in the shower, Sasha prepared them both hot cups of tea. She looked into the refrigerator but didn't find anything more than drinks and fruit. Shaking her head, she grabbed the fruit, and some cheese to prepare a fruit platter. When she was done, she picked up the phone to call in a delivery, making a mental note to pick up a few food items for the bachelor.

Shortly after hanging up with the carryout, Sasha watched as Jerome re-entered the room wearing a black silk robe and pajamas. She handed him the cup of tea and placed the fruit platter on the coffee table before him. He took a couple of sips of the tea and popped a few grapes in his mouth. "Thank you, baby," he said before he leaned back in the seat. His eyes closed wearily. She walked behind the sofa and slid his robe down to gently massage his shoulders and back.

She paused briefly as her cell phone began to ring, but she

decided not to answer it. This was a special night, and she wasn't going to be interrupted. Ignoring the phone, she continued her ministrations while Jerome sat with a look of pure contentment.

After a few more minutes of the sweet pleasure, he spoke half-seriously. "I could lie down; that would be even more relaxing."

Sasha smiled. She was just about to respond when her phone began ringing in her purse again. At the same time, the doorbell chimed. She headed for the door.

A young man not much older than twenty-one stood on the other side of it holding a brown paper bag. "That will be $17.63."

Sasha handed him a twenty from her pocket and took out an additional five dollars to give him. "Keep the change."

She closed the door and turned to see Jerome staring at her. "Impressive. If you keep this up, I'll be spoiled beyond repair."

"I can't think of anyone who needs to be spoiled more than you," she said earnestly. She walked to the coffee table and placed the bag on it, next to the fruit platter. With her hands now free, she pushed him to lie down on his back. Then she climbed on top of him, smiling down at him. She relished the shocked but pleased expression on his face for a moment before she leaned down to kiss him. He pulled her skirt up to bunch around her waist, leaving only his silk and her lace as barriers between them. Their lips just met when her phone rang again, causing her to take a deep, irritated breath.

Jerome laughed at her exasperation, but the material of his silk pajamas had already tented. He held her pressed against his arousal as each of his hands held its half of a soft cheek. He kneaded the globes in slow, seductive, semicircles that caused a deliciously light friction between their bodies. "That must be really important. You should get it so they can stop calling, and we can get back to what we're doing."

More than a little disgruntled with the never-ending phone calls, she considered just turning the damned thing off so they could continue their love-play. But just as the phone stopped ringing, it started all over again. As their friction mounted, her eyes already passion glazed, Sasha disengaged with a sigh. She would get rid of whomever was ringing her phone and back to her main objective. This night was special. She was in love with him. Four months ago she'd met him, and her life had not been the same since.

When she slid off the couch, Jerome got a flash of pink lace before she inched her skirt down and scurried across the room to grab her purse.

She pulled out her phone and answered without checking the number. Her irritation was evident in her voice when she spoke. "Hello!"

The voice on the other end of the line was just as irritated. "I've been trying to call you for the past three-quarters of an hour." The clipped voice spoke. "I am on the way home, and when I get to the house, you had better be there!"

She didn't want to leave. She shook her head and looked at Jerome, her pupils constricting with panic. Life hadn't always been so full of difficult decisions for her. She'd never before had a boyfriend that her dad didn't approve of. And of all the guys her dad had approved of, she'd never felt as strongly about any of them, as she felt for Jerome. She never would have thought she'd have fallen so hard for him when she met him as a surprise for her birthday. She couldn't stop her thoughts from travelling back there even as her father subjected her to this embarrassing tirade.

## FOUR MONTHS EARLIER

It was a wonderful birthday! Sasha's family had taken her out to dinner, and her dad had given her a shiny new silver BMW set up with satellite radio, voice command, Wi-Fi, and fingerprint to start the ignition. That morning he'd taken her to the dealer to imprint their fingerprints to the vehicle and set up the voice command system. They'd left to get the rest of the family, with the dealership promising to have the car delivered to their home by the end of the day. Once they picked up her mother and sister, they'd gone to Maggiano's, her favorite restaurant. The day couldn't have gotten any better!

Okay, so she was spoiled. She could admit that, but she was also the model daughter. She'd been an honor student through high school and had graduated at the top of her class as valedictorian.

She'd received her bachelor's, majoring in culinary arts, and minoring in finance management, and graduated summa cum laude. She'd then gone to Paris to spend the next eighteen months studying at Le Cordon Bleu. She returned four months ago at her father's behest, but spent time taking more classes and having fun with her friends. Someday she would own a bistro or something, but for now, she was content with being a daddy's girl. At the age of twenty-five, she knew it wouldn't last much longer.

Her dad was proud of her. He always was because she made certain she did what made him proud. She climbed into her new car and decided to take it for a drive. Loving the feel of the soft leather and the aroma of that new car smell. She touched the start button for the ignition and pressed her thumb on a small screen on the door panel, and it purred to life.

She drove off with no particular destination in mind, but just thinking about her life. Ten months into her time in France, her long-distance boyfriend, Malcolm, had broken up with her. He called her and said, "Paris is too far away for me to keep the relationship constant and in good standing."

Whatever the hell that meant, Sasha translated it to mean the bastard found himself another girlfriend, and she was right. Sasha and Malcolm met when she was finishing her sophomore year while attending classes at Princeton. They'd been devoted while she was there. He'd studied business too, and planned to become a financial adviser.

Malcolm was clean-cut and good-looking. Her dad had loved him instantly. When they'd broken up, her dad was probably more upset than she was. Although their relationship for the first two years had been hot and heavy, it had grown cool when she went to France. She'd realized they'd grown apart when their series of long-distance and Skype calls slowly fizzled away. She wasn't surprised when the breakup occurred, in fact she had been anticipating it.

She was not, however, okay with him dating someone else while they were still an item. For that reason, she'd given him a piece of her mind. With her looks, she could have any guy she wanted, but she kept herself faithful to him and had expected the same. She wasn't conceited but did consider herself beautiful. Her hair fell just past her shoulders, and her skin was a soft, flawless, toasted caramel brown. She had big, almond-shaped eyes that dazzled with an exotic upward slant.

At five feet nine inches, she was considered a brick house. Her thirty-four-D bosom always garnered immediate attention, not to say her other assets didn't. Her behind flared out from a narrow waist and softly rounded over, long, shapely legs. She'd turned down many men in Paris, hunks with sexy accents, because she had a boyfriend in the States. But after the breakup, she'd swiftly rectified that with the next hottie that asked her out.

Eight months after her breakup with Malcolm, she'd finished her Cordon Blue course, and extended her stay to a four month tour of France. Then her dad called and told her he found a nice location in DuPont Circle for her to look over in consideration for her bistro and he wanted her to come home. She came home and decided that since she was going to be home, she may as well take classes to become a certified nutritionist. She could design a healthy meal option list on her menu. She took a look at the building and thought it was nice, but her dad had changed his mind. He'd decided they should look around a bit more. She thought he probably just used it as an excuse to get her home.

She turned on Route 29 and quickly reached Interstate 66. She began to think about the friends she'd left behind when she went to college, mainly Bonnie. They'd been friends since junior high school and were still the best of friends. After her return home from France, they'd become even closer. Finished with breaking the car in, she made her way back to Route 29 to head home. She spoke to her car. "Call Bonnie."

The phone rang twice before she heard a perky voice announce, "It's Bonnie!"

"Hey, girl. It's a car!"

"You're freakin' kidding me!"

"Sure not. Hey, you want me to swing by? We can go for a drive."

"Tomorrow. You can drive us all when we take you out for your present from us!"

"Only if you tell me where we're going?" She inquired hopefully for what must have been the hundredth time.

"Nope. It's a surprise," Bonnie taunted. She knew how much Sasha loved surprises, and this would be a good one!

"Not even a hint?"

"Not even."

"I'll just call Shelly. She'll tell me."

"Ha. Not on threat of death. And just so you know, I did threaten her."

"You suck."

"Maybe you will. That was your hint, by the way."

"That was not a hint."

"Course it was."

"What kind of hint is that?"

"The kind that makes it impossible for you to figure out the surprise," she teased again.

"All right then, I give up, I'm home anyway. I'll talk to you later."

"Okay, sugar, happy birthday."

They disconnected the phone just as Sasha pulled into the drive of the family's sixty-five-hundred-square-foot colonial.

When she stepped out of the car, the pleated skirt of her sea green chiffon summer dress fell into place around her knees, and her silver strappy sandals made clicking sounds on the hardwood floor as she entered the foyer. Joslyn, her older sister, and her parents were sitting in the family room, so when Sasha called out, "Where is everybody?" Joslyn called her into the room.

Joslyn had news that she wanted to share with the family but wanted to wait until after Sasha's birthday celebration, so her news didn't overshadow Sasha's day. Once Joslyn had everyone in the family room, she excitedly burst out, "Everybody, Ethan asked me to marry him, and I've accepted!"

Their dad was ecstatic. Their mom jumped up to hug Joslyn, and then Sasha took her turn, whispering, "Congrats, sweetie. I'm so happy for you."

Joslyn smiled with tears sparkling in eyes, almost identical to Sasha's almond-shaped eyes, and the two sisters hugged again, both on the brink of tears. Ethan was a wonderful man who would make Joslyn a fine husband. Their dad knew that. He'd been the one to start the wheels turning to put the two of them together.

It was for that reason that Sasha had been certain Ethan and Joslyn's relationship wouldn't work. Joslyn was very strong-willed. She and their dad had very explosive arguments upon occasion. Joslyn loved him dearly, but she just didn't agree with everything he said or did and had no problem letting him know when she did disagree. They always ended their bouts with one or the other giving in, or else agreeing to disagree.

So when their dad introduced Ethan to Joslyn, Joslyn was primed to *not* like him *because* she and their dad were such disagreeable creatures at times. Sasha, on the other hand, was the exact opposite, she did whatever their dad asked of her without question, and valued his opinion on all things. She sometimes wondered why he'd never tried to play matchmaker with her, but she reasoned that since they were so much on the same page so often, whomever she chose would likely be perfect.

Joslyn often told her she needed to stick up for herself with their dad, but she didn't see any reason to when she didn't dispute his superior experience on this earth; so she continued doing the things that made him happy, and he continued to spoil her outrageously.

# CHAPTER 3

$\mathcal{J}$erome sat in his dressing room studying. It was a great way to keep his thoughts away from his upcoming performance. The initial dance of the night always seemed to make him nervous. He and his siblings had taken dance lessons as long as he could remember, his mother thought it was a good way to get them into something positive as well as help their posture. His dad countered the dance lessons by putting them in martial arts, disputing that when the other boys learned they were dancing, they would need to know how to defend themselves.

Sin entered Jerome's dressing room. At six feet with a caramel complexion and soft, curly hair, they could almost pass for brothers. Sin looked like an older version of the kid from *The Last Dragon*. Sin was a good twenty years older than Jerome in physical age, and light-years ahead of him in street smarts. Sin was the name everyone called him. No one knew his real name, and that was by Sin's choice. Sin had a ring to it. At least Sin thought so.

Jerome smiled as Sin walked over to him, the deep dimples in his cheeks making an immediate appearance. Sin tapped Jerome on the back almost affectionately. "It's going to be another packed house tonight, Romy. I hope you drank your Red Bull."

"Don't worry, I've got it under control. I'm gonna rock the house tonight; when am I on?"

Sin walked to the door, "In an hour," he answered.

"Great! That gives me a little more time to study."

Sin turned back to face Jerome, he couldn't understand his fascination with those books, "Why do you waste your time with that? With all of the money you make here, I don't see why you would want to leave."

"I told you, Sin—this is just temporary. I have goals, and I certainly don't want to be a stripper for the rest of my life." Jerome opened a folder and started writing.

"An exotic dancer," Sin corrected.

"Whatever," Jerome joked with a shrug.

"If you don't like dancing, why not find something else? I'm sure there are other things you could do to cover your tuition."

"I never said I didn't like it. It does have its perks," Jerome said, thinking of the bevy of women who offered themselves to him on a regular basis. The only problem for Jerome was, the job's pros were its own cons because, for him, working in the profession for three years and having so many women offer themselves on such a regular basis made him a bit cynical. He began to feel it was his title as an exotic dancer that made the women show such an avid interest in him, not that they wanted to get to know him on a personal level. As a result, he'd found it difficult to develop a serious relationship with anyone.

He wouldn't have minded a serious relationship, but between school and work, he found little time to meet anyone outside of the club; and in his experience, the women inside of the club were not interested in anything but finding out if his hips moved the same in bed as they did on stage. He continued, "It's just not what I want to do for the rest of my life. I want to be a doctor, it's what I've always wanted. Maybe someday get married, go back home, and open a private practice. Nothing else will pay me near as much as this. Believe me, I've looked. I need the money for more than just my tuition and bills, but to take care of my family also. I make more than enough money here to do all of that, and I am grateful to you, believe that."

"Yeah, well, you've more than earned your keep. You're the best dancer here, and you rake in more money than any of the other guys," Sin replied briskly, but it didn't matter, because Jerome was already absorbed in his studies.

"Right," Jerome said distractedly.

Shaking his head, Sin quietly exited the room, leaving Jerome to his books. Sin remembered Jerome when he first came to work for him three years ago. He'd taken one look at the boy and wanted to hire him. When he found out that Jerome had never performed as an exotic dancer before, he'd almost changed his mind, but there was just something about him. When he later learned that Jerome had taken Latin ballroom dancing as a youth, Sin knew it wouldn't be too difficult to train him, and for a kid with a face and body like his, he was more than willing to take the chance, because he knew what kind of money he would generate for the establishment.

Sin had been a dancer in his younger years. He could command a crowd with his deep brown eyes and strong physique, so he knew what to look for in a dancer. He'd seen a softer side in Jerome of what his life could have looked like with proper care and nourishing from good parents. That hadn't been his lot in life, however, because he'd had a mother who was an addict. She'd had no clue who his father was, he never tried to find out. All he knew was, he was biracial, and he suspected the same of Jerome by his similar features.

Sin's ethnicity had been a major contributor to his unhappy childhood. Both children and adults mistreated him, because of his ethnicity. His mother hadn't cared enough to do anything about his bullies. Her biggest concern was never for her child's welfare, but always for her next fix. So he'd learned to fight so others would leave him alone, and he fought his way through his adolescence. The moment he finished high school, he left his mom and the crap-hole tenement he'd essentially raised himself in. He slept on the streets until he had enough money to board a room.

It was after he met the person who'd taught him to dance that he began to appreciate who he was. He saved most of the money he earned as a dancer, and after ten years, Sinclair Fuller had recreated himself, and saved enough money to open his own club. The Sinful Pleasure.

Sin reached the dancers' lobby. It was a sitting area for the dancers, with comfortable, charcoal leather furniture, end tables covered with magazines to interest a man, a large-screen television to pass the time, and a bar with a bartender. Sin called this room the 'dancers' entertainment lounge.' Sin spared no expense for his boys. They were, for the most part, a great work group. They knew their craft well, bringing an outrageous amount of money to the club. There was a doorway in the lounge the dancers used to access the stage. From the doorway, a large portion of the club could be seen. Sin checked to make certain everything was running smoothly before heading to his office.

Before he hired Jerome, his club had been doing well. When Jerome came with his knowledge of books, his dance background, and a great business sense, along with his dependability, Sin's business began an up-rise. The first year Jerome worked at Sinful Pleasure, the club went through a major change. Jerome learned the moves, perfected them, and enhanced them, and then he began changing the structure of his routines. The women had loved it. He was hired to spotlight in Vegas, New York, California, and Florida, meeting other spot-lighters along the way. Together they formed a male review, touring once every three months for two weeks. That popularity followed him back to DC, and into The Sinful Pleasure.

By the end of that first year, Sin's club was packed, and couldn't hold capacity. He moved, at Jerome's urging, to a better location. Using the money he earned from Sinful Pleasure, he purchased the new spot, made Jerome his featured entertainer, and paid him to train newer dancers. Jerome had by far been the best investment he'd ever made. Sin was now a millionaire.

∽◦◡◦∾

Sasha couldn't believe she'd let her friends talk her into this. She'd never been to a male strip club in her life! But they said, "Girl, you need to let loose a little, and since it's your twenty-fifth birthday, why not?" If her dad knew, he would kill her. She decided that she would leave as soon as it was polite to do so. She just hoped none of the sweaty dancers tried to single her out because her reaction would not be pretty.

They entered the club's waiting area. It resembled a large vestibule. To the right and left of the room were steel blue leather sofas and love seats artfully positioned to provide a welcoming atmosphere. Rounded end tables held brochures for patrons waiting to gain entrance into the club to leaf through, or to take home as mementos.

Standing before Sasha's group was a half-naked, hard-bodied man waiting to receive his guests. He greeted them, and while her friends took care of confirming their reservation and making payments, Sasha walked to one of the end tables, curious as to what was in the brochures. She picked one up and immediately dropped it. It was a man even more naked than the one taking money from her friends just as unconcerned about his nudity as anyone could be. The brochure told everything about the man in the picture. *Nice looking, though,* she thought to herself.

The host ushered them into the dimly lit club, and Sasha took a moment while her sight adjusted to the room. What she saw was not the sleazy place she would have expected to see, but a club that was very well put together in a masculine way. There were tables of differing sizes with cushioned leather chairs of steel blue at one table and charcoal at another, the variance in color very subtle. The music was loud, but not so loud that one could not hear another speaking. The chairs were all positioned for a bird's eye view of the stage.

"I can't believe I came here," Sasha muttered to herself.

"What'd you say, honey?" Sasha's best friend, Bonnie, replied. Tonight Bonnie resembled a black Barbie doll, with her long legs, purple minidress, and matching stilettos. Her chocolaty brown skin and plump lips were a perfect setting for the purple matte lipstick and eyeshadow she wore. All-in-all she looked like a basketball player's trophy wife.

"I said I think I'm ready to go home now. This was a mistake," Sasha spoke a little louder so the other four girls would hear, too. Regina, Jennifer, Shelly, and Leeza were the other culprits responsible for her being here.

"Oh, don't be silly, you *will* have fun, or I will kill you," Leeza said while grabbing Sasha's arm and bringing her to the seats that the host was leading them to. A waiter came, introduced himself, took their order for drinks and walked away, his muscular behind covered by a pair of black tuxedo trunks.

Shelly followed the waiter, returning shortly with the waiter in tow, skillfully balancing a platter full of drinks on his palm.

While the waiter placed their drinks, Sasha distractedly looked around. Along the sides of the far right of the club was a row of rooms. She watched as a hot-bodied Adonis escorted women into those rooms. She shook her head. *Is this a club or a brothel?* She thought to herself.

"I just heard that Dr. Romy is in the house, y'all!" Shelly said excitedly, craning her neck to search him out.

That earned her attention back. "Who is Dr. Romy, and why would he be here?" Sasha asked perplexed, as the waiter expertly handed out the proper drink to its owner.

Laughing at her naiveté, Jennifer replied, "He's not a real doctor, it's his stage name. I'm pretty certain it's short for Romeo though," she quipped, tongue in cheek.

As if on cue, the announcer introduced in an excited voice,

"Ladies, is anyone hot? Somebody need to call the doctor! No? Well before the night is over, someone will need a doctor … from a case of heart palpitations! Someone will need the doctor, of, love. Dr. Romy!"

The dancer came out in a cloud of fog as the screams of the audience became deafening. Sasha sat up a little when she saw his face, it was different from the man on the brochure. This man was delicious with beautiful tawny brown skin, soft curly hair cut short at the temples and neatly tapered. He was about six feet two, and, oh goodness, his dancing *was* making her … hot. Without even realizing it, Sasha began to fan herself. Then his white lab coat came off, and she had to remind herself to breathe. *My goodness*, she thought, *those abs were made for a woman's lips.* He bent over and grabbed his shiny black pants from the ankles and ripped them off. Her eyes followed them as they hit the floor, returning immediately to his perfectly toned body.

Sasha suddenly felt very thirsty as she watched him remove his stethoscope and lower it to his thong-covered erection. His hips made enticing little circles as he pushed his arousal in and out of a circle he'd made using the stethoscope's tubing, just before tossing it aside. She picked up her drink and began to sip it. In an attempt to compose herself, she looked around. Every woman she saw seemed mesmerized by the sleek-bodied god. Her eyes paused on Jennifer. She panted softly, her mouth slightly open. She looked as though her lips had replaced that tube.

Sasha decided she had two short-term goals to fulfill. One was to stop gawking, and two was not to look as desperate for him as just about everyone else in the place. He was probably so used to women throwing themselves at him that he didn't even have to work for it. She was willing to bet he'd take to bed whichever one got to him first, and that would not be her. Her daddy raised her better than to throw herself at some stripper just because he had a face so beautiful it was almost pretty, and, wait, were those dimples? She closed her eyes for composure.

Jerome was dancing for crowd participation. He learned long ago that connection was what brought in the money. He never got too raunchy by grinding his pelvis in some girl's face, although it was allowed, and some of the guys definitely did, especially when their hard-on started to go soft. Jerome would just think of something that really excited him at the time it happened, and there it was, instant rejuvenation.

Halfway through the routine, Jerome noticed a girl sitting in a group near the stage. She was beautiful. Sipping from a drink looking almost … bored? Her hair was pulled up into a ponytail that was near childlike considering where she was, but the dress she wore was too tight for her to be as underaged as her hairstyle suggested.

She looked up at him, as if sensing him looking at her, but quickly looked away. She didn't want his attention. *Hmmm, interesting.* Still watching her as he finished his routine, he stepped off the stage and headed directly toward her, dancing around her without touching her. When the music came to a stop, Jerome asked Sasha, "Would you like a private dance?"

"No, thank you," Sasha replied in a clipped tone, wanting him to go away.

"Are you sure?" Jerome asked in disbelief that he had asked in the first place, but even more that she turned him down.

"Positive," Sasha responded, turning her head to look in the opposite direction.

Jerome sighed dramatically, causing Sasha to turn back around to look up at him, a frown marring her beautiful face. The other girls were all looking in fascination, and Leeza was on the verge of touching him while her eyes ate him up.

"That's too bad," he almost sounded disappointed. "It would have been so good, and for you, I'd have done it for free."

"You're not my type, so I wouldn't want your free dances, and I doubt it would have been so good for me." *Liar, he's any woman's type with his strong-looking muscles and tight rippling abs.* She

30

tried hard not to notice those abs were moving in and out while his breathing returned to normal. His hands were neatly manicured and beautiful, with graceful fingers, she saw when he put his hand on the table next to her. His lips appeared soft, kissable as they framed a row of dazzling white teeth. Teeth all the same length with the exception of his canines, which pointed at the tips to make what promised to be an irresistible smile, and his eyes were a nearly transparent, light brown over a straight nose. He was just beautiful, but what kept her looking away was his body part standing half-mast, and showing itself off in that G-string, he simply had no shame. She shook her head.

"What is your type? Maybe I can be it," Jerome heard himself say, very intrigued by this woman who didn't find him to her liking, and wanting to know her on a more personal level because of it.

"My type is someone who uses his brain to get what he wants out of life instead of his body," Sasha replied with disdain.

Feeling a little put off by her snobbish attitude, Jerome opened his arms wide and looked around, and then asked, "Then why are you here?"

Sasha looked around as well to see men in all fashion of sexy underwear. Some were carrying drinks, and some dancers were mingling with the crowd to procure private sessions. Then she looked back at Jerome, "I'm here against my better judgment with my friends."

"Riiight," Jerome dragged the word out long to show his disbelief, then smiled at her look of irritation.

*Damn, those are dimples, as if he needs them,* Sasha thought before saying rather rudely, "Please stop harassing me, don't you have other things you should be doing?"

Jerome started to negate the question, he knew what he wanted to be doing, but the cue for the dancers to clear the floor sounded by way of the MC announcing the next dancer. "I'll see you later."

"I'm counting on it," Sasha said sarcastically.

# CHAPTER 4

She hadn't returned. He found himself repeatedly looking into the crowd for her over the weekend, but he never saw her. For some reason, the girl affected his concentration. He couldn't seem to think of anything else but her, and everything he tried studying just hadn't stuck … damn.

Monday morning he sat in class daydreaming about her. He thought about her skin; it was like toasted caramel, and it looked so soft that his fingers had itched to touch it. She had full, juicy-looking lips that appeared slightly swollen, like she'd just been passionately kissed. She'd been wearing some shiny stuff on them that made him want to feel them all over his body. Her eyes' exotic slant was emphasized by the makeup she wore that night, and he could only wonder what her body looked like under that tight little dress.

While he sat imagining her nude in his bed, he missed a portion of the lecture. Disgusted with himself, he scooped up his books and dumped them in his backpack. His plan was to make a hasty departure as soon as class was over, but Professor Sherman called out to him.

"Mr. Jacobs," he called in his deep bass, "Let's have a talk."

"Damn," Jerome muttered under his breath. Carefully holding his backpack, he made his way to the professor.

"I wanted to talk to you about your seeming lack of focus and motivation lately. I know you to be an excellent student, and can only surmise that you are in need of a pep-talk. Your grades have slipped, marginally, but now is the time to be proactive—"

He wanted to pay attention to what the professor was saying, really he did, but at that moment he had the most embarrassingly uncomfortable stiffy that for the life of him wouldn't go away, so his immediate goal was to get far away.

"—don't wait," The professor finished.

Jerome realized Professor Sherman was finished, and that he missed a portion of the 'pep-talk.' The professor was staring at him intently, as though waiting for his reply; so with his backpack covering his suddenly out of control body, he told the professor, "You're right, and I'm working on it. I really have to go."

At the professor's imperial nod, he rushed off as quickly as he could. Friday, he lost the keys to his favorite motorcycle. He spent the weekend getting around on his older bike. He finally found his keys on Tuesday. On Wednesday, he had an exam. He'd just gotten his grade for it, he hadn't done well. He needed a retake to keep his GPA where he wanted it.

He sat atop his motorcycle as he rocketed through traffic on his way to work. His last two weeks had been a lesson in frustration, brought on primarily by this sudden obsession. He couldn't stop thinking about that little beauty at the club. He was usually the one pursued, which created a certain level of detachment; he could take what he needed when he needed it, and not have his studies suffer from it, but this girl threw him for a complete loop.

When he left the club that night, he'd almost expected her to be waiting for him outside of the club, simply because he'd seen her attraction to him in her eyes and thought she was just playing hard to get. It wouldn't have been the first time a girl waited for him outside of the club, but she hadn't been waiting, in fact she hadn't been back.

He reached the club and entered through the back alley to

avoid the patrons coming through the front entrance. He was thinking about her *again,* so to take his mind off of the girl, he walked to the entertainment lounge and looked out at the Iceman as he performed. He then scanned the crowd to get an idea of how busy they would be tonight, and there she was with her five friends again, sipping drinks and watching the show. She looked … disinterested; he got excited all over again. *Well, it'll work for my performance,* he thought to himself as he stood fixed to the spot, just staring like a boy with his first crush.

Sin and Red Hot, a Latin American dancer with black as night shiny curls, that always had some woman's hands in it, walked up to Jerome, who was so transfixed by whatever he was watching that he never turned around. They looked out into the crowd to try and find what had his attention so raptly.

"You should be getting yourself prepared, Romy, you're up in fifteen," Sin advised.

"Hey, Sin, can you send someone else out right now?" Jerome responded, never taking his eyes off of whatever he was looking at so intently out there.

"Why? You can't make any money standing back here looking crazy. What are we looking at anyway?" Sin spoke with amusement in his deep voice.

Jerome pointed her out with a finger, giving the other two a bit of a shock, because no one had ever seen Jerome so interested in a girl before.

"Nice, very nice," Red said admiringly.

"Yeah. Buy me about thirty minutes, Sin. I'm going to do a private dance."

Both Red and Sin looked even more surprised by that and exclaimed at the same time, "But you don't do private dances, Romy!"

Jerome smiled and began to walk away from them, "I do for her." Jerome walked from backstage and approached the women. He looked at Sasha as though he was a starving man, and she, a seven-course feast. "Back so soon? You must have missed me bad, huh?"

Her heart sped up. *Yeah, couldn't stop thinking about you,* she thought, which was why she'd *let* the girls convince her to come back. "Yeah, couldn't sleep thinking about you," she gave herself a silent pat on the back when she managed to make that sound sarcastic.

Jerome purposely let that bit of sarcasm fly over his head, and with a smooth rotation of his hips, he replied, "Me neither. You know my offer from the other week still stands. I'm yours for the next twenty minutes."

"No thanks." *Liar.*

"Are you sure?"

"Positive." She'd done that with such a straight face that she was proud of herself.

"Okay, but just so you know, I was really looking forward to all the things I was going to do for you in that room over there." He tilted his head in the direction of the only room along the wall without occupants. "I'll be available until two o'clock if you change your mind." Jerome walked away to prepare for his show, but in truth there was not much preparation he needed to make. He was already erect.

They all watched him leave, but it wasn't long before Shelly burst out. "You must be out of your mind! If he offered to give me a private dance, you could kiss me good-bye!"

"Why don't you go get one then?" Sasha inquired, genuinely puzzled.

Bonnie answered the question for Shelly. "Because he doesn't give them; he doesn't need to. He makes a rack load of money being the featured entertainment in this place, and from what I hear, a couple of other places, too."

Sasha leaned forward in her chair. She was more interested than she wanted anyone to know. She asked, "Why would he offer to do something he doesn't do?"

"Maybe he would have?" Regina answered, but she didn't make as big a deal over Jerome as the others. He was sexy, and a great dancer, but she had her own little secret she'd never told the others that made Jerome completely off-limits to her.

Jennifer spoke with almost longing while looking in the direction of the stage. "Girl, I wish he would offer himself to me like that. I would take him to the nearest bed and tear him up with his fine self. Why don't you like him anyway?"

The conversation froze as their ridiculously gorgeous Demigod in the guise of a waiter came to the table to deposit their drinks. Everyone took a moment to appreciate his skill, while Sasha's thoughts remained on the god-like specimen who'd been there ten minutes prior.

When the waiter was gone, Sasha continued as though no time had passed, "It's not that I don't like him. I don't even know him. I just don't want what probably half of the women in this club has already had."

Regina spoke out. "I don't know about them, but I sure haven't had him. Neither has anyone at this table, so, statistically speaking, I wouldn't say half."

"It didn't take long for the statistician to start blurting numbers," Shelly quipped at Regina.

Regina rolled her eyes playfully at Shelly. Her smile was quickly hidden behind her glass as she took a sip of her drink.

Leeza chimed in, "I've seen the way these women look at him."

"So?" Sasha questioned, stirring a straw in her own drink.

"It's the same way we look at him." Sasha stared blankly at Leeza, prompting her to say, "It's not a look of knowledge, but want."

He began his performance as the lyrics, *"Ain't this what you came for, don't you wish you came, oh, girl what you're playing for,"* seemed to taunt. They all watched in wonder of the man dancing so erotically. Sasha shook her head, unable to stop thinking about Leeza's words. *Damn, why can't I be like other women and just take him up on his offer? Instead I over analyze everything,* Sasha thought through feelings of self-doubt. *Didn't they just say he never offered private dances?*

She spared a precious millisecond-long glance at the row of rooms along the far wall. She was getting tingly just thinking about what Dr. Romy would do in one of them. So as his dance came to an end, and before she could talk herself into accepting that private session that she knew would entail more than just dancing, she decided it was time to go. "Hey guys, I think I'm ready to leave."

Bonnie argued, "He still has a couple more dances."

"He always saves his best routines for closing," Leeza cajoled.

"Girl, sit down. You're not fooling anyone. You know you want to stay," Shelly said, sparing a glance at her before returning her attention to a more worthy subject.

Determined, she left with an, "I have to get up early in the morning, and it's already so late."

Jerome watched her go, feelings of disappointment consuming him. She took the easy road by leaving before he could come back to her table. He finished his routine and walked off stage, letting the cleanup boy gather his tips. He was upset, thinking about how this might affect his next week, considering how her rejection had affected the two weeks prior. *I just have to not think about her,* he thought to himself as he walked down the hall to his dressing room. *I mean, I couldn't have been more obvious about my desires, so the ball is in her court. I'll leave it there.* Jerome was so deep in thought that he almost walked into Sin.

"Hey, you okay? If I didn't know any better, I'd have thought you were blind."

"Yeah, I'm fine. Just giving myself a mental pep talk so I can realign my priorities."

"Anything you wanna talk about?"

"No, I can handle it. Thanks, though."

"Well, I have a problem, too. Poison didn't come in to work, so I need you to cover one of his time slots."

"I don't understand why you keep that dude around. He's just so unreliable."

"Yeah, that's Poison. Hey, when he's good, he's good, but when he's bad, he's really bad. He's the quintessential bad boy. That's why I need you both in this place."

"What do you mean?"

"Well, you're strong. You don't need anyone. You're always in control." He shrugged. "I hear the ladies talking about how much they love that aura of strength you carry about yourself. Now Poison, he's so broken and needy that he makes a woman feel like she can fix him. It gives her purpose. They love that crap. You guys both bring to this establishment a different demographic, and that, my dear boy, is great for business."

# CHAPTER 5

*P*rofessor Sherman stood at the front of the classroom handing out graded midterm papers. Jerome hung back. He knew that his grade wasn't as good as usual. After the last student grabbed his paper, Jerome walked down to retrieve his. Jerome rolled his eyes at the C- on his assignment and then turned to leave, making a mental note to make up this grade before the end of term.

The professor watched him take a couple of steps and decided to have another pep-talk with him. He genuinely liked Jerome and knew he would someday become a wonderful doctor. He stopped him by calling out, "Jerome, I would like to have a word with you, if you can spare the time."

The professor's deep, cultured voice stopped Jerome in his tracks. He felt dread down to his toes because of the *word* the professor wanted to have with him. He took a couple of deep calming breaths and tried not to look as put out as he felt. He then turned around and walked back to the professor, placing his heavy backpack down before him. Jerome felt the need to clear his throat a couple of times and wished he had a glass of cold water to cure his sudden feeling of extreme thirst.

"I want to talk with you about that," the professor said, pointing at the paper Jerome was holding in his hand. "You were always one of my most promising students. I've known you would make a great doctor someday, but not if you keep getting grades like that. On top of that, you've been late for my class so many times that I begin to wonder if you have forgotten what time it starts." He looked paternal for a moment. "Jerome, I'm concerned about you, is everything okay?"

"I'm fine, just working late hours. I know I've been distracted lately, but I'll pick up my grades."

"Good, I'd hate for you not to get into a good residency program because of your grades, when you have less than a year to finish here. You've entirely too much potential."

"Thanks, I needed that. I'd better go, or I'll be late for my next class." Jerome hefted up his backpack and ran out of the room, and right into someone just outside the class.

Jerome dropped to his knees trying to catch and pick up a floating, steady stream of papers as they drifted to the floor. He never looked up to see through the raining paper, just began apologetically, "I'm so sorry, I'm not usually so clumsy."

Sasha also dropped to her knees immediately, trying to gather as much of her paperwork as quickly as possible. She was irritated now, because she would be late to see the professor. She spoke at the same time as he'd begun his apology. "You need to watch where you're going. You could have given me a concussion or something," she fussed, then looked up, recognizing Jerome with a look of surprise. "Oh!"

Jerome paused in his apologies when he realized that at the same time he was apologizing, he was also being upbraided for running into her, but the softly muttered, "Oh" had him wondering why.

"Wait, what?" Jerome looked up, recognized her, and smiled sensually. "Well, fancy meeting you here."

"Are you stalking me?" she asked with a frown.

Jerome snorted at the absurdity, "Not that desperate to resort to stalking, so you can take those kinds of maggots out of your brain. Besides, I was here first. How do I know you aren't following me?"

"You attend class here?" she asked without bothering to acknowledge the statement.

"Try not to sound so surprised. I do have goals, you know. I don't intend to use my body to make money for the rest of my life," Jerome threw Sasha's words back at her. "Despite what you may believe." He handed her the paper, then looked at his watch and accepted the fact that he was going to be late again for another class. He got up from his squatting position and helped her up, and then he turned to walk away.

"Hey!" Sasha called out to him. Was this the same guy who came on to her every time she stepped foot into the club? He was wearing a Ralph Lauren, dark green, short-sleeve ribbed T-shirt, with dark blue relaxed fit jeans, and a pair of Timberland boat shoes. She was impressed by his sense of style, and the smooth grace with which he carried it.

Jerome stopped to look back at her and was reminded of how attracted he was to her. Her pants clung lovingly to her long legs, a white peasant top bared her shoulders and played peek-a-boo with her stomach, and a pair of heeled sandals revealed soft pink polish on manicured toes. *Focus,* he thought to himself. If she was not interested, then he would not push it. There simply were too many available women.

"Maybe if you're still offering, I'll take you up on that dance," Sasha spoke almost in a whisper.

Jerome was shocked but he didn't let it show. Instead he replied. "I'm not, I gotta go, I'm late for my next class." Jerome smiled and turned to run, disappearing down the campus hall and leaving Sasha in doubt as to whether he was serious or not.

Sasha watched him run until he was out of sight, not quite sure what to make of that exchange. She shook her head, feeling they were playing a game of cat and mouse. She decided she needed to find out a little more about this guy. It felt strange seeing him here.

Mostly because he was all she could think about in the last three weeks, but then also because that was the first time she'd seen him fully dressed, and he looked good … damn good, dressed or not. He'd just come from the professor's lecture room, so maybe the professor could tell her a bit more about him. She smiled to herself as she went into the room, suddenly excited about this visit with her dad.

# CHAPTER 6

$\mathscr{J}$erome walked into his apartment deep in thought about the little beauty. He realized he still didn't know her name, and vowed to learn it the next time he saw her, but wow, what a turn of events! He smiled to himself thinking about their run-in earlier that day. She actually *wanted* to see him dance? Impossible. For as long as he lived, he would probably never understand—

"If I'd known you were doing this good for yourself, I would've come to stay with you a long time ago. How can you afford all of this and send money back home too?"

Jerome's head jerked up midthought, shocked to hear a voice in his apartment. His smile turned to a look of surprise as he saw his younger brother, Eric. His expression quickly changed to a frown, and he cut him off to sharply ask, "What are you doing here?"

Eric's features closely matched Jerome's. He was tall, at just over six feet, his brown eyes crystal clear with a hint of amber flecks near the pupils. A dazzlingly perfect smile and tawny golden brown skin covered shoulders that, although not yet as broad as his brother's, were themselves impressive.

Eric had been standing behind Jerome's island fixing himself a drink, but when Jerome came in, he began to prepare another.

Finished, he walked to Jerome and handed him one. "I had a fall-out with mom," he answered, then waved his hand back and forth and began to impersonate their mom in exaggerated falsetto. "You need to be more like your brother; you're too immature."

The brothers exchanged a brief hug before Jerome invited Eric to sit. After getting himself comfortable, he took a sip of his drink. "Well, I wouldn't call you immature, just spoiled. How'd you get in here anyway?"

"Mom gave me the key. So as I was saying …." Eric looked around at the opulence of the penthouse apartment—the expensive furniture; the huge kitchen with stainless steel appliances and an island with bar stools perfect for entertaining, which also served as a divider between the spacious living area, and the kitchen. The dining area that rounded the corner was not quite visible from the angle of the plush, off-white living room suite. A huge flat panel television was anchored on the wall over a fireplace. The place was immaculate. Why had he been keeping this a secret? And why was he suddenly looking so … guarded? Eric was determined to find out.

"So, then, what are you doing to be able to afford all of this?" Eric persisted, gesturing to the apartment with his drink in hand.

"Promise me you won't tell mom?"

Holding up two fingers, and with a look of pure solemnity, Eric replied, "Scouts honor."

"I entertain," Jerome murmured on an exhalation of breath.

Eric looked around the space again, completely getting the wrong idea about his older brother's entertaining. His misunderstanding showed on his face when he incredulously replied, "In what capacity?"

Jerome ran his hands over his face, stood up and circled the sofa, and then returned and sat down. He looked at his brother, then at his drink as if he'd find inspiration there. If this had been someone else's situation, having to explain how they could afford the penthouse apartment, expensive furniture, and money to take care of their family, to their younger brother who'd had no previous idea, Jerome would be rolling on the floor. Just that look on Eric's face would've been enough to get him going, but it wasn't someone else, "Damn, Mom is going to kill me if she ever finds out about this." He looked up at his younger brother, "I've been an exotic dancer for the last three years."

Eric looked shocked and worshipful at the same time, "You make this kind of money *stripping?*"

Jerome corrected Eric with a bit of irony in his voice, thinking of the conversation he'd had with Sin not too long ago. "Exotic dancing."

"Whatever; I want in!"

"No way, not in a million years! Hey, look, it's bad enough that I'm doing this without bringing you into it. And you're supposed to be here to straighten yourself out, right?"

"Mom did say to be more like you." Eric laughed loudly at the idea of his perfect older brother being the one in trouble for a change. "My God, this is priceless. Man, you must get paid a lot of money to afford all of this! Please, let me stay here with you? I can look around and, you know, get used to the idea of going to college and decide what I want to do with myself. That *is* why I'm here, you know."

Jerome grimaced, "All right, make yourself comfortable. I need to study before I go to work tonight. I'm falling behind in my grades, and I have to get more focused if I want to get into a good residency." He stood up, picked up his backpack, and walked up the hall toward his study.

Eric was excited about the idea of going to the club to see exactly what Jerome was doing to afford him such luxuries, "You have to work tonight. Can I come?"

"No!" Jerome yelled, closing the door behind him.

∾◡◠

Eric waited standing beside his motorcycle at the side of the building. He took a brief step back as the headlights from another vehicle flashed while exiting the garage. A beautiful, sleek, cobalt-blue BMW motorcycle with Jerome sitting on top turned out of the garage and zoomed out of sight. Eric quickly followed behind, keeping a discreet distance.

An hour later, Eric stood at the back of the club. He was fascinated as Jerome performed, and had some pride in the fact that his brother was the featured dancer in the club. A waiter walked toward him holding a drink tray and offered him one. "Would you like a drink?"

"No," Eric answered after shaking his head, barely able to take his eyes off of his brother, "but, you can tell me how to get to Jerome's dressing room."

After giving Eric a strange look for asking, the waiter responded, "I don't think he goes that way."

The waiter gave him his directions after Eric shot him an irritated look, pulled his ID from his back pocket, and showed it to him before saying, "He's my brother."

Jerome sat at his dressing room table dressed in the robe that all of the entertainers of Sinful Pleasure wore after their performances. He couldn't seem to stop thinking about that girl. For some reason, he thought she'd show up tonight, but he hadn't seen her after the first two performances. So he'd stopped looking.

Jerome looked up into the mirror before him as the door opened. First astonishment, then anger registered on his face when his younger brother sauntered into his dressing room as though he hadn't specifically told—no ordered—him to stay home! "What the hell; I told you to stay home!"

Eric put his hands up in an act of surrender, still looking at Jerome through the mirror with an expression of hero worship on his handsome face. "I know, you told me to stay at the apartment, but I just had to find out what in the world you were doing here. Come on, let me in on this. I could save up and go to college."

"No, I told you, I won't have my baby brother doing this. Besides, if Mom found out, she'd kill us both, starting with me. Go home!"

"If Mom finds out what you're doing, she'll kill you anyway," Eric said in a tone of voice that suggested he would tell.

Jerome looked at Eric in disbelief. He stood and turned toward him. The little fool was trying to blackmail him, infuriated from the implication, he stepped into Eric's face, his superior body mass quite evident as they stood facing one another. He spoke through clenched teeth, "Are you threatening me?"

To Eric's credit, he didn't back down from the menace on his brothers' face; he was saved by a knock on the door. They both turned toward the door at the sound and for a pregnant moment, silence reigned before Jerome spoke, "Come in." Jerome's look of anger turned yet again to surprise upon seeing who this visitor was.

Sasha stepped just inside the room, looking at Jerome as though he was the only man alive. "I heard voices in the hall. I hope I'm not interrupting."

"Not at all," Jerome replied, shock still showing on his face. He cleared his throat and continued, "What brings you here? I thought I was the last person you wanted to see."

She smiled enticingly, "Now what would make you think that?"

His out of control body reacted immediately, "It could have something to do with you sneering at me every time you see me."

"I haven't exactly sneered."

"I just get the feeling when you look at me that you find me wanting. It's not very encouraging."

With a provocative come and get me if you can look, Sasha replied, "Well, be encouraged."

As the interlude played out, Eric watched with obvious

captivation, his head turning back and forward between the two. Unbelievable how his big brother was just on the verge of tearing his head off a few moments before, and now Eric would bet every dime of Jerome's hard-earned money that Eric carried in his pocket that very moment, that Jerome had a happy boner. In fact, he had all but forgotten Eric was even there. Eric smiled to himself, *time for a cold dunking.* Eric spoke to remind Jerome that he was still in existence. "It's getting hot in here. Would you guys like a little bit of privacy, a fan, a room with an ice bucket?"

Jerome looked at Eric, his frown confirmation for Eric that Eric certainly was at that moment equal to a bucket of ice water.

Jerome started to speak, "Go—"

"Yeah, yeah, I know. Go home, Eric." He paused. "But don't you think you want to introduce me to your lady first?"

"No, and I swear, when I get home, if you're not there, so help me—"

Eric threw up his hands again, "I'm going, I'm going." Eric smiled to himself as he walked out of the room, the door closing behind him. He knew when he had a reprieve.

Jerome watched Eric as he left, then turned to look at Sasha, who had come more fully into the room to stand before him, his interest in her showing clearly in his eyes. Standing in front of him, she was taller than the average girl, but that was good because at his height, Jerome needed someone he didn't have to break his neck to kiss. She was soft in all the right places, with high breasts and a round little butt. She drew him out of his inspection of her when she spoke.

"I just wanted to tell you how great you were out there tonight." Sasha appeared uncomfortable with that statement.

Jerome raised an eyebrow. His look incredulous, "Really?" All the skepticism he felt portrayed itself in that one word.

"Why are you looking at me that way?"

"I'm just wondering if you lost some sort of bet."

"What do you mean?" She questioned.

"Well, a few weeks ago you looked at me like I was the inventor of the plague, and now you're here telling me how good I was?"

Sasha looked at him for a long moment, letting the silence fill the space before responding, "Can't a girl change her mind?"

"What? Next, you'll be asking me out on a date?" he lead.

"Would you like to go out on a date?" she followed.

"When?"

"Tomorrow?"

"I'm sorry, but weekends are bad for me. Is Monday okay?"

"Yes. What time do you get off?"

"Monday?"

"No, tonight."

"About two," he answered, "Why? Are you looking to have that dance?"

Sasha laughed as she walked to the door, opened it and took a step out. Jerome watched her from the same place he'd been standing since she'd entered the room fifteen minutes earlier, her silver and black striped strapless dress lovingly hugged her curves, and his eyes devoured them.

She turned back around, "I'll wait for you."

The door closed softly behind her, leaving Jerome to wonder what had changed her mind so suddenly. He didn't have much time to dwell on it, though, because he was due on stage in ten minutes. As he quickly disrobed to refresh his costume, he was thankful that at least he didn't have to work too hard to get the erection he needed. It was already there.

# CHAPTER 7

*a*t about four in the morning, Jerome and Sasha entered his apartment building. They'd been hanging out having drinks since two when he got off, so they were both a bit tipsy. The corridor was dimly lit by wall sconces that brought a certain ambience to the immaculate apartment structure.

Jerome fumbled with his keys in the lock, and Sasha giggled as he mumbled to himself. Finally separating the key from the lock, they both entered, and Jerome closed the door behind them. He approached Sasha, who'd stopped in the middle of the room. She was slightly shocked by how beautiful his place was.

The walls were a very neutral soft champagne color to set the stage for the off-white plush furniture with overstuffed throw pillows in shades of white, beige, and olive green. The polished wood side tables held sculptured lamps of a goddess holding a lighted globe, all set on gleaming hardwood floors, and the walls held a quartet of paintings depicting the changing of seasons.

Just ahead, and slightly to the left, was an island separating the living area from the kitchen. Around the corner to the right appeared to be another room, but she couldn't see what kind of room it was from where she stood.

Sasha turned toward him as he came closer and placed her hands on his shoulders, then leaned upward for a kiss. The kiss was explosive on contact, sending a jolt straight to Jerome's toes and back up to settle in his groin. This was the first time he'd reacted to a mere kiss from a girl in forever. He whispered the name he'd finally learned a few hours before, "Sasha."

Sasha was reeling from the kiss. She clung to his broad shoulders for dear life. His lips were soft as he opened and closed them, gently urging her to let him in. She pulled back instead, needing to catch her breath. This was going too fast, and she could feel her nipples harden into tiny little buds, aching for his touch.

Jerome stepped back, not wanting to push her too fast. He took into consideration how long it had taken her to even speak to him, let alone let him kiss her. And he knew that she was not the kind of girl he could have for a booty call, not that he wanted to anyway. *It would be better to move away from foreplay*, Jerome thought.

"Come, make yourself comfortable and have a seat. I'm so glad you decided to wait for me," he spoke softly, aware that Eric was in the spare bedroom. Jerome sat on the sofa next Sasha after she sat in the spot he indicated for her to get comfortable.

"I had a really good time," Sasha said, all the while staring at his soft lips. "It's very nice to know that you have a head on those ..."

Sasha's words trailed off breathlessly as Jerome leaned in to claim another kiss, this one hotter than the first. She opened her mouth this time, and Jerome's tongue immediately slipped inside to duel with hers, and then withdrew, only to have hers follow his inside of his mouth. She ran her hand down his chest and stomach, feeling the hard muscle jump beneath her fingers. She stopped at his erection ... In a voice so husky she barely recognized it, Sasha asked Jerome, "How about that dance?"

"Shh, not so loud. My brother may wake up. Let's go to my room," he whispered. He stood and reached for her hand, then led her down the darkened hallway to his bedroom. He closed the door behind them and led her farther into the room, then walked away, leaving her in total darkness for ten seconds. When he turned on the light, it released a soft, dimly set glow. Sasha turned in a full circle. These walls were done in soft beige. Slightly lighter in shade than the living area.

His king-sized bed was covered with a silver, blue, and beige comforter. A set of beige reclining chairs sat against the far right side of the wall, where he led her to sit. An unlit fireplace sat between the two recliners. On the opposite wall was a large flat panel television and what appeared to be a radio system beneath it; all of it was set into a wall mount that looked like a hanging entertainment system. Across the room was a set of double french doors that led to his bathroom.

The room was very impressive, and her admiration showed on her face. Jerome walked toward her with a knowing smile on his face and leaned forward to plant a chaste kiss on her lips. He then walked away and without a word walked toward a nightstand and pushed a button that slid open a panel holding four small remote controls. He took out two and lightly pushed the panel, which slid smoothly back into place.

The first remote turned on the fireplace. The second remote turned on the radio set in the wall. Immediately Lilo Thomas began singing, *"Baby please don't go, stay a little while,"* and with the dim glow of the light framing his body, Jerome began to undulate. He lifted his shirt so slowly she could count the muscles dissecting his abs two at a time. Next his pants slid from his body like warm butter.

His torso glistened with a soft sheen of sweat as he moved before her clad only in a pair of black sport boxers, his hips making a figure eight. She reached out, but he stepped back before she could touch him, and continued his erotic torment. She was now breathing in soft, heavy pants, more aroused than she'd ever been in her life as she watched his hands caressing the waistband of his underwear. He was taking an eternity coming out of them, and the more he prolonged, the more excited and tensed she became.

The core of her throbbed, and squeezed out its moisture so she tightened her thighs, and then relaxed them in an effort to gain relief from the persistent tingle there.

It didn't work. As she waited, staring with her lip tucked between her teeth, she finally realized what she hadn't noticed in her distracted state, when impatiently she looked up into his eyes. They glittered at her through the firelight as he teased her, drawing out the moment by keeping the underwear on. Sasha stood, walked over to him, and hooked her finger inside the waist of his underwear, and then pulled him forward. She kissed him on the neck, working her way down to his chest.

Jerome stopped teasing Sasha the instant she reached out and grabbed the waistband of his boxer briefs. This was something he'd wanted for weeks now, so his private dance became a slow dance as he wasted no time sliding her dress off to reveal her very sexy underwear.

Together they continued their slow dance in their underclothes as Lilo's serenade reached a crescendo. When it was done, he picked her up and carried her to his bed, then laid her down. He took a moment to gaze reverently at her body before lying on top of her.

Sasha opened her legs automatically to receive his weight, and to feel his arousal press urgently against her core. She moved her hips up and down, enjoying the feel of their friction, his body easing and heightening the tingle she needed to rid herself of. *Mmm, feels so good*, she thought, but the friction was turning her once tingle into a full-out throbbing, and her panties were soaked.

Jerome was enjoying what she was doing to his body with her slow grinding, and going by her heavy panting, he knew that she was fully aroused, and if he didn't do something fast she would find her own fulfillment this way. He reached down and slid his fingers inside of her panties noting how wet she was, he could feel his erection grow painfully to reach its fullest. He was at his limit.

Drawing on everything he knew about the female body, he

slid two of his fingers into her warm slick moisture; she groaned in pleasure; he groaned in agony. He curved his fingers, creating friction against the roof of her inner walls where he knew the core of her pleasure would be located.

Her pleasure intense, she began bucking her hips against his fingers, not noticing her panties slide off. Nothing had ever felt better for her. She was so caught up in the delicious sensations he created with his fingers that she didn't noticed his position shift either; and then she felt his tongue on the cleft between her folds. It began slowly circling the hardened little nub, gradually picking up speed until she thought she would scream from the pleasure of having his fingers working their magic inside her, and the warm, rough texture of his tongue doing wonders on the outside. When he stopped doing that twirling thing with his tongue, she did scream, "Please don't stop!"

Sasha lifted her legs to give Jerome better access, and when she did, he took it. He sucked the little nub into his mouth, all the while still creating that friction with his fingers, and it was where she reached her pinnacle. Her muscles began to contract in a supremely delicious way, first slowly, and then they built into the most power-ful breath-stopping orgasm she'd ever experienced. She screamed out her pleasure as a floodgate of juices came spilling out of her to wet his fingers. She'd barely recovered when Jerome entered her with so much force that she almost came off the bed.

Jerome was in a state of mindlessness after witnessing her climax. He slid into her the moment her screams had subsided. He could feel her muscles still contracting around his shaft when he entered her completely. He stroked her hard and fast. He didn't mean to, but the way she gushed all over he and his bed, com-pletely snapped his control. Finally he came to his senses enough to feel her nails digging into his back and hear her screams of … pleasure or pain? He wasn't too certain, so he slowed down and asked her rather breathlessly. "Are you all right? I'm not being too rough, am I?"

Sasha answered with a negative shake of her head. Barely able to speak, "I am so good, but I just can't seem to quiet down," she responded in a raspy pant.

Jerome slid out of her, causing her to protest, so he grunted, "Turn on your stomach," and handed her a pillow. After she took it, he entered her again, this time a bit more in control. And with smooth, measured strokes he pleasured her body, changing his speed while at the same time rotating his hips, then returning to his original stroke. Jerome was on the verge, and could feel his release building within. He leaned forward to whisper close to her ear, "I'm gonna cum."

Sasha shivered hearing that soft, sexy whisper. *So was she,* she thought to her surprise, *again,* but she wanted to see his face when he did. She lifted herself to her knees and moved forward, dislodging him so that she could be on her back again. She then guided him back into her core, and he immediately began to stroke in a long, upward direction, once again hitting the roof of her inner walls. Her second climax sizzled through her body, causing tingles that began in her toes and traveled across every nerve ending before settling in her groin.

Jerome saw it coming and understood why she wanted to be on her back. He leaned down, taking her lip into his mouth as she screamed and grazed her nails down his back, up his waist, and across his nipples, and then she sucked his upper lip into her mouth.

He let out a grunt of pleasure as his impending release tightened his muscles on an inhale. Its exhale sent his seed shooting from him and ripping a groan of undiluted pleasure from his lips. He wrapped his arms tightly around her and rolled onto his side, taking Sasha to her side with him without separating their bodies. They both fell asleep that way.

∾♉︎∾

The next morning, Jerome walked Sasha to the door, Eric watched the two while sitting at the island drinking a cup of coffee. She turned to kiss him and he leaned down for the kiss, "Don't forget our date on Monday. I will meet you outside the campus at three thirty?" he reminded her.

"It's a date." Sasha opened the door, and then turned in for another kiss.

Jerome pulled out of the kiss to ask, "Are you sure you can't stay a little longer?"

"No, my dad will be concerned that I didn't come home as it is, but I'll see you on Monday." With that and one more kiss, Sasha left, closing the door quietly behind her.

When Jerome turned around, he noticed Eric sitting at the island with a cup in his hand. Eric said in amusement, "You look like someone who's just gotten rain after a very long drought."

Jerome smiled thinking of the night before, *rain*. "I've wanted that girl from the first moment I saw her, but she never seemed overly interested. I don't know what made her decide to give me a chance, but after last night, I'm so glad she did."

Eric offered Jerome a cup of coffee, which Jerome declined with a shake of his head, "I'm gonna get some much-needed sleep," Jerome said, heading back toward his bedroom.

# CHAPTER 8

*T*hat night, Jerome went to work feeling better than he had in a long time. He'd woken in the afternoon well rested and ready for the world. He'd felt so good, in fact, that he'd done something that he hadn't done in a very long time. Jerome choreographed some dances. One of the reasons he did so well in the club, was that until he'd left home for college, his mom had taken his siblings and he to dance lessons. So he'd quickly mastered the style of dance needed to make the money.

Jerome wanted to let Sin know that he'd made some changes to a couple of routines, so after entering Sinful Pleasure, Jerome headed straight to Sin's office. He walked down the hallway with name stenciled doors on either side of him. When he reached Sin's office, he knocked and then entered at Sin's, "It's open."

Jerome entered with a smile of both excitement and contentment. "Hey, Sin, I have some new dance moves that're going to make the crowd—" Jerome's smile quickly froze as he noticed who was standing in Sin's office. "What the hell are you doing here, Eric?" Jerome growled out.

"This is my newest dancer," Sin said, momentarily oblivious and not noticing the resemblance. "Hey, you two know each other?"

Jerome glanced at Sin, but his eyes turned stormy as they

returned to glare at Eric. Through gritted teeth, Jerome spoke. "I absolutely forbid it, Eric. I thought we already agreed that this is not for you."

"No, Romy, we didn't agree; you did, and my thoughts are that I want to make some of the money that you're making."

"No. Eric, I'm serious. I forbid it!"

"First of all, the last time I checked I was a grown man; second, you're not my father, and third, it's too late, I already have the job!"

Jerome turned to Sin. "This is my baby brother, Sin. I don't want my brother working as a stripper."

"It is not your decision to make, Romy," Sin replied calmly.

"Like hell it isn't!" Jerome exploded. "I'm the one who's been supporting him! He's staying with me right now. I'm feeding him." Jerome pointed at Eric's expensive clothes. "I paid for those clothes he's wearing, right down to the underwear, and contrary to what the little ingrate has said, I'm the closest thing to a father he's had in the last four years!"

Sin shrugged, seeing now the resemblance as he looked between the two. Although Eric was tall, he was at least an inch and a half shorter than his older brother. He was more slender too, not having filled out in the chest and shoulder area yet. He still had that immaturity of youth on his handsome face, but their tawny brown complexion was almost identical. The hair texture and smiles bore strong resemblances too, now that Sin thought of it, even though neither brother was smiling at the moment. "If that be the case, then I say it's about time he got a job and started taking care of himself. Hey, I just had a great idea! You two could be a duo!"

Sin turned to leave the office, then stopped and looked back at the brothers appraisingly. He nodded to himself as though making a confirmation, "Yeah, you two will make a killing together with your looks. Jerome, why don't you teach him those moves you were so excited about?" Sin left on that remark.

Jerome turned his head to look at Eric, who was trying unsuccessfully to hold back a smile. Jerome felt too angry to speak, so he turned around and walked away.

After Eric saw how genuinely angry Jerome was, he followed behind him. He had to nearly jog to catch up to Jerome's fast pace. He reached out and grabbed his arm in an effort to slow him down, "Hey, Romy, I know you want to protect me and all, but I'm not a baby anymore. I could really love this."

"You don't understand," Jerome argued, "I've been doing this for over three years so I could take care of you guys and make sure you'd never have to do something like this to make a living."

"Something like ... okay, you might not enjoy it much, but I think I would have a lot of fun."

"Fun? There are other ways to have fun. This is a job, Eric! A means to an end, and you're a kid, so you have no idea of the kinds of trouble you could get into in a place like this! You know I can't always be around to protect you."

Eric walked up the hallway alongside his brother, a look of incredulity showing on his face. "A kid? Oh yeah, you're so much older than me by," Eric held up his fingers to count, "what, five years at best? Listen, I'm not a kid. I can take care of myself!"

They reached Jerome's dressing room and entered together, leaving the door ajar. Jerome walked over to a wall with double doors and opened them, revealing a closet filled with costumes of different color, texture, and role play. He grabbed one of the costumes, not really caring which, brought it to his dressing table, and began to prepare himself for the show he was to perform in twenty minutes.

"I can't believe my ears right now, seeing as you're the one who came to me just yesterday needing a place to stay," he reminded Eric, yanking off his shirt. He continued to disrobe during his outburst, "But you tell me you can take care of yourself; and, yes, I may be older by only five years, but in experience, little brother, I have a lifetime of wisdom on you. You see, while you were still able to maintain your childhood and grow at your own pace, I had to face the realities of life and become the man of the house I was expected to be, and that meant doing whatever I had to do to make certain you were taken care of!"

There was a knock on the door. Through the mirror, Jerome saw the face of the very good-looking yet slightly dissolute Poison, as he poked his head through the crack in the door. Poison's smooth milk chocolate complexion, hazel green eyes, and impossibly white smile gave a perfect balance of contrasts that kept him pursued by partying women all over the greater metropolitan area. Poison was slightly older than Jerome. He'd been working at the club since before Jerome started, and from the looks of things, he had no intention of doing anything else.

"Hey, Romy there's a party happening next weekend. You in?"

"No, thanks, Poison." Jerome knew about the kind of party Poison would be going to. He'd been naïve enough to attend one of them when he'd first come to work for the club. Parties were the side gigs of exotic dancers, and a great many of them made the bulk of their money that way. This one had been thrown by a woman newly divorced and celebrating with her friends. She'd hired Poison, and was willing to pay $1,500 to him along with any other two guys he could get to come for entertainment purposes. Jerome had jumped at the chance to make a fast $1,500. Jerome later found out that Poison got paid a little extra for bringing the other two, but he hadn't cared, he needed that money to pay the mortgage.

Jerome went to the party with Poison and another dancer who went by the name Blaze, with the intention of putting on a stellar performance. The instant they entered the mansion, a drink was shoved into his hand, and he and the guys were steered to a room with a table covered with drugs. Poison and Blaze dove in but Jerome declined, and went to perform. An hour into his performance, he'd turned down five propositions, with one woman offering him $500 to have sex with her.

It wasn't long after that proposition that he'd realized he wasn't at a party to give a show, but to be a stud. Jerome had promised to stay three hours, but after two hours, countless offers of sex for ridiculous amounts of money, and one woman drunkenly attempting to perform oral sex on him right in the middle of a performance, even after he'd turned down her proposal twenty minutes before, Jerome was ready to leave. It hadn't escaped his notice that he'd been dancing primarily solo for the pack of horny, high off their rockers, women. Poison and Blaze were too busy being breathing blow-up dolls in other rooms of the house, to entertain any other way. He found Poison, collected his money, and left not caring that he hadn't stayed the entire three hours.

Poison nodded his head in Eric's direction. "Who's this?"

At the same time Eric gave his answer, Jerome was giving his, "My kid brother."

"I'm Eric. Just got hired on."

Poison looked at the two and then spoke to Eric. "I hope you don't plan to use Eric as your stage name. So are you in for the party?"

Again the brothers responded at the same time with opposing answers. "No," Jerome said forcefully.

"Sure, why not," Eric said with a shrug of his shoulders.

Poison looked at Jerome, and then back at Eric with a smirk on his handsome face, "A bit overprotective isn't he?" Poison left after the observation.

Jerome watched through the mirror as Poison disappeared from view, and then he looked at Eric through the mirror. "For your own good, Eric, stay away from that one."

"Why? He seems pretty cool to me."

"Because trouble follows him wherever he goes. It's not just for stage purposes that we call him Poison. The guy has never met a drug that he wouldn't try."

Jerome gave himself a look-over, and satisfied with his appearance, headed out of his dressing room and walked up the hall, Eric alongside him. When they reached the entertainment lounge, Jerome stood back to wait for his cue. Eric took a seat to watch from the lounge.

               ∽◎〜

Sasha entered the club. She just could not keep away. After the night before, she wanted to see if Jerome would look at her the same as he had before. Jerome put in a star performance while Sasha enjoyed every part of it, and when he finished work at two, they started out for an early breakfast but ended instead making love on his motorcycle in the park.

Jerome wanted her from the very first time he'd laid eyes on her, and he couldn't seem to keep his hands off of her long enough to learn about who she was, but he would, he promised himself, as soon as he sated his hunger.

Sasha was in paradise. He looked at and touched her with an almost reverence, as though she was the only woman in the world. She knew that she was not the only girl he was sleeping with, just looking at him told her he had lots of girls, but the way he made her feel was priceless. She promised herself that tomorrow they would get to know one another on a more personal level, since it was obvious they were sexually compatible.

# CHAPTER 9

*J*erome was the last person in line to receive his graded essay on Monday at the end of class. When he saw it show a B he smiled, grabbed his paper, and turned to walk away. The professor stopped him to say, "I'm glad you have been getting yourself back on course."

Jerome turned back around to look at the professor, "Thank you, Professor Sherman."

The professor smiled, "I don't know what you did to my daughter, but she has really taken a liking to you."

Jerome looked at the professor in puzzlement, because he didn't even know the professor had a daughter, let alone one he'd made an impression on. "I'm sorry, Professor, you have a daughter?"

"Yes. She asked about you the other day."

Jerome didn't know this girl, "And what did you tell her?"

"That you were one of my most promising pupils, very intelligent, and would make a very gifted doctor someday."

Maybe she was a groupie, "What was her reaction to that?"

"It seemed to be confirmation, so to speak. You know, she's very picky about who she deals with."

Jerome was more perplexed by this puzzle than ever. He didn't have a clue who this person was. "What's your daughter's name?"

Now it was the professors' turn to be puzzled, and it showed on his handsome face when he replied, "Sasha Sherman. You do know who she is, don't you?"

Jerome had an instant boiling feeling in the pit of his stomach as flashes of the statuesque beauty writhing in his bed filled his head, "Oh, yes, I know exactly who she is. I met her a few weeks ago, I didn't know she was your daughter though." Jerome thought for a second, "I ran into her here one day earlier last week."

"That was when she asked me about you."

Jerome was starting to get angry. Something about this didn't sound right to him.

Along with Jerome's growing anger was the professor's growing confusion. The professor said then, "Did I say something wrong?"

"No. I'd better get going, or I'll be late for my biology class. Can't go messing up now that I've gotten myself back on course, can I?" Jerome went through the rest of the day simmering. *Unbelievable* was the word that kept replaying through his mind. It explained so much about his amazing weekend and her abrupt change of mind.

Maybe if he hadn't been so angry, and maybe if he'd spoken with her immediately after that conversation with the professor to clear the air, instead of carrying the anger with him for the rest of the day, what happened that afternoon may not have occurred.

Jerome stepped out of the college campus with Monty and Ronald, and instantly spotted Sasha standing at the bottom of the stairs waiting patiently for him. A jazzy little backpack sat heavily on the ground beside her feet. He watched as Sasha looked up and smiled as she spotted him exiting the building. Monty and Ronald both waved in greeting, and she responded with a smile and tilt of her head.

Seeing that interchange just tipped the scale for Jerome, and the anger that had been simmering all day rose to boiling. But rather than get into an argument in the open, Jerome disengaged himself from the others and walked briskly down the steps, not stopping to acknowledge Sasha.

Sasha was upset by this. She stood rooted to the spot for brief seconds staring at him with a dumbfounded expression on her face, but she refused to let him walk away from her without an explanation, so she picked up her pack and walked quickly to catch up to his long-legged stride.

They were still in close enough proximity that the others could hear when she spoke. "So what, you don't know me now that you've gotten what you've been wanting all this time from me?"

By now Dillon and Jeffery had exited the building to join the others standing outside, and silence reigned because everyone wanted to know what the commotion was all about.

Jerome growled low in his throat, "You have some nerve to say something like that to me after what you did!"

Sasha had no idea what he meant by that remark, so she asked him, "What the hell are you talking about?"

"I'm talking about you being a stuck-up little—" Jerome stopped himself, on the verge of calling her a name that he couldn't take back, all the while he'd been walking as fast as he could to get out of earshot of their little audience. He looked at her contemptuously and finished with an improvised, "Money grubber."

Sasha grabbed his arm to make him slow down. He stopped, turning to look at her furiously. She was trying to catch her breath after having to practically run to keep up with him. "Now I'm really confused. When have I ever asked you for anything?"

"I couldn't figure it out no matter how hard I tried. I couldn't seem to understand what made you change your mind about me, but then I wanted you so much that I really didn't care, and so I decided not . . . not to look a gift horse in the mouth, but now I wish I had. I should have known it was just too good."

Confused, she asked, "What was too good?"

"Everything!" Jerome fired, "You coming to my dressing room and smiling so sweetly, you coming on to me, you waiting for me, and you going out with me after my shift was over. You having …" *the best two nights of lovemaking he'd ever experienced,* he thought. He ran his hands up his face as though he could wash away the anger he was feeling. "You know what, never mind. Let's just pretend that night never happened. Let's pretend the last two nights never happened, and go back to the way it was before, with you looking at me like I'm the scum of the earth."

"This sounds like the ramblings of a madman, and I can't make heads or tails of what you're talking about. What do you mean? What made me change my mind?"

"I'm talking about you not liking me, about how I came on to you for what … weeks? How you turned me down with a sneer every time and let me know that I wasn't worth your time because I'm an exotic dancer, but as soon as you found out I'll likely be a doctor someday, I suddenly became so special that you could not only consent to speak to lowly me, but invite me into your bed too! Or should I say invite yourself into mine?" he said with a sneer.

Sasha felt the hurt those words were intended to deliver. With tears in her eyes, she balled her hand into a fist, landing a blow hard enough to leave an immediate imprint on his face, and ran away.

Jaw clenched, Jerome watched her run away. He also felt the pain of his words, as well as her right hook. The guys walked to him. Ronald looked back to see Sasha disappear around a corner.

Dillon asked, "Dude what was that about?"

"I don't know why, but I thought she was different." Jerome spoke softly.

"What's going on?" Monty queried.

"We went on a couple of dates, but before that she seemed not to like me much. I didn't know what changed her mind," Jerome answered absently.

Ronald exclaimed, "You went on a date with her?!"

"Yeah. Why?" Jerome answered turning to look at Ronald.

"She's just so stuck-up," Ronald stopped talking when Jeffery elbowed him in the ribs.

Monty changed the topic, "She's been interested. She asked about you last week."

Jerome didn't respond to Monty's revelation, but he had a feeling it had been after she'd spoken with her dad about him. That just made matters worse.

# CHAPTER 10

$S$he called three days later. Jerome was sitting at his desk in the study poring over some books when the phone rang, and Eric answered it. Eric brought the phone to the study and handed it to Jerome. Jerome asked, "Who is it?"

Eric answered, "Sasha." Jerome shook his head and continued to study. Eric spoke into the phone, "I'm sorry. Jerome can't come to the phone." She said something on the other end that caused Eric to say, "Jerome, it's an emergency, at least give the girl a chance to make things right."

Jerome had been in a state of anger for days, but this heated his anger past the boiling point. The little traitor was sympathizing with the enemy. He growled, "Just hang up the damn phone and be done with it."

"I won't hang up the phone, because you need to talk to the girl!" Eric yelled, handing the phone to Jerome.

Jerome kindly accepted the phone. Eric smiled, thinking he'd won that exchange. He turned and headed for the door. The phone came flying over his head to crash into the wall, landing in a broken heap by the door.

Eric ducked to avoid the flying missile that passed inches from his head. When he turned in complete shock to look at his brother, it was to see him sitting behind his desk calmly studying as though nothing out of the ordinary had occurred.

The following week, Monty and Jerome sat in Jerome's apartment with a case of beer. They were waiting for the others to come over and watch a few games. It was Sunday, and Jerome had taken the day off.

Monty asked, "So what's the deal with you and the professor's daughter?"

Jerome looked surprised, "You knew she was his daughter?"

Monty raised his brows, "You didn't?"

"I guess not," Jerome grimaced, and then took a swallow of his drink. Monty looked at him expectantly. He answered Monty's silent query, "I met her at the club about a month ago. She was so beautiful, I was instantly attracted, but she didn't want anything to do with me. Then two weeks ago, she started dropping hints. Next thing you know we're in my room having the best night of sex ever. Monday the professor is like, 'You made quite an impression on my daughter.'"

The other guys came in and headed for the refrigerator, grabbed some drinks, and settled in front of the television. Ronald asked, "What are we talking about?" His honey brown skin and deep brown eyes would have been an attention-grabber on their own. But he was quite metrosexual, so his look was always sharp. Ronald philosophized that there were very few women he could not get.

Jerome answered, "Sasha Sherman."

She was one of the few he couldn't get. "Oh, the stuck-up one."

Dillon laughed, "You only say that 'cause she turned you down."

Jeffery said, "She is stuck-up, though. How'd you meet her?"

"At my job," Jerome answered, taking a swallow of beer.

"Oh, at the hospital?" Ronald perked up.

"No," Jerome answered uninformatively.

"Yeah, so tell us about your other job," Jeffery asked. "And why didn't we know about it?"

Jerome looked at Monty in accusation. Monty shrugged as if to say, "I tried." Jerome cleared his throat. "Well, I mean …"

Monty took over. "He's waiting tables. He didn't say anything because he was embarrassed."

Everyone looked at Jerome for confirmation.

Jerome stared at Monty incredulously. "Umm, yeah, you know, just kinda been waiting tables to help since my dad died. It's no big deal."

"And you didn't think you could tell us? Seriously?" Dillon asked.

Jerome went to the kitchen for another round of beer. He handed them out, then joked, "What can I say? I didn't want to cheapen your worship of my esteemed self."

The guys laughed and settled to watch the game.

∽❧∽

The following week, Jerome and Eric began practicing a routine that Jerome choreographed. Within three days, Eric was of the firm opinion that if he didn't get those two in front of each other to hash out their differences, his brother would kill them both trying not to think of her, which was impossible, fine thing that she was.

Their bodies were covered in sweat as they danced the number to perfection in front of the wall-sized mirror. When the music stopped, Eric dropped to the floor, Jerome walked to the corner of the room where there was a radio and a few bottles of water. He took a sip from one of the bottles and then said, "Let's do it again."

"Come on, Romy, you've *got* to be kidding me. I'm too tired, and I can't do it again. Besides, it was perfect!"

"If you can't handle it, you can always quit," Jerome said without sympathy, "You're supposed to be having fun." He turned the music on again, and they began the dance all over.

Eric started making plans for a run-in with Sasha.

Everything else over the next two weeks went by in a blur. Jerome got his graded finals from the professor with a look of approval. He was rounding off his first year as a physician's assistant at the hospital. He had taken the job to increase his experience in the medical field, but it was sometimes hard juggling his good-paying job, classes, studying, and the job at the hospital.

One evening Jerome watched Eric have his first performance from the lounge. He finished with a round of applause and dollar bills being thrown onto the stage. Those were bills that Jerome knew firsthand were not singles, as this was a high-end club, and the ladies tended to have more money to spend.

It was Jerome's turn, and he performed well. As he came to his finale, he received a standing ovation, and bowed. He looked up at the audience, and as the crowd settled down, there she was. Their eyes locked for a brief instant and in hers, Jerome could see the longing she felt, but he turned to exit without further acknowledging her presence.

That night Sasha went home and cried, Jerome went home and drank, and Eric hung out with Poison, drinking and getting high. Eric stumbled into the apartment in the early-morning hour still high from the past night's excess.

# CHAPTER 11

$\mathcal{I}$t had been four weeks since the altercation with Jerome outside the campus, and he seemed to immerse himself in work and school to keep from thinking about her. She knew he knew that she called because Eric told her Jerome could hear Eric when he spoke to her.

Sasha walked with her dad toward the parking lot for staff members, hugging one of his briefcases to her chest.

Her dad spoke. "I must admit I'm a bit surprised that you waited for me today. You seemed to be in your own world these last few weeks."

"I needed to talk to you about something and I … I don't know how to …"

The professor's attention was caught after Sasha's stuttering announcement. They reached his car. It was a black Mercedes fully equipped. The professor started the car using a remote, and then he unlocked the doors to place the briefcases inside. Once he was done, he turned to give her his full attention.

"What is it, Sasha?" he asked her softly.

"Well, remember when I asked you about Jerome?"

The professor nodded his head affirmatively, "I wondered what happened with that. I'm sorry, but he did seem a bit upset when I mentioned it to him."

"Well, nothing happened. After that day he won't even come within shouting distance of me. I don't know if you know how I met him, but it was in a strip club."

The professor's expression showed his utter shock by that revelation. But Sasha continued. "He offered to give me a lap dance, but I turned him down."

"Okay, that's not funny," he said.

"It wasn't meant to be."

"You mean Jerome is a strip dancer? Are you out of your mind, girl? I have not raised you to be the plaything of some stripper!"

"Well, technically, Dad, he's an exotic dancer."

That indifferent reply got a frown out of the professor. "What's the difference? He takes his clothes off for money. You know, come to think of it, that would explain a lot. He didn't even know you're my daughter, did he?"

"I don't think so, and now he thinks the only reason I decided to like him is because he's going to become a doctor someday, and he won't even talk to me. He called me stuck-up," Sasha said with all the pain and dejection she was feeling.

"That's fine with me. I don't want you getting caught up with a stripper."

"Okay, wait a minute, we're talking about Jerome here, the guy you couldn't stop singing the praises of a few weeks ago. This is not fair, Dad, and you know it."

"A few weeks ago I didn't know he was a stripper. You deserve better than that. I won't see my daughter hanging out with that caliber of person."

The unjust persecution her dad was throwing on Jerome made her mad. It didn't occur to her that this was the exact reason Jerome was now not speaking to *her*, because she initially thought the same thing of him. "If that isn't the most bigoted thing I think I've ever heard in my life! He's no different now than he was before you knew he was a stripper!"

"Nevertheless I don't want you with him! I absolutely forbid it!"

Sasha's eyes began to water. She realized she should never have told him, but she'd been desperate for the words of wisdom her dad would normally give when she needed them. Sasha could feel the air blasting from her father's car as she stood vainly trying to figure how to convince her dad that Jerome was not a bad choice for her. She needed his approval, because the weekend she'd spent with Jerome let her know that he was all she wanted, and she would do whatever she had to do to get him back. Tears began to spill down her cheeks because she knew she wouldn't get the approval she needed, and for once she was going to commit outright defiance. "I'm a grown woman, and you really couldn't stop me if I decided to continue to date him."

"I can, and I would," he promised.

"This is all wrong, Daddy. You like Jerome," she reminded him imploringly.

"You know how I feel about him, so I won't even lie. He's a wonderful kid with a great head on his shoulders, but the fact still remains that he is stripping for a living, and the world he now inhabits is not the world you were raised to live in." The professor looked at his watch and seemed to dismiss the conversation. He climbed inside his car and then closed the door. Sasha stood on the outside looking utterly miserable.

The window rolled down. "I need to get going, Sasha, but remember what I said. You can end things with him, or I will, but I don't want you to carry this any further than it has already gone." The professor frowned while he thought of something, and then he looked back at her. "What were you doing in a strip club anyway?" He drove out of the parking lot without waiting for an answer, leaving Sasha standing alone.

She walked to her car. Before she could get inside, her phone began to ring. "Hello?"

"Hi, Sasha, this is Eric."

Sasha looked at the phone, and then put it back to her ear, not completely understanding why he was calling, but her heart jumped in her chest, "Hi, Eric. What's up?"

"Well, I just wanted to invite you to the club tomorrow night. Jerome and I are doing our first duo, and I thought you might like to see, or maybe participate in it?"

Her heart was now thumping. "How could I do that?"

"Well, you would have to be willing to be on stage with us both—"

Sasha interrupted, "I don't think I want to do that. I mean, he doesn't want anything to do with me."

"I disagree. He misses you like crazy, and he's driving *me* crazy as a result, but the only way you're going to be able to influence him, is by putting him in a situation that he can't easily walk away from. He was the one who choreographed our dance, with me pulling someone from the audience, and I choose you. So are you in?"

*This is it,* she thought excitedly. "Tell me what I need to do."

Jerome was putting the final touch on his costume when Eric walked into his dressing room. Jerome looked up, a slight frown of concentration on his face.

Eric said, "You look mean as hell, and, to be honest, you've looked that way since you let that little cutie go."

"You need to be less worried about me and more on keeping your moves straight. That is, if you can with all those drugs and alcohol in your system."

"Quite the bear tonight, aren't we?" Jerome frowned even harder, which made Eric shrug. "I've been doing fine all this time. So tell me, have you spoken with her, or are you still giving her the silent treatment?"

Jerome walked out of the dressing room, not wanting to talk

about her, but Eric just fell in step beside him, and together they headed to the entertainment lounge to await their cue.

"No, I haven't spoken with her. There's no need to because it's done with. What have you been doing with the money you've earned?" he asked in a no-nonsense tone.

"I've spent some and saved some. You know you're in love with her. Might as well stop trying to fight it, and kiss and make up."

Jerome gave Eric a frown of disapproval for that observation, "That's ridiculous. I don't even know her."

"Don't frown at me like that when you know I'm telling the truth. She rocked your world that night, and you know it, and what's really upsetting you is you can't control the way she makes you feel, regardless of whether you know her or not."

Jerome stopped at their designated waiting spot, ignoring that last comment of Eric's. "I want you to take some of the money you have saved and pay for a semester at the college."

Eric looked out into the crowd and spied who he wanted to see, and then he turned to Jerome smiling mischievously. "You talk to the girl, and I'll enroll for the next semester."

Jerome didn't know that Sasha was in the club or that Eric had spotted her, so he jumped at the bait. "Deal, and I want you to stop hanging out with Poison. You don't know how much trouble that guy is gonna get you into."

"I think she's in love with you. Will you talk to her as soon as you see her? And if I'm wrong about Sasha, I'll stop hanging out with Poison, but if I'm right, you'll stop nagging me about hanging out with him. Deal?"

Jerome crossed his arms over his chest, irritated. He frowned at Eric's lack of attention to this serious matter. "Fine, but I'll only hold my tongue as long as you enroll and not get too out of hand with Poison."

"Stop worrying, Romy, I'm fine. I hang out with Poison because he's fun, so relax; I'm in control. Oh, yeah, once you've made up with Sasha, you may thank me by way of a monetary contribution."

"Oh, so that's why you came stumbling into the apartment at the crack of dawn the other night, 'cause you were so in control? Eric, I wouldn't give you any money right now because I don't know what you'd do with it."

They both turned at the sound of laughter behind them to see Poison standing with a smile on his handsome face. "Gee, Romy, I'm beginning to think you don't like me."

"I have nothing against you. I just don't want my baby brother getting mixed up in the vices associated with your name, not with the potential he has to do so much greatness."

Poison smirked, "Can't a person have a little fun and still do greatness?"

"Not if they're strung out, or worse ... dead," Jerome replied seriously.

Eric spoke in feigned disgust. "My goodness, Romy, that's a little extreme, isn't it? I begin to wonder how on earth you've become such a big success in this industry being such a stick in the mud."

"You know, I've been wondering the same thing for the longest time." Poison laughed at his own quip, and since Jerome didn't see any of the humor in the conversation, he turned his back to Poison to look at Eric.

"I won't have any problem calling Mom and sending you back home if I think for one second that you're getting out of control."

Eric threatened, "What, and risk tarnishing your squeaky-clean rep? Now this I would have to see."

"In a heartbeat I would risk it to keep you from turning into Poison, if you think for one second that I would—" Jerome stopped in midsentence upon hearing the announcer, who was giving them their cue to take their positions.

"Ladies, may I have your attention. Tonight we're doing something a little different, and you get the honor of saying you were the first to see it here! Because for the first time ever, our very own Jerome 'Dr. Romy' Jacobs will be dancing with Eric 'Love god' Jacobs! So buckle your seatbelts because this is going to be one hot and sexy ride!'"

The music began to play and the brothers started their dance. They were both wearing silver-blue shirts with pants that looked like denims and soft silver boots that resembled a boxer's boots. The dance began with them side by side as their hips rotated in unison, and then Jerome stepped behind Eric continuing a series of movements. Jerome's hands grabbed Eric's shirt from around his waist and ripped it off.

The crowd went wild! Next it was Jerome's turn, except Eric took off his pants. They danced a while longer before Eric whipped off his own pants, which left him in his thong, and Jerome in his shirt and thong. It was time for Eric to pick a woman from the audience for their finale.

Jerome looked around to try and see who Eric might choose, and saw Sasha sitting in the crowd with her friends. Jerome flashed Eric a look of disgust as with the same mischievous smile he'd shown behind stage earlier, Eric headed directly to Sasha and pulled her on stage. For split seconds Jerome danced solo, as was rehearsed, until Eric returned with her. With another disgusted look aimed toward Eric, Jerome proceeded to finish the dance.

Sasha saw the exchange between the brothers. She knew that Jerome didn't want her there, so she was determined to take full advantage of his being forced into this intimate position. With them all but sandwiching her, Eric began to do a booty pop behind Sasha while Jerome did slow hip rotations in front of her, slowly pulling off his shirt.

Sasha touched Jerome every chance she could get. She loved every response his body gave. She was then turned to face Eric and smiled in delight when she felt Jerome's erection against her backside. In an act of boldness, when Eric turned her back around to dance from behind her, she dragged her tongue across Jerome's chest, smiling to herself when she heard him suck in his breath.

When the music came to a stop, instead of letting her go back to her seat, Jerome grabbed her hand and pulled her offstage while Eric enjoyed the standing ovation as flowers and money was thrown onto the stage.

Jerome stepped behind stage, pausing only long enough to grab the robe that a young man, whose sole purpose was passing robes to the dancers after their performances, handed him. Jerome was unmindful of pulling Sasha so fast down the hallway that she was practically running to keep up with him as he stalked to his dressing room. Red looked up in surprise as they passed him down the hall, and when they reached Jerome's room, he pulled her inside and closed the door behind him.

He immediately turned around to face her, saying, "What's your game, Sasha? Because whatever it is, I'm not about playing." He shoved his arms into the robe, and then focused his full attention on her, his beautiful face looking cold and unwelcome.

Sasha spoke with all the calmness she wasn't feeling. "Do you have any idea how much I've missed you? That was really closed-minded of you not to accept any of my phone calls." She walked to him and kissed his neck and chest between the openings of the robe.

Jerome was highly affected, even though he didn't want to be, his body responded on cue. He stepped back from her to create space for himself in an attempt to not be so affected. "I can't see what you would want to talk to me about."

"I'm sorry for hurting you, it wasn't my intention. You just seemed to me to be another oversexed playboy using your popularity here to get laid. The last thing I wanted was someone to come on to me one night and move on to the next pretty girl the next night."

"But you changed your mind after you found out I was in med school," Jerome said cynically.

"Not when I found out you were in med school, but when I found out that you never offered private dances, that I was the only one you'd ever offered to do that for. When I asked my father about you, he could only sing your praises, but what I wanted to know was not what kind of future you have in front of you. I wanted to know if he'd ever seen you with a lot of girls, and if you *were* the oversexed playboy I thought you to be. When I finished talking to him, I asked who your friends were because I wanted to find out about you from a more personal standpoint. You know what they told me?"

Jerome shook his head, and Sasha took one step forward. "In a nutshell, they said they rarely see you with any girls and had wondered upon occasion if you were gay, except they never see you with any guys either." As though she was approaching a wounded animal, Sasha cautiously took another step forward.

Jerome cleared his throat softly, and when he spoke, his voice was very gentle, but his expression hadn't changed; it was still cold. "So what does that say to you about me?"

"That maybe I was wrong about you, that maybe you're not a playboy, and that you might just be able to make me extremely, deliriously happy."

"Well, I guess there's only one way to find out about that," Jerome whispered, absolutely mollified, and grabbed her arm, pulling her toward him. Once she was close enough, he leaned in for a kiss. Sasha placed her hand over his mouth just before their lips touched.

"Uh-uh, not so fast, big boy. I believe you have some groveling you need to do after the way you treated me that day and since."

"You're right. I'm sorry for acting that way. I guess being in a place like this for so long can make you a little cynical, but I'll make it up to you, if you let me. Will you do me a favor though? In the future when you want to know something about me, come to me."

"If I'd done that, then you'd have known I was interested."

Jerome smiled, conceding defeat, and once again leaned forward to kiss Sasha, and once again was stopped just short of his mark when the door flew open, and Eric came bursting in oozing excitement. Jerome released a loud sigh of frustration as Eric, not even noticing what the occupants of the room were doing, began to ramble.

"Oh, my goodness, can you believe that crowd? I think I had at least five requests for a private dance, and Sin said ... he ... wanted ... oh, my damn! Hey Romy, did I interrupt something? How are you, Sasha?"

"Eric, it's a pleasure to talk to you face to face."

Jerome interrupted a little impatiently. "What did you want that was so important that it couldn't wait 'til later?"

"Well, gosh, Romy, what's your hurry now? I mean, you've had the girl waiting all this time, so a few moments more isn't gonna hurt much." Eric tapped his temple playfully. "You owe me something, don't you?"

"No, *you* owe *me* something, and I want to see those enrollment forms in two weeks. Now why don't you go do a private dance or something?"

"Can't; don't have time. We're up for round two," Eric informed with glee on his way to the door, then looked Jerome up and down, noticing he was still in his robe and thong. "I hope you're not wearing that back out there," he said, closing the door behind him.

Jerome went to his closet and grabbed a change of costume, hurrying to get into it. His opening the door caught Sasha's attention, and she looked away from Jerome briefly to look at the buffet of color and texture. When she turned back around, he was completely nude, and she was transfixed. Sasha realized that although they had been intimate, she'd never seen this part of him before. While it was true that he probably knew her body like the back of his hand, she'd been a receiver and enjoyer of every minute of it.

So she stared as though trying to memorize the shape and size of his penis. It was the same shade of tawny brown as the rest of him. It was very nice to look at, although not very imposing, and then he pulled his G-string up ever so slowly; all the while it began to grow without him even touching it. Its niceness became *fierce*, and her body responded. She looked up, and their eyes met. Hers with want, his with promise, both unmistakable.

Jerome shook himself as though from a daze and continued to dress, and once again with the help of Sasha, he was ready for his show.

# CHAPTER 12

When Eric left the room, he almost ran into Sin. Sin was just about to knock on Jerome's door when Eric came rushing out, as was the way of youth. "Where's your brother?"

"Inside there," Eric gestured with his thumb.

"Man, you guys were amazing out there! Let me go talk to him quickly."

Eric hadn't left the front of the door, and before Sin could reach past him to touch the knob, Eric spoke. "Uh, you might want to wait."

"For what?"

"He has a girl in there."

Sin laughed a little because Jerome never brought girls back there. In fact, he was so discreet with his women, that Sin hardly ever saw him with any. Jerome just didn't bother to make the time for a full-on relationship. "Yeah, right. Good one, Eric."

Inside of Jerome's dressing room, he checked himself in the mirror, running his fingers through his soft curls, and then he turned to look at Sasha. "Don't leave, okay? Will you wait for me here?"

"Not even. I won't miss this round two, because round one was hot!" Sasha said with a mock shiver.

Jerome smiled as he ushered Sasha out of the door and ran into Eric's back. Eric's grunt captured his attention, and over Eric's shoulder, Jerome made eye contact with an astonished Sin.

∼⧸𝒬⧹∼

After Jerome left work, he and Sasha went back to his condo, while Eric went out with Poison. "To give you guys some time alone," Eric had whispered to Jerome before disappearing off into the crowd.

Immediately after entering the condo, they began kissing passionately and taking off one another's clothes. Jerome picked Sasha up and carried her to the counter. After sitting her there, he quickly divested her of her remaining garments and then leaned down to kiss her hardened nub, sucking it between his lips.

Sasha moaned, her hips moving backward and forward while he made love to her with his tongue, but this time she was determined to give as much as she got, and so before her body reached its peak, she stopped him. She jumped down from the counter and kneeled before him, pulling his underwear off as she descended. She licked the tip of his manhood as soon as it sprang free, and then took as much of it into her mouth as she could fit. She moaned, loving the feel of it between her lips.

Jerome moaned at the hot, wet suction. His hips began to move, stroking in and out of her mouth. Afraid that he would release any moment, he pulled back and said, "Not like this," in his soft deep voice.

Her remedy was to pull Jerome onto the floor with her, where they lay with their bodies facing one another's in sixty-nine fashion, and as Jerome began suckling her again, he started to hum, creating a vibrating sensation. Sasha reached her orgasm almost instantly and continued to suckle Jerome through it, sucking harder and longer, causing him to spill his seed.

They lay on the floor, both temporarily replete. After a few moments, Jerome rose and pulled Sasha into his arms, carrying her to his bedroom.

∽⌒∾

The next day, Sasha and Jerome decided it was time to spend some time getting to know one another. They went to see a classic movie about a little girl with the ability to make fire. Jerome laughed through the entire movie even though it wasn't a comedy. When the movie was finished, they went to an ice cream shop.

They left the shop to walk together toward Jerome's condo with Sasha drinking a milkshake and Jerome licking an enormous three-scoop ice cream cone. On the way there, they reached a little park. Jerome grabbed her hand and steered her into the park. Sasha watched Jerome, entranced as he licked the melting ice cream. Her eyes followed the trail his tongue took. Jerome finally looked at Sasha and noticed the look on her face, and then he smiled knowingly.

Sasha looked away then. In an effort to take both of their minds away from the path hers had set, she started asking him questions. "So tell me about yourself."

"What would you like to know?"

"For starters, where are you from?"

"Connecticut. I was born and raised in the same house in a town called Manchester."

"What was it like growing up there?"

He shrugged, "Fair. We had a good upbringing, and our share of fights. I wanted more than fair for my own family though."

"When did you decide you wanted to become a doctor?"

"When I was in the third grade, my class had a career day. One of the students had his dad come to tell about his job. He was a doctor who made being one sound so exciting. When I was a little older, I had an occasion to go to that kid's house. They lived on the other side of our school zone. Their home was amazing to me. I knew I wanted that for myself, so I decided to become a doctor when I grew up. I knew it wouldn't be easy, so I worked hard to keep up my grades, and I got a partial scholarship to Johns Hopkins University to study premed. I've applied at the hospital for my residency too."

It was a typical humid August day and the trees were heavy with green leaves, so his ice cream was melting faster than he could eat it. Jerome stopped talking long enough to lick away the new melted cream. Sasha looked away, trying not to notice the way he looked doing something so seemingly innocent, but then she saw how many other girls in the park noticed him too, and was struck anew by how utterly gorgeous this man walking beside her really was. With his soft, even-toned skin, deep dimples, almond-shaped eyes, and head full of soft, loose curls, he had the exotic look of a biracial man, and she made a mental note to ask him about that because even though she knew he was not completely black, she couldn't really tell what he was mixed with.

Although Jerome had a napkin he could have wiped his hands with, he was really enjoying what he knew his licking was doing to Sasha, so he licked each of the fingers on one hand clean one by one, while the ice cream began to soil the hand he'd transferred it to.

He gave her a sideways look, and one of his dimples appeared, making her realize that he was doing it all on purpose. "Will you please stop it? People are watching."

He stopped teasing her and picked up where he'd left off with his information about himself. "While he was alive, my dad took care of my necessities, and the things that my scholarship didn't cover. I finished premed, and was just getting settled here for med school. I was to begin in the fall that year when my dad passed away. At that point, he'd been paying for over 75 percent of my finances." Jerome gestured to an empty picnic table under a shade of trees, and they sat down, each finishing their treats before Sasha asked any more questions.

She frowned in sympathy, "I'm sorry about your dad, but why didn't you get financial aid?"

"What, think I didn't try? Believe me, I tried with everything, but you'd be surprised to know that not a lot of students can get financial aid so far into their studies, especially when they're half-way through. I can still remember the conversation I had with the dean when I came back to school after my dad's funeral."

"What was that like?" She asked, completely absorbed in his story.

"Well, I was sitting in Dean Winston's office with the financial aid officer, and they were trying to figure out how to get emergency funding for me to keep me from having to drop out of college. I remember her name was Martha, because he kept calling her by her given name. She said, 'It's almost impossible to be given a grant this late in the semester, but even if we could get you any, it wouldn't cover everything, and you no longer qualify for a scholarship.'"

Jerome deepened his voice in an imitation of the Dean's gruff-sounding voice: "Dean Winston said, 'What's he supposed to do then, Martha? This advanced into his studies, am I to tell the boy he has to quit school?' He asked her, so she said, 'I'm not saying he has to quit, but he may want to look into getting a job to help pay for his classes. Also, it may not be completely out of the question to get an approval from a bank for a loan.' So Dean Winston goes, 'We both know no bank is going to give a loan to a student, especially when they can't receive repayment for it any time soon.' Then he said, 'Well, Martha, there must be something we can do for a kid with his level of academic achievements.'"

What Jerome didn't know was that her dad and Dean Winston had known one another for years. Sasha laughed because Jerome's affectation of her father's old friend was spot-on. "Then what happened?"

Jerome continued, "Martha clicked around on her computer for a little while, then said, 'We can give him a one-time dean's choice award,' so the dean asked, 'How much Martha?' So she goes, 'fifteen thousand.' So the dean said, 'That won't cover one year, but it will take care of now.' Then he looked at me and said, 'How many more semesters can you pay for on your own?' I told him two, but they would only cover the classes and dorm. So he told me, 'Then I would suggest you get yourself an off-campus apartment and use the money you would have used for your dorm room to pay the rent up as far as you can pay it. Then go job hunting. You'll be able to save up a bit with having your rent paid up. Try finding a job as a waiter, they tend to do pretty well in tips. There are a lot of professionals who have paid their way through school doing just that. Let me know if you need any assistance.'"

Sasha was still chuckling when Jerome finished his one-man tell-all. He smiled at her smile. She rested her chin on her left hand while her right hand rested on the picnic table. Jerome reached out and grabbed her hand, he rubbed his thumb across her knuckles, marveling at how much he felt for her in such a short time. He barely knew her, but that didn't seem to matter to his heart. He raised her hand to his lips, planted a kiss on each knuckle, and admitted to himself that his infatuation with her began the moment he'd seen her in the club. It had never gone away, but had gotten stronger since.

He felt a need to close the space between them. He stood, walked to her side of the bench, and sat beside her. He sat staring at her for such a long time that she leaned over and nudged his shoulder with hers.

She asked, "Tell me more about your visit with the dean?"

"He patted me on the back as he walked me to the door, but I remember the look they exchanged between each other when they thought I wasn't looking."

"What kind of look?"

"It was like a, this kid is doomed look." He glanced at her as if he had a dirty secret.

She smiled. "What?"

"Okay, so the look they exchanged made me wonder what was going on with them, so I stuck around and eavesdropped a little when they closed the door."

"You eavesdropped?" she asked, sounding scandalized. At his nod she asked, "What did you hear?"

"Something that made me even more determined to succeed. The dean said to Martha, 'That young man has a tough road ahead of him. It's going to take great perseverance to see him as the doctor he wants to become, and with so many obstacles he has to overcome, I don't know if he is ready to face those challenges.' So Martha goes, 'Maybe his desire to become a doctor will help get him the stick-to-itiveness he's going to need to get through this.'" Jerome looked up at the sky. "They were both right, I didn't have a clue how hard it would be."

She laid her head on his shoulder, "But you've done it." But she did wonder about one thing, and decided to ask, "Why didn't your dad have any money saved to pay your tuition?"

"He'd saved as best he could, $40,000 to be exact, and you know that doesn't last long in college, but he didn't know that. That money was gone in two years, and if not for my scholarship, it would've been gone before then. So by the time he died, he was paying with money he'd gotten as a loan from his job. He'd been there for a long time, so they had no problem giving it to him and just taking back a small amount to pay themselves back with from his paychecks, and then, of course, he had Eric and my two sisters to see to as well. Jessica, my sister just younger than me, was in college too."

"So there are four of you, and you're the oldest?"

"Yes. Then there is Jessica, who is twenty-four. Eric is twenty-one, and Liana is seventeen. Let's head back. I'm feeling sticky from eating ice cream in August."

"You didn't seem to mind five minutes ago." He smiled impenitently as he stood. They began walking, and once again she noticed the women's stares as they passed them by. She also noticed Jerome's lack of attention to the constant looks of admiration he received. His eyes seemed to be for her only. He kept looking at her like she was the only woman in the world, and that look was intoxicating to her. As they headed back to his apartment, Sasha was too intrigued by the window into his becoming a dancer that he'd opened for her to let him stop. "So what got you into stripping?"

"The money."

"A regular job could have gotten you money."

"Yes, but not enough to pay my way through med school, pay for an apartment, and send money home to my family."

"So your mom depends on you?"

"Not entirely now, but when my dad first passed she did. She'd been a stay-at-home mom. She'd left her job to take care of us, and hadn't worked in years. She told me she needed me to come home and get a job to help out. She figured with the bachelor's I already had, that I should have been able to get a pretty decent job to help with my sisters and brother, that I really didn't have to go to med school. I'd gotten further than my dad had, and in her eyes that was good enough."

Her heart was bursting with emotions for this man. He'd been burdened with so many obstacles in his quest to become a doctor, and he'd met them all head-on. She marveled at his strength. She knew she wasn't that strong, knew that if she'd come to the same circumstances with her dad that he'd come to with his mom, she would have quit. She'd have done whatever her dad told her to do. "Did he not have a life insurance policy then?"

"Sure he did. It paid off most of the mortgage." He began ticking the list of debtors they were obliged to pay with the insurance money. "The debt he owed, including his employer for my schooling, my next two semesters in school, and my first six months payment on my off-campus apartment. It was cheaper than staying in the dorm room. It also bought me more time. So with that time, I went to find a job, and so did my mom, and my sister Jessica."

They entered the apartment with Jerome heading to the kitchen to prepare refreshments while Sasha looked around. After she was done looking at the portraits, she came to the island to watch him.

"So this is the off-campus apartment you got after leaving the dorms? It's very nice."

"Actually no." He smiled, "The apartment I had was not so nice, but then I was looking for a roof at that time, and was desperate enough to sleep in a shack if I had to, to keep from dropping out of college and giving up my dream."

"So you went into stripping?"

"Well, I tried out a few other things, but none of them paid me what I needed to make to be able to stay in school, and then one day while I was at my job as a waiter, I had this customer, he was a big tipper, good-looking guy, and I knew he wasn't much older than myself. So I asked him what he did to be able to afford to tip like that. It was bold of me, I know, but what did I have to lose, right? He told me he was a dancer and then asked if I was interested in giving it a go."

Finished preparing them both cups of tea, he ushered Sasha into the living room to sit on the sofa. Jerome waited for Sasha to get settled, and then he handed her one of the mugs before he seated himself next to her. Then he continued with the story he'd only told a couple of other people, one being his closest friend, Montgomery.

"I told him that was not my thing, and he said, 'Suit yourself. You certainly have the look for it,' and then he said, 'A guy with a face like yours could make a killing, that is if you have the right body to go along with it.' So what kind of body is that? I asked him, and he said, 'The kind with no flab; you know, tight abs, nice pecks … it wouldn't hurt if you were packing a little bit too.'"

Sasha kicked off her shoes and curled up on the sofa, laying her head in his lap.

He stroked her hair and continued, "So I told him that was definitely not my thing and that I'd take my chances at the restaurant. Then he asked me, 'How much money do you make here?' When I told him what I made in a week, he laughed and said, 'Dude, I could make that in an hour.' I went to meet his boss the next day and started working the day after. I got this place the following year." Jerome stopped talking to look at her for a while, and then he said, "So enough about me. Let's talk about you."

Sasha sat up and took a sip of her tea and then, holding the mug balanced on her knee, she looked at Jerome and said, "Just so you know, my dad was not happy to find out you're a stripper."

"That's not a surprise. Most people's attitudes change when you tell them something like that, especially if their daughter is considering dating the guy."

"Well my dad's was no different. He wants me to stop seeing you all together."

"What do *you* want to do?"

"I want to love you."

"Now?"

"Now works for me."

"No. First we'll get into your head and find out some things about you," he said, kissing her neck. His hand trailed down her stomach to get lost in her pants.

She cleared her throat. "Well, I'm the younger of two girls. My dad is a professor here, as you know, and he was a reconstructive surgeon for some years before he decided to retire," she gasped out.

"What made him decide to retire?" Jerome asked, watching the look of pleasure on her face as his finger made circles on the tiny nerve-filled nub between her thighs.

"Just got tired and wanted a change of pace. I think my mom had something to do with it too. She was tired of hardly ever seeing him because he was always on call. He was retired for all of a year when he started driving my mom crazy, because he was bored, so she suggested he take a side job. Dean Winston hired him, and he's been there since. So what kind of doctor are you going to be?"

"A neurosurgeon. I have a lot of interning to do, though, so I really won't be making a lot of money for a while."

Her hips started moving. "You make pretty good money dancing, I take it?"

"Oh, yeah."

"Approximately how much?"

"Let's put it this way. It's been three years, and I own this apartment, and my mom now owns the house. I have practically paid Jessica's college tuition, and I have money saved for Liana when she's ready for college."

"Wow, Romy, that's a lot of money. So how much?"

"More than I will make as a neurosurgeon. Now can we stop talking about this?" Jerome leaned forward and kissed her, slowly sliding his hand up and under her shirt. Her moan told him when he had the right spot, and his slow perusal became a mutual quick disrobing that ended with Sasha straddling his lap and riding him with wild intensity. They never left the sofa.

After they'd exhausted their passion, it occurred to Sasha that she had not asked him about his ancestry, so she asked, "What's your nationality, Romy?"

"Does it matter?" Jerome asked curiously.

"No, I was just interested because of your pretty face."

"Pretty face, huh," he said with a frown. "The last person who said that to me got a black eye. I was in fourth grade, but I'm sure I could do it again."

"Are you threatening me?" she said laughing.

"Just in case you take the notion to say that to me again, you might want to remember that."

"Well, you do have a pretty face."

He grabbed her and tossed her on her back on the sofa and then straddled her, holding her arms with one hand and tickling her with the other.

She laughed and squirmed until tears came out of her eyes, and then she conceded defeat with an, "I'm sorry. I'll never say it again."

He released her then, looking awfully proud of himself, which made her laugh even harder.

After they settled back down, he answered her question. "I'm primarily black. My father's dad was half black and half white, and his mom was half black and half Indian. And my mom is half black and half Puerto Rican. So I guess if I had to put it into percentages, I would have one half black, one fourth Latin, one eighth white, and one eighth Indian. Wow, I've never done that before. Those are a lot of cultures to keep up with."

"Have you?"

"No. My dad used to take us to the Indian powwow every summer, but outside of that, we just lived, not really concerned about our race."

"You don't have to be concerned to know your heritage, Romy. It is a beautiful thing, all of the cultures you carry, and they blend well 'cause hot damn, boy, are you fine."

His smile was warm, then he changed the subject, "Tell me what you want to do when you grow up."

Sasha told him all about her plan for her Bistro, and Jerome's fascination with her grew.

## CHAPTER 13

*E*ric and Poison went to one of Poison's favorite spots. The drinks and drugs came fast and ready. Poison passed a joint to Eric, and after Eric accepted the joint, he took a long drag then handed it back. Poison then handed him a shot of liquor, and Eric tossed it down.

"Oh, man, this is good stuff." Eric could feel his head going foggy. He noticed a pretty girl across the room, so he danced his way over to her. When she looked at him, he spoke somewhat drunkenly, "Hey, beautiful, how about you come and dance with me?"

The girl smiled at Eric and walked with him onto the dance floor.

After a few rounds of dancing, drinking, and drugs, Eric, Poison, and the girls they picked up left the club and rented a motel room for a couple of hours. After their time was finished in the motel room, they all left. Eric and Poison had to get ready for work.

Jerome didn't see Eric that evening until it was time for them to perform, and by that time Eric had gotten himself under control, so he was functioning with some semblance of being sober.

Nirvana would be the word Jerome would use to describe the following couple of weeks. He had the girl of his dreams, his grades had vastly improved, and Eric was spending a little less time with Poison. Jerome was sitting at his office desk studying when Eric walked in with some papers in his hand.

He sauntered to Jerome with the papers and playfully waved them under Jerome's nose. "Guess what these are?"

"What, top paper?"

"Ha! Very funny, jackass, it's my notice that my application was received and that they'll be contacting me soon to let me know if I'm accepted or not."

"Hey, let me see that!" Jerome was so excited he jumped out of his seat and grabbed the letter from Eric, scanning it quickly, and then he grabbed Eric into a bear hug. Eric extricated himself from his brother's strong arms, feeling a little embarrassed by the display of affection, to say, "See, I told you I'd do it. You know, just because I party a little doesn't mean I don't want to do something with my life."

Jerome was looking at Eric with a smile of accomplishment, but after he finished that statement, began to look at him with skepticism plain on his face. There were some things he could say about that, but he decided not to because he was in too good a mood, so he snorted, picked up the phone, and dialed. "Let's call Mom; she'll be so—" Jerome was cut off from what he was saying when someone on the other line answered the phone. "—Liana, Hey, girl, how are you?"

Liana sat down in a chair to talk to her oldest brother. He was her hero, and she loved her conversations with him. "I'm fine. I started putting in applications for college. How's Eric? I miss him so much."

"He's fine. Hey, what am I, chopped liver?"

"No, it's just that you've been gone forever, so it's natural not to see you. Eric has only been gone for a couple of months so …"

"Yeah, so?"

"So I'll go get Mom."

While Jerome spoke to Liana on the phone, Eric went to answer the door after hearing the doorbell ring. He opened the door to see Sasha and smiled his warmest smile as he invited her inside. "Come in and get comfortable. Romy will be out in a few minutes. He's on the phone with the home-front."

Jerome listened to Liana as she spoke of everything that was important to a seventeen-year-old girl until she passed the phone to their mother. He could hear Liana say, "Mom, the phone is for you."

"Who is it?" their mother asked Liana.

"Jerome, and he sounds really happy. I think he has some good news. Maybe he's getting married."

"Oh, that's rich," Their mother took the phone, laughing, and placed it on her ear, "Hey, Jerome, what's up!"

Jerome smiled to himself thinking how nice it was to hear his mother laugh again. "I just thought you would be happy to know that your son has finally applied for college and will likely be starting with the next semester."

"Shut up! Are you serious? How are you going to pay for all of this? Is that going to be too much?"

"Eric has his own job, so he'll be paying for most of it. He's decided to start hanging with some riffraff, though, and I'm a bit concerned about that, but I think once he starts classes he won't have time to think about the partying."

"You know that was one of my main concerns here. He was just getting into too much. It's not that he's a bad kid. He's just too fun-loving to take anything seriously. That's why I wanted him there with you, so maybe he could pick up on your self-discipline."

"Yeah, well, don't hold your breath, I'm just taking this one step at a time, and right now, I'm happy to have him getting into college. Once he's there, we'll concentrate on keeping him there, and out of trouble, restless soul that he is."

Eric knocked on the study door that he'd closed on his way

out of the room ten minutes past. Jerome looked up just as Eric's head popped into the opening as he pushed the door open a little. "We got tired of waiting for you to stop gabbing." Eric opened the door with a flourish and ushered Sasha inside.

Jerome, on the phone, spoke in response to a question his mom asked. "Yes, that's him now." He paused, listening to what his mom was saying on the other line. "Hold on a minute." Jerome passed the phone to Eric. "She wants to talk to you."

Eric took the phone and placed it on his ear. "Hey, Mom, how's my favorite girl in the world?" Eric paused to listen to whatever his mother was saying on the other end. "Of course I'm not giving him a hard time. Did he tell you that? (Pause) Yep, got a job, a good-paying one, too (pause) in a club (pause). Oh, god no mom. It's very classy—in fact, it's where Jerome met his new love, the daughter of a college professor."

Eric paused again, listening to his mother, and then he feigned a scandalized look. With laughter in his eyes and mock surprise in his voice, he said, "You mean he didn't tell you? Well, I can't imagine why, as much as he talks about her, it's always Sasha this and Sasha that. Why it's enough to make you wanna puke. (Pause) Sure, but what about our talk? (Pause) Why? Did you want to meet her? Yeah, she's standing right here with the ever-frowning doctor. (Pause) Sure, hold on a minute."

Eric smiled impishly as he handed the phone to Sasha. "My mom wants to meet you."

Sasha took the phone from Eric and placed it to her ear, all the while never taking her eyes from Jerome, who was frowning angrily at Eric. "Hello, Mrs. Jacobs, it's a pleasure to meet you, and I hope that maybe someday we can meet face to face." Sasha took a seat, smiling at whatever Jerome's mom was saying on the other line. Jerome shoved Eric out of the room and pushed him down the hall and out of earshot.

"Why did you do that?" Jerome asked Eric once they reached the living room.

"Took the spotlight off of me. I told you not to be trying to bust my chops like that, Romy, especially when you've got so much dirt to uncover."

"I did what I had to do to support my family! It's called responsibility. I don't regret it and neither would I change it if I could. I warned you about trying to blackmail me. Don't forget that I'm still the man of the house and the one supporting this family, and I can and will make your life a living hell if you pull another stunt like that."

Eric put up his hands, and replied with feigned severity, "You're the man; no one's contesting that. Gosh, do you have to be so dang uptight about everything? You really need to lighten up sometimes. You constantly make me wonder how you can be such a headliner with that stick up your butt, and what really surprises me is that no one has noticed it yet. I mean, how do you bend over without one of your groupies seeing it?"

Jerome began to laugh, unable to remain mad at the incorrigible scamp. He replied with a smile, "With great finesse, dear boy, with great finesse."

The ringing of Eric's cell phone halted their conversation. Eric answered his phone and listened to the person on the other line for a few seconds before hanging up. "I gotta get going."

"Hanging out with Poison again tonight?"

"Please don't start nagging again, Romy."

"I'm not nagging. I'm just saying this dude is bad news, and you need to heed my warning before something really bad happens, and it's too late. You aren't getting all strung out like him, are you?"

Eric grabbed his keys on the way to the door, opened the door, and then turned to Jerome long enough to say, "I've got this under control. Stop worrying about me. I'm a big boy and I can handle myself. I assure you I'm not doing anything here with Poison that I wasn't already doing."

"Oh, yeah, that's reassuring!"

Eric left the apartment, closing the door softly behind him. Jerome turned to head back to his study and straighten up his classwork when he noticed Sasha standing quietly in the entrance to the living room, leaning against the wall with her legs crossed nonchalantly. Jerome walked to her and leaned forward to kiss her.

Sasha indulged herself in the all too consuming kiss, because there was something she wanted to say to him, and she didn't know how he was going to take it. She wrapped her arms around his waist, pulling him closer and coming into contact with his erection. She had to stop before this went too far. Sasha pulled back from the kiss, and when she looked into Jerome's eyes, she saw the question there. She didn't wait for him to ask it but went straight into what she'd wanted to say, hoping he would be open-minded about it. "I think you need to stop treating Eric like a child. He's grown, you know."

"When he starts to act like an adult, then I'll treat him like one."

"Well maybe he'll start acting like one when you start treating him like one. He's a very intelligent man, and I don't think you give him enough credit for that. He looks up to you too. It must be hard living in your footsteps, first with your mom, and then she sends him here so you can "turn him into a man," and you're constantly ragging on him. Show him that you trust his judgment and that you respect him as the man he has become, and stop looking at him as the baby brother whom you've been responsible for, for the last four years."

"I do trust him. I just don't trust his choice of friends, or some of his life choices, so I just figured I'd tweak him in the right direction."

"Essentially what you're saying is you don't trust your brother. Hey, listen, not everybody knows from birth what they want to do with their lives like you did. Some people need to play around with a few ideas first, maybe even enter the school of hard knocks before they have an epiphany. I believe Eric is one of those people, he'll get it together."

"So what you're saying in layman's terms is I need to back off and let him make his own mistakes?"

"Yes, and I'm sure you raised him right," she joked, "so he'll see the light and probably become a great success at whatever he chooses to be in life."

"How did you get to be so smart?"

"My dad's a surgeon. Remember?" They both smiled, Jerome leaned forward to claim a kiss, but Sasha held him off once again.

He looked confused. "This talk isn't over?"

"I want to talk about something else that's been bothering me."

"You talk," he said, leaning forward to plant tiny nibbling kisses on her earlobe.

"Jerome, I'm serious."

He pulled back, took a deep breath, and ran his fingers through his hair, "Okay."

"Define our relationship."

His brows shot up. "Huh?"

She pointed her finger back and forward between them. "What are we? Is this a fling?" He shook his head. "Are we in a relationship?"

"I thought we were."

"Are we exclusive?"

He stared at her for a brief moment. That last question finally clued him in. She wanted to know if he had any other women. He smiled.

That smile looked guilty to her, and it hurt. She hadn't even known him long. She'd been in a relationship with Malcolm for three years, and it hadn't hurt her to find out he'd been cheating. Angered, yes, but hurt, no. Their relationship wasn't even defined, yet the thought of him with another woman tore at her insides. "You asshole," she turned away.

He reached out and grabbed her arm. "Hey, there's no one else."

"Liar. You're telling me, as many women, beautiful women, you deal with on a regular basis, that you aren't hooking up with any of them, and you want me to believe that?"

"Yes," She looked unconvinced. "Why would you ask the question if you weren't going to believe my answer?"

"Because I thought you would tell the truth about it."

"Okay, the truth is," he let a long moment go by before pulling her to him to finish, "that you are the only woman I've been with since the first time I met you."

She smiled a little, almost placated, "Really? Why?"

"Simply put, no one else would do." That statement, spoken so matter-of-factly, led them to a kiss that led into the bedroom, where they spent the rest of the evening until it was time for Jerome to prepare for work.

# CHAPTER 14

*O*utside of the apartment building, Eric had just stepped onto the curb when the SUV Poison owned sped up. The tires screeched to a halt just in front of the building. The tinted window of a Lincoln Navigator slid smoothly down, "Hop in, dude. It's time for some fun."

Eric shook his head laughing and jumped into the car, and placed his seatbelt across his lap just as the car sped away with tires screeching. "You know, I've always wondered how you could afford to keep this car."

"I make really good money at the club? Not as good as your brother, though." Poison handed a little packet to Eric. It was filled with thin purple-colored strips. "Here, try one of these. Those things are so good they'll have you going forever."

"What is it?"

"They're called lightning. They melt on your tongue and buzz you so fast you feel like you've been hit by lightning."

"No man, that's too much for me. I'll stick to what I know."

"Oh, come on, don't tell me you're gonna go all Romy on me."

"Hey, I got my limits. There's things I just won't do. I'll leave the experimenting to you."

"Hey, suit yourself," Poison said just before he pulled one of the wafer-thin strips from the bag, preparing to place it on his tongue.

Eric grabbed Poison's hand just before it reached his mouth, causing Poison to look at him curiously. "No lightning while you're driving, eh? I wanna live to see my next birthday."

Poison looked at Eric in mock horror as though he was seeing the devil himself. "My goodness, you are getting Romy on me."

Eric rolled his eyes.

Fifteen minutes later, they pulled up at the front of a house. Two young women came rushing out. Eric stepped out of his seat and opened the back door preparing to seat himself with his date, but Poison had other plans, because at the same time Eric was getting out of the car, Poison was opening his door to step out.

Poison grabbed one of the girls and kissed her hard before looking up at Eric to say, "You drive this time while we play around a little back here." After getting settled into the car, Eric pulled off with his girl for the night beside him. Poison sat in the back seat with his girl for the night. She was already unbuttoning his shirt. "Hey, sweetie, you ever try lightning?" Poison asked. He pulled out two of the little strips and placed one on his tongue and the other on hers.

With the music pumping in the car and half of the occupants high on lightning, the group sped along to their destination, which was toward whatever trouble they could get into.

Jerome and Eric came in to work together, each on their own motorcycles. They walked toward the stairs to enter The Sinful Pleasure, but Jerome paused when a group of women stepped out of their car prepared to party, and walked toward the building. The music was loud enough that it could be heard from the outside, as the club was just waking up. When one of the women noticed Jerome and Eric, she tapped the others to turn their attention, gesturing toward the handsome brothers walking their way.

Jerome noticed the interaction, and in an effort to avoid the pawing that he knew would come if they attempted to maneuver through a group of tipsy, horny women, he grabbed Eric's arm and pulled him in the opposite direction toward the alley, leading to the back of the club where most of the entertainers entered.

Eric allowed himself to be dragged in by his brother but couldn't resist asking him as soon as they reached the back door of the club, "Dude, what was that all about?"

The sounds of music and laughter filled the air as the brothers entered the club and began walking down the hall toward their dressing room. "I didn't feel like being the wildebeest caught in the middle of those lionesses. They looked hungry."

"Well, maybe you didn't want to, but I certainly would've loved it," Eric grumbled just loud enough for Jerome to hear. Then he asked, "So, have you asked her to marry you yet?"

Jerome looked at Eric with a cross between amusement and disgust on his handsome face. "What gives you the idea that I would do something like that?"

"It's obvious that you're in love with her. She makes you happy, and for the first time in a really long time I actually see you being young again. You know that's something you haven't been able to do since dad died, and now I realize how much strain you've been under trying to support us all."

Disregarding the latter statement because he didn't want to look at the truth behind it, and the enormous responsibility that he was even now still carrying on his shoulders, Jerome elected to tackle the former statement because it was easier to think about. "It's only been a few months, Eric. You don't ask someone to marry you after only three months of dating."

"Hell, I don't see why not."

"It's just bad protocol. Not only that, but it smacks of obsession."

Eric laughed as Jerome rolled his eyes while letting loose a brief show of dry wit. His brother actually had a great sense of humor when he wasn't being the responsible man of the house that it really wasn't his responsibility to be. Sometimes he thought their mom had done Jerome a disservice by heaping such a heavy weight on the shoulders of the man-child he was, and forcing him to grow up overnight. "You know she would say yes, 'cause she's in love with you, too."

"Yeah, well, I don't know, not with her dad disapproving of us."

Eric shrugged, "You guys do seem to have that forbidden love thing going on."

As they neared Sin's office, he stopped them calling them inside. He gestured for the brothers to be seated, waiting until they were both sitting before he handed them envelopes, and then he began his brief speech. "I wanted to show my appreciation by giving you guys that. I also wanted to ask you to become a permanent duo, dancing together three nights a week."

Eric opened his envelope and looked at the check inside. His eyes opened wide with shock upon seeing a $15,000 bonus check. "Holy crap, I'm in!"

Eric leaned toward Jerome to show him what the check had written on it. Jerome nodded his head in acknowledgement, not bothering to open his own check. He'd been down this road with Sin before, and although his generosity was appreciated, it always came with a price. Jerome turned back to look at Sin, his face inscrutable.

Sin knew Jerome knew his game, so he came straight to the point. "It's just a little bonus, probably a bribe too." Sin turned to Eric then, addressing his next comment to him. "That's how I keep Jerome here with me and away from all of the scouts who're constantly trying to sway him to their clubs."

Jerome finally spoke to Sin. "A bonus like this means we did even better than I at first thought."

Sin looked at Jerome for a long minute, and in that time the expression on the young man's face never changed. He didn't even blink. Sin knew he needed to be completely honest with him. It hadn't always been this way. When Jerome had first come to work for him, he'd been so happy to have gotten the job and been making the kind of money he was making that he never questioned anything asked of him. He was then a lot like Eric was now. Just give him a bonus, and he was in.

But Jerome and his performances had been what turned Sin's place around. He'd employed spot-lighters before, but Jerome came in with an enthusiasm that was just what the club needed to hit the top, and as a result he owned the number one club in the metropolitan area. People came from miles around to view his dancers. Even Jerome doing special performances in Vegas, California, and select clubs in the Northeast region brought in more business for Sinful Pleasure.

He'd begun to have Jerome train other new dancers to the club, which made them hot commodities too, but most of them came and went, and he was certain that one of the main reasons Jerome was so sought-after was because he was so hard to get. So Sin did whatever was necessary to keep him. Sin answered Jerome in all honesty. "You more than doubled your original audience, and the house take went through the roof."

Without changing his tone or the look on his face, Jerome spoke. "Wow, then shouldn't we get a bit more than we're getting? I mean, I understand the bonus and all, but that's a one-time deal. You, on the other hand, are profiting every time we do this duo, and now you want us to do it even more."

"It's really your audience, Romy."

Jerome lifted his eyebrow in a gesture of skepticism. It was his audience, and he was constantly bringing in new clientele, but he was getting tired of the constant bids for his work, tired of the pawing women; tired of people thinking they had a right to his body because of what he did; tired of hiding, tired of the whole thing. Sure he earned a lot of money doing this, but he'd also made Sin a millionaire. If he knew when he first started what he now knew, he would be one along with Sin. He'd learned a lot about the business working at the club, and touring, and he was transcending. He was ready for the next level. He wanted to get Eric to that point now before he reached a point where he was tired of the whole thing too. "Here by popular demand ... hmm, that's telling."

"Oh, come on, Jerome. I take good care of you, and you know it. I mean, I've seen your apartment."

"I've worked very hard for that apartment, and I know you've taken good care of me, but don't mistake the fact that everything I've earned in the last three years has not come solely from you and this establishment. What I also know is that I, along with the gaping Eric here, am now responsible for more than 60 percent of the club's earnings."

Sin did not try to negate that last statement. He just resignedly asked, "What do you want me to do?"

After a few moments of silence, Jerome replied, "Let me think about it and get back to you on it. In the meantime, I'm in for the extra work. It'll give Eric a leg up on that college tuition, but can we make it twice a week instead of three, just for now?" Jerome's next comment was accompanied by mischievous glee. "Oh, and just for a heads-up, I'm thinking about a percentage, maybe even a co-ownership. Think about it too, will ya?"

Sin was shocked by his request but wasn't certain if he joked or not.

Eric had been so busy thinking of all of the things he could do with the money that he hadn't paid much attention to the conversation. Hearing Jerome mention tuition brought his attention to the proceedings. "Huh? Oh, yeah, tuition, but can't I spend some of it? I mean, fifteen grand."

"Sure you can spend some," Jerome said as he ushered Eric out of the office, "after you deposit some into your account, and after you get yourself a new costume." Jerome smiled at the disgruntled looked on Eric's face. "Gotta represent, and after you send some home to Mom."

Sin could hear Eric grumbling about how little money would be left after all of that, and he laughed to himself. "He's going to make a man out of him yet."

Sin sat down at his desk to look at some reports concerning his business ventures. He thought about Jerome's proposition and decided he was willing to grant him just about anything he asked for, simply because he knew the quality of work Jerome displayed. A man would be a fool to let him go to any of his competitors. His train of thought was interrupted by a noise outside of his office. It sounded as though someone had fallen. Frowning, he stood up and walked toward the door. He heard the sound again and sped up his pace.

Sin looked into the hallway and saw Poison stumble, right himself, and stumble again. Sin shook his head as Poison, obviously under the influence of some unnamed narcotic, continued his stumbling gait up the hall. When Poison finally reached Sin's office, Sin grabbed Poison's arm as he almost stumbled again, this time into Sin. Poison, in his intoxication, allowed Sin to assist him into the office, leaning on his considerable strength. After Sin steadied Poison, he shoved him into his office, causing Poison to stumble yet again. Sin was angry, and he wanted Poison to know it.

"Damn it, Poison, I told you not to come here like this again! What the hell have you been taking that you can't even stand up straight, and what the hell am I supposed to do with you?"

Poison slumped down on the same couch that Jerome and Eric vacated ten minutes earlier, his bloodshot eyes opening wide at the anger in Sin's voice. Poison's words slurred so that he was barely understandable, "Just let me rest and I'll be fine in a little while." His eyelids closed slowly as though being pulled by lead weights, and in the brief silence, he began to fall asleep.

Sin was not just angry; he was incensed, and he yelled, "Hell, no! You're supposed to be preparing for a show, and if you're not gonna dance, then you need to go the hell home!"

Poison jumped at Sin's yell. Why didn't Sin understand that he did his best work this way? He just needed a little more time to come down. "I *am* gonna dance, Sin. I just need a little time. Can't you stall for me and just buy me an hour?"

"You don't make enough money with your strung-out self to buy an hour!"

Jerome and Eric were both in Jerome's dressing room preparing for the night's entertainment when they heard Sin yelling. Jerome looked up from strapping his black leather pants together, wondering what was causing Sin to yell so furiously but not bothering to go see.

They heard Sin again, and this time Red came to the door, opened it after a brief knock, and said, "What do you think that's all about?"

Jerome responded by shrugging his shoulders.

Eric closed his belt, replying, "I don't know, but I'm going to find out," as he headed to the door.

"I'm right with you, buddy," Red said, starting down the hall.

Jerome followed behind almost as curious as the other two. They all reached Sin's office in differing stages of undress. Jerome stopped at the door while Eric and Red stepped inside. Sin stood over an obviously high Poison, who was passed out on his sofa. Jerome looked at Sin. Sin looked as though he was ready to do Poison bodily harm, and not for the first time he wondered about the background that Sin kept such a closely guarded secret.

"What's all the commotion about, Sin? We could hear you yelling all the way down the hall," Red said.

Jerome knew already what the answer would be. Poison had come to work high off of his rocker again.

"This fool just came stumbling in here high and probably

drunk too, and then he goddamned passed out on my lounge!"
Sin spoke in agitated tones.

Red looked at Jerome after resting Poison on the arm of the
chair to keep him from falling forward. "Hey, Romy, you might
wanna take a look at him real quick. He doesn't look too good."

Sin nodded in agreement with Red. "Yeah, you may need to
give him a diagnosis."

Jerome shook his head, grunting in disapproval, "None
needed. What he does need is to go to a detox center and then
maybe a twelve-step program."

Eric began to laugh at that diagnosis and covered his mouth
to stop the full outburst.

"It isn't funny, Er. You keep hanging around this loon, and
you'll be in the same condition in the not too distant future."

After making his prediction, Jerome walked inside of Sin's
office and hunched down to take a good look at Poison. Jerome
grabbed his wrist and looked at his watch at the same time. He
released his wrist, staring at Poison's chest to count his breathing.
He opened his eye to check his pupil. Finding all of his vitals much
lower than he would be comfortable with, Jerome tried to wake
Poison. He shook him vigorously a few times, calling out to him.
"Poison, can you hear me? Poison, if you can hear me calling you,
I need you to open your eyes."

When Poison didn't respond, but just lay there in his drug-induced state of unconsciousness, Jerome stood and turned to Sin.
"I don't know what he's been binging on, but I'm almost certain
it's been a medley of things. He's just on this side of an overdose,
and, to be honest with you, that can change at any time, because
we don't know what he's taken or how much of it has taken effect
yet. He'll need to be watched for the rest of the night until whatever's in his system has worn off. If I were you, though, I would
send him to the ER and let them bring him down and keep him
monitored. Unless, of course, you want to nurse him and make
certain he doesn't flatline."

"Hell no, I'm not nursing him! He'll be lucky if he has a job after this stunt!" Sin pulled his phone out of his pocket and called emergency to report a possible overdose.

Twenty minutes later, the commotion of a group of uniformed men rushing through the back halls of Sinful Pleasure, brought the other dancers out of their rooms to watch. There were four medics in all and they carried with them a gurney to transport Poison from the club to the ambulance. As the paramedics began to examine Poison, Jerome filled them in with the same info he'd given Sin, but with the medics he included Poison's vital statistics as of five minutes ago. As this all happened, one of the medics took his vitals as another wrote down the information. In rapid fire, the medic taking Poison's statistics called them out to the medic writing them down. "Pulse is fifty, respirations eight, blood pressure one hundred over sixty. Pulse oximetry is at 90 percent. Let's begin oxygen respiration."

The medics placed Poison on the gurney and put an oxygen mask on his face. Finally one of the medics separated himself from the others to ask, "Who's responsible for this guy?"

Sin's anger hadn't subsided, so his answer was given more sharply than he'd intended. "He's a grown man and therefore responsible for himself."

The medic holding the clipboard and writing suddenly stopped and looked up at the anger in Sin's voice. "Then you won't be going to the hospital with him?"

"No. I have a business to run. It was his decision to go get himself all strung out like that. He didn't ask for any help then, so why should I be the one to suffer for it now?"

"I see no reason why you should."

Eric looked around at all the faces of the people they worked with and saw that no one was willing to help. He swore under his breath, and then took a step forward. "I'll go with him."

Sin negated Eric's offer, "No, you won't. It's bad enough I'm now short by a dancer, and everybody's gonna have to pick up the slack for that. If you wanna go see him after work, that's on you, but right now you're on my time."

The medics rolled Poison to the door. Jerome cleared a path for them, then he gestured toward the departing group with Poison lying passed out on the gurney and said to Eric, "See that? That's the life of a jun—"

Eric held his hand up to stop Jerome from finishing his sentence. It was sad that Poison had come so close to outright overdosing, and it was a lesson that Eric was learning he didn't want to experience firsthand. "I'll stop hanging with him, Romy. Just don't rub it in right now while the boy is fighting for his life."

Jerome nodded his head in compassion for his brother's upset and patted him on the shoulder consolingly, then quietly exited the room.

As the crowd of onlookers dissipated, Sin took a deep breath, rubbing the back of his neck, and then turned toward Eric. "I guess you'd better get yourself ready, kid. You and your brother are in for a long night. You'll both have two extra dances to cover Poison's absence."

Eric nodded and walked down the hall toward his dressing room.

The ambulance screeched to a halt in front of the emergency entrance of the hospital. The attendants in the front of the truck jumped out and quickly moved to the back and opened the door to move the gurney with Poison still passed out on it. They entered the hospital, and immediately a flash of light and sound permeated the air. The sound of people and babies crying, and people talking, could be heard as the paramedics quickly rolled Poison toward the admittance section.

The medics stopped in front of the admittance desk used for emergency patients delivered to the ER. Jason, one of the medics, began filling in paperwork while Drake, the other, began to explain Poison's condition in a no-nonsense tone of voice.

"He's a dancer at The Sinful Pleasure nightspot. The owner called in about 10:00 p.m. complaining that he had come in and passed out in his office."

"What are they saying caused him to pass out?" Natalie the admittance nurse asked as she began to write down what would be pertinent information for the doctors on call.

"One of the dancers speculated it to probably be a medley of drugs. He says he's famous for trying just about anything he thinks will get him high. He's likely going to need a pumping as well as something to offset the high level of drugs in his system."

"All right, we'll get right on it." Natalie picked up the phone and pushed a button calling for an orderly to take Poison to an observation room. After doing this, she signed the necessary paperwork. A nurse came and took Poison up the hall to the room. This was all done in an efficient five-minute time frame.

As Drake and Jason turned to leave, Natalie stopped them to ask, "How did the dancer know he was not just having a really good high?"

"I don't know, but I could swear I know that guy from somewhere," Drake answered a bit puzzled, as though he had been trying to figure out from where he knew him for a while.

"How do you figure?" Jason asked.

"He just looked too familiar," Drake answered absently, still puzzling.

Natalie and Jason exchanged laughing glances before Jason decided to have a little fun. "So have you been hanging out in male strip clubs lately?"

"Oh, ha-ha, everybody's a comedian. You guys can laugh if you want to, but I know I've seen that guy before. You just don't forget a face like that."

With even more laughter, Jason ribbed, "So this guy really caught your fancy did he?"

Drake began to laugh with them, and he swung his clipboard at Jason after that last comment, tapping Jason on the shoulder with it. Laughing, they both waved bye as they headed out the door.

∽ℯ∼

Sinful Pleasure was busy beyond belief that night. The lounge was full almost to capacity as women and some men sat at tables in very comfortable-looking chairs, waiting for the night's featured entertainer to be announced. Scantily clad male waiters wended their way through the crowded room with trays full of colorful drinks. VIP tables were set up for reserved parties, and women out for a night on the town had their money ready.

When the night was at its end, Sasha met Jerome in his dressing room. He smiled tiredly when he saw her and walked to her, enveloping her in a warm and gentle hug. "Are you coming home with me tonight? If so, can I just hold you while I sleep? I'm beat, and I have to be at the hospital at eight in the morning, which leaves me about four hours to get some rest."

"What time will you get off?"

"At about five, and that will leave me about four hours before having to come back here."

"Okay, you go home and get some rest, and I'll call you later this evening, okay?"

"That sounds good to me. I'll walk you to your car." Once they reached Sasha's car, Jerome kissed her long and passionately before he deposited her into the car and watched her drive away.

# CHAPTER 15

Jerome walked through the halls of the hospital along with Dr. Heath, who was one of the senior attending physicians he worked under. Dr. Heath was an internal specialist and overseer of the residents in training on their rotations. Dr. Heath told Jerome on numerous occasions he was quite impressed with his drive, and knowing where Jerome was headed, he didn't mind giving him a leg up. Although Jerome knew he wanted to be a neurosurgeon, he found it gave a wealth of hands-on experience to work under Dr. Heath until he finished med school, and then began his own residency.

They entered Poison's room, where he sat in a reclined position caused by the angle of the hospital bed, to see him sipping a hospital-issued juice.

Jerome pulled the folder that was uniquely Poison's from a plastic container placed on the wall just inside of the room for the sole purpose of holding the patient's information for the doctors as they changed shifts.

Dr. Heath stood just inside of the room and observed Jerome's patient care. He kept himself available in case his charge needed anything. He was confident leaving the work in Jerome's capable hands. Jerome walked to Poison's bedside while reading his hospital reports. When Jerome reached Poison, he looked up at him and spoke to him in a tone so professional, and matter of fact that one would never know they were previously acquainted. Shaun Langley was the name on the file. Jerome didn't think he'd ever known Poison's given name. "Good morning, Mr. Langley. I'm PA Jerome, and this is Dr. Heath," he gestured to the doctor standing back watching. "Dr. Heath will ensure accuracy in your treatment today." Dr. Heath nodded, but continued his observation of Jerome's interaction with the patient.

Poison was connected to an IV unit, which served the dual purpose of keeping him hydrated and medicated to keep his system from going into shock after the large dose of drugs was removed the night before. Jerome read through the chart to get an update.

"From the look of things, Mr. Langley, you were just on this side of dead when you were brought into the hospital and admitted last night, going of course, by all of the things that were needed to be done to keep you breathing on your own. You're lucky that you survived your latest overdose." Jerome's voice changed to one of quiet concern with his next words. "I'm wondering how long you're going to live like this before you kill yourself or someone else does it for you." Jerome looked him directly in the eyes.

"Don't start in on me with that, Romy. Hey, how did it go without me at the club last night?" He adjusted himself in the bed.

Jerome checked Poison's stats on the monitors, writing the information in the folder to update it, and then he performed a physical exam, also logging the info in the chart. Once he was finished, he addressed Poison's response to his drug abuse. "Is that really what you want to talk about, seriously? Okay … it went fine. We made lots of money that probably would have been yours. You'll be held one more night for observation and released in the morning. In my professional opinion, you should check yourself immediately upon your release into a rehab center. I will leave some pamphlets for you to look into."

"No need to. I'll be quitting anyway. I think this time was too much for me. It really scared the hell out of me."

Jerome looked doubtful about Poison's words of quitting and said, "It's difficult enough to quit taking drugs with a good clinic to help you, let alone trying to do it by yourself. I have to get my rounds done, so get some rest; you look horrible." Jerome walked to the door, and as he reached for the knob, Poison called out to him. Dr. Heath was halfway out of the room when Jerome started toward him, so he continued out as Jerome turned around in response to Poison's call.

"I just wanted to thank you for everything. If you hadn't been there, Sin would probably in his ignorance have let me sleep it off, and I would never have woken. I think that's the part that scared me the most. Anyway, I wanted to say this outfit fits you so much better than the ones you use at the club." The last was said from Poison with a gesture toward Jerome's lab coat, slacks, and expensive loafers.

Jerome smiled at Poison as he headed out of the door, closing it behind him. He walked to Dr. Heath, who was waiting in the hall and itching with curiosity. "I'm not sure if I should want to know exactly how you know that character, but from the sound of things, you know him from a club that you make money in?"

Jerome was amused, he was certain that the club Dr. Heath was speaking of was nowhere near, in the doctor's mind, the same kind of club Jerome and Poison made money in. As they walked up the pristine white hall of the hospital, Jerome debated shortly whether he should tell the doctor. It seemed, of late, that his secret wasn't much of a secret anymore. First Eric, then Professor Sherman, and now Dr. Heath. Maybe it was time for him to stop hiding from the censure of others. Some people would accept it openly, others grudgingly, and still others not at all. It was best he learned how Dr. Heath would react now, because this hospital was his second choice for residency, and the doctor could make his residency really good, or extremely bad.

He began to explain to the obviously curious Dr. Heath exactly how he knew Poison. "Yes, actually we work in the same club … as exotic dancers." Why was it easier to tell him than it was to tell his friends? Jerome wondered.

Dr. Heath's mouth dropped open, most probably without him even noticing it. Jerome saw his shocked expression, covered his mouth with his hand, and coughed discreetly to cover his amused laughter. But he was now enjoying himself enough to shock the doctor a little more, so he said, "That's how I've been paying my way through med school. It's very expensive, you know."

Dr. Heath nodded, and Jerome nodded back, still amused at the doctor's sudden loss of speech. They reached the next room on their rounds and went inside, exiting five minutes later.

Dr. Heath looked at Jerome expectantly. The bombshell he'd dropped before they entered the room had been all he could think about the entire time they were with the patient.

Jerome saw the doctor's look and knew what it meant. He'd known he couldn't say something like that and leave it unfinished, so he continued, "No matter how hard I looked, and, believe me, I looked very hard, no one could pay me the kind of money I needed to see my way through school and support my family."

Dr. Heath found his voice enough to inquire, "Is the money that good?"

"For me, it's great; it was good the first year. Then I learned the best moves and began a male review tour in Las Vegas, New York, California, and a few other places. After word spread about me there, and my popularity increased, *good*, which was about two grand a week, became *great*, which was about four grand a week."

Dr. Heath looked at Jerome sharply, unsure that he had heard him correctly. "You make about four grand a week dancing, and you want to become a doctor?"

Jerome gave the doctor a measured look and decided to ruffle his feathers a little more by audaciously replying, "I wouldn't dare dance for anything less than five thousand per week. When I'm on the road, it's not unheard of for me to make five thousand per night." The two of them reached the nurses' station, and Jerome immediately picked up a folder that had just been placed in the section for patients requiring emergency assistance. The nurse looked up and smiled invitingly at Jerome. This was not lost on Dr. Heath, who'd noticed in times past how the handsome young man seemed to attract girls all over the hospital, including some of the patients.

"Good afternoon, Dr. Jerome."

"Afternoon, Sammy," Jerome spoke kindly.

"So when are you going to take me out on a date?"

Jerome looked up from the file and gave the nurse a noncommittal smile, then turned and headed for the outer room in search of his newest patient. Together he and Dr. Heath walked briskly up the hall toward the observation room.

Dr. Heath couldn't believe he'd just witnessed one of the hottest nurses in the hospital get turned down. "You have got to be kidding … I mean, you are kidding right? Did you just blow off one of the hottest nurses in the whole hospital? Do you really have that kind of swag?"

Without breaking his stride, Jerome shook his head, more shocked to hear the doctor use words like "swag," and "blow," than Samantha's infatuation with him, although he shouldn't have been. The doctor was cool for someone in his fifties. They reached the observation room, and Dr. Heath walked inside while Jerome took a moment to gather the information that had been left by various other nurses, and added it to the file, then handed the file to Dr. Heath.

Dr. Heath scanned the file as they both entered the room. He spoke to the patient. "Good afternoon, Mister …," Dr. Heath paused to check the patient's name, "Jordan, I'm Dr. Heath, and this is my PA, Jerome Jacobs. We're just going to take a quick look at your injury here." Dr. Heath spoke to the man sitting on the examination table. His pant leg was torn and bloody from his wound. Dr. Heath removed a thick white pad that had been placed to staunch the flow of blood, but it was already beginning to bleed through the top layer.

Removing the pad revealed a cavernous wound in his leg about six inches long. The doctor gestured Jerome over to take a look. Jerome examined the wound, and then he began to write as the doctor interviewed the patient about his injury. "How did you get this?"

"I was working at the steel mill when a sliver of hot iron cut through it. It was pretty sharp on the count that it had just been heated through, ya know. By the time I actually felt the pain, the damage was done. Cut through there like butter."

Jerome and the doctor exchanged a look of long-suffering before Dr. Heath spoke to Jerome, "PA Jacobs, we're going to need to suture him, if you will page the anesthesiologist and have an operation room readied for us." Turning back to Mr. Jordan, he said, "I think you should thank God the iron that cut you was hot. It probably kept you from bleeding to death with a cut like this."

The poor man looked so confused by that statement that Dr. Heath gave a short explanation. "Although it cut long and deep, Mr. Jordan, it was the heat that helped keep the wound from bleeding too much; it cauterized the wound for you."

Jerome sent a page to the anesthetist while the doctor made his explanation. They exited the room in a hurry to prepare for the surgery that would put the man's leg back together. Jerome was shaking his head when he said, "Cut through it like butter, huh? I can't believe how nonchalant the man is about that gaping hole in his leg."

"It could be worse."

Jerome looked at him in question. Dr. Heath smiled and shook his head. "He could be crapping the bedsheets too, and we'd have to contend with blood as well as feces."

Jerome smiled at the doctor's humor. They reached the OR

prep area and began to sanitize themselves in preparation of surgery.

"So you make an average of twenty grand per month, and you're giving it up for this?" Dr. Heath gestured around with his head, indicating the sometimes crazy world of the ER.

Jerome smiled to himself as he scrubbed his hands and arms. He'd known the doctor wouldn't be able to leave it alone. "Everyone knows it's just a temporary thing when they go into it. I promise you that guy we just left makes nowhere near as much as I make, and he's been doing it twice as long. Eventually this face and body will no longer be so appealing to young women, and then where would I be? I'd be a washed-up, has-been begging for a gig while watching all the up-and-coming showstoppers make the money. I would never in a million years give up the steady career of being a doctor for that."

Jerome and Dr. Heath finished fixing Mr. Jordan's leg by removing the seared flesh. They then used two layers of over one hundred stitches to close the open wound. They were just removing their soiled outer protection when Dr. Heath received an emergency page, and the two rushed to the admittance area.

Drake and Jason were wheeling in their first call of the night—a pregnant woman shot in the shoulder and leg, who was in shock. They rushed her to the OR to stabilize her as quickly as possible in the hopes that her unborn child would suffer no ill effects from the mother's blood loss. While Drake breathed oxygen into the woman's lungs, he rode on the side of the gurney as Jason pushed.

Jerome jumped onto the other side without the moving bed ever coming to a stop, and took over the task of getting air into the woman's lungs. Drake was in the process of telling the doctors what he knew of the woman's injury, but when Jerome jumped onto the bed, he lost his train of thought. He looked hard at Jerome, pausing in his explanation, and then he looked at his partner to see if he realized now who this man was. Jerome noticed the exchange and cleared his throat to get the attention back on the lady.

Drake finally regained his tongue and started over with his information. "Uh, we received an anonymous call about a pregnant woman who'd been shot. When we got there, the police were already on the scene. From the look of things, they believe it may have been a case of innocent bystander. Her vitals are on the low side of normal."

They took the woman into the OR. Dr. Heath did a cursory examination of the woman while Jerome called for the house OB. He arrived within moments of the call and immediately connected her to a portable ultrasound machine to listen to the baby's heart rate.

Determining the baby was strong enough at the moment for what must be done, he connected her to a fetal monitor and allowed the two to remove the bullets.

Outside of the operating room, Drake and Jason walked back to the admittance area, where Samantha and Natalie were changing shifts. Drake looked at Natalie and Jason and said, "I told you I'd seen that guy before! Now we know from where." Drake shook his head in bemused confusion. "A stripping doctor. If I live to see a hundred years, I don't think I will *ever* understand that."

"I'm not sure I want to," Jason said.

Natalie was clueless when she asked the two, "Who are we talking about here?"

"The stripper I told you guys seemed familiar to me last night? Well, it turns out he works here."

Samantha overheard the conversation and wanted to know to whom they were referring, so she cut into the conversation. "Who works here and works at a strip club?"

"That's what we're trying to figure out," Natalie said while looking directly at Drake. "What's his name?"

"I don't know, but he's tall, kinda light brown skin, curly hair, and dimples? He was working with Dr. Heath."

Samantha lit up with the description that sounded like the same person she'd had endless happy dreams about. "You mean Jerome? I mean Dr. Jacobs? Are you saying he's a stripper?"

"He looked like one to me."

"Where at? I can't believe this. He's too reserved, too conservative." She gushed in shocked excitement, almost jumping in place.

Jason answered, "At The Sinful Pleasure. We saw him there ourselves."

"I have to see this for myself," Samantha said, and beamed.

"Not without me, girl, I've often wondered what he looks like under those scrubs and lab coat myself," said Natalie, who was just as shocked as Samantha was.

## CHAPTER 16

*J*erome left the hospital feeling exhausted. The day was one of the longest he'd seen, with constant blood and gore. He was carrying a briefcase as he headed toward the parking garage for staff members. He looked up and saw Sasha standing in front of his motorcycle. She walked to him and greeted him with a deep kiss.

"Why don't I give you a ride home? My car is just outside the garage ..."

Almost an hour ago Sasha had offered to give Jerome a ride home, and now she stood in his apartment, holding her phone while her father spat demands out at her in a tone he'd never used with her before. He barked through the phone, "I'm on the way home, and when I get there, you had better be there!"

Sasha's senses were in a riot as she tried to figure out what to do. She watched Jerome sit up from his reclining position. He'd either heard her father from where he sat, or was alarmed by the look of panic on her face. She could smell the aroma of Szechuan chicken as it wafted through the brown paper bag. The scent, mixed with her nerves left an acrid taste in her mouth. She opened her mouth to speak, and had to clear her throat before saying, "Dad, I'm not coming home right now, I'm—"

"With Jerome Jacobs I know! Go home, Sasha, now!"

Sasha took the phone away from her ear and looked at it as though it was a snake. She then replaced it on her ear, cradling it between her head and shoulder. She crossed her arms over her chest in a defensive motion, "Dad, I'm an adult who can make my own decisions. You can't just tell me what to do with my life like that."

The professor's anger soared. He exploded. His voice became louder with each word he spoke until it reached a near shout. "As long as you live under *my* roof, and *I* am paying for *your* tuition, and you are all around dependent on *my* money to take care of you, then damn it, I will tell you how to live your life! And—you—will—live—it—without—Jerome—in—it!"

Jerome could hear the professor's voice through the phone from where he sat. He stood and walked to where Sasha stood frozen to the spot. Tears in her eyes.

The professor cursed softly and continued in a more reasonable tone of voice. "I told you before to end things with him before they got too complicated. Now since you either wouldn't or else couldn't, I will have to do it for you. Put the phone on speaker."

"Dad, please just listen to me—"

"Just do it!"

Sasha took the phone away from her ear and pressed the button for speaker. The professor's voice could be heard throughout the room when he spoke next. "Jerome, can you hear me?"

"Yes, sir, I can."

"Good. Because I know you to be a sensible young man, I'm telling you what I've already told Sasha. I don't want you to see any more of one another. I've asked her to leave there now, and now I am asking you to respect my wishes."

Jerome asked him in a respectful tone, "What if I don't want her to leave?"

"Then I will come and remove her physically, and let's not forget who grades your papers and gives you release for your credits. It would be a shame if you could not take your MCAT2 exams."

Jerome exploded over this new bit of blackmail, which was so much different from what Eric would usually do; Eric's would anger his mother, the Professor's would stall his career and potentially affect his admittance into a good residency program. "That's bull! You can't put a hold on my grades and credits because of some personal vendetta you have for me for dating your daughter! I just can't believe the same man whom I've looked up to for the last three years would do something so underhanded and selfish!"

"Send my daughter home." The phone line went dead after those words were spoken.

Sasha was now crying in earnest. Jerome grabbed her upper arms and turned her to face him. He could see the look of futility in her eyes and it frightened him. It prompted him to say, "Oh, come on, baby, don't look like that. Don't cry like its over?" His heart pounded so hard, he could hear it in his head, which is why he initially thought he was hearing things with her next words.

"Jerome, you heard him. He has all the power. He's talking about your career. I mean, do you really want to have to repeat an entire semester because you failed this one because of me? My dad is a very powerful man. He's friends with the dean, not to mention the fact that he does support me. I'm completely dependent on him."

She was serious. He could suddenly feel his pounding heart drop into his stomach, "Then you can come and stay with me. I'll take care of you. Just don't let him decide our fate for us. Unless it's what you want too," he implored.

Sasha pulled away from him and grabbed her purse, taking a few steps away. "No, but for now it's the only way. I can't let you take care of me like that, Romy. You have enough responsibilities as it is, and I would only become a burden."

Jerome walked slowly toward her as though he was approaching a frightened mare. He stopped just two feet away from her and held out his hand to her, silently beseeching her to take it, to trust in them. "Please, we can work this out. Just don't do this to us."

Sasha backed away with tears streaming down her face and reached for the door.

Jerome called out, "Sasha!" When she stopped, he spoke to her words he'd never spoken to a girl before. Very softly he whispered, "Please, I love you, Sasha."

She opened the door and turned, taking one last tearful look at Jerome, and then she walked out.

"Sasha! Sasha!" Jerome followed her to the door, watching forlornly as she stepped inside the elevator. He slammed the door shut, and once it was shut, he pounded his fist into it.

# CHAPTER 17

*J*erome had never been in so much pain before. Not the pain from ramming his fist into the door, but the feeling of his heart shattering in his chest was a completely new experience that he was not particularly fond of. He knew he should have left her out of his life before. If he had, then he wouldn't be feeling such pain now. He sat brooding in his dressing room nursing a chaser full almost to the rim of VSOP.

Eric walked into the dressing room and stopped in shock when he saw Jerome with the liquor. "It's a rare occasion when Jerome Jacobs is caught with a drink in his hand, and the evidence of many before that. Are you drunk, Romy?"

Jerome was affronted. He didn't get drunk, maybe a little mellow, "Of course not! I never get drink, I mean drunk."

Eric hid his laugh behind his hand. His brother wasn't drunk, he was soused. "What's the occasion?"

Jerome sat looking at his drink almost hypnotically as it swirled around in his glass and sloshed over the side. In a painful whisper he said, "It's over, for good this time."

Eric stopped smiling at the pain he heard in his brother's voice. He walked to him and hunkered down to look at him eye level. Reaching out to take the glass from him, he asked, "Are you sure? I mean, what happened?"

Jerome's words were slightly slurred when he answered, "Her dad called earlier tonight, and pretty much gave her an ultimatum."

"And?" Eric asked after it seemed Jerome wasn't planning to say more.

"She took it."

"She was probably just overwhelmed. She'll come to her—"

"Don't make excuses for her!" Jerome nearly shouted, cutting off Eric's words midsentence. "She's a grown damn woman who let her father intimidate her into leaving me! She chose to be spoiled rather than loved, so it's over, her decision!" Jerome grabbed the drink back from Eric and downed half its contents, then stood and walked to the door with admirable ease. He turned to look at Eric. "Let's go dance."

Two weeks after the forced breakup, the Sherman family had still not been back to normal. Sasha only spoke to her dad when absolutely necessary, but most times she just avoided him altogether. She was miserable, and everyone knew it. She entered the formal dining room of the family residence to everyone already seated. This was a traditional Sunday in the Sherman household, but this day they had a guest. A young man in his late twenties, he was distinguished and good-looking and obviously from a wealthy family.

He was just the kind of guy Sasha would normally have been attracted to with his polished good looks and Ivy League persona. But she knew what this was all about. In fact, this was the second man in as many weeks her dad had brought home in an attempt to get her interest going in any other direction than Jerome Jacobs.

She walked slowly to her seat, and as she approached, the young man automatically stood and assisted her in getting settled.

She knew he would do that. *So predictable*, she thought, but what came out of her mouth was a polite, "Thank you."

Professor Sherman cleared his throat. "Sasha, I wanted to introduce you to Miles Langford. He is the middle son of Claire and Huntley. Do you remember them?"

Sasha looked at her father coolly, and then turned to acknowledge the introduction by nodding her head to Miles. She then turned toward her mother to ask, "Will you pass the salad, please?"

"Certainly, dear." Mrs. Sherman passed the bowl of salad to Sasha before turning to cast a 'what are you doing' look to her husband.

Miles spoke, "I really want to thank you for inviting me over, Dr. Sherman. My mom and dad send their best."

"Such great people, your parents. And how are your brother and sister?"

"Just fine; Justin is now working as a scientist at NIH, and Suzanne just accepted an assistant manager position at Grayson and Fields Department Store."

"And what of you, Miles?"

Miles wiped his mouth with his napkin and placed it on his lap. He looked up at Sasha. She was eating and looked completely disinterested in the conversation. Seeing her indifference, Miles cleared his throat and answered, "I am currently working as assistant DA here, and after two years I will apply for DA, if the position opens, and if not, I will go a little further upstate. My goal is to run for Senate in about fifteen years or so."

"Did you hear that, Sasha? Professor Sherman spoke like he was falling in love with him himself. "A prosecuting attorney."

Sasha looked up from her plate at her father with a blank stare, and without acknowledging that he'd even spoken, she turned to her sister with a polite smile and asked, "So, Joslyn how are things going with you and Ethan? Have you guys set a date yet for the wedding?"

"No, but when we do, I want you to be my maid of honor. Will you do it for me, Sasha?"

"Of course, sweetie. I would be honored."

The conversation between the sisters was cut off by her irritated father. "Sasha, in case you haven't noticed, we have a guest, and you are being a bit rude by pretending he isn't here."

Sasha placed her napkin on the table, having lost what little appetite she had, and slowly looked up at her father. She knew what he was doing, and thought, mistakenly, that if she didn't encourage it, maybe he'd stop. She knew now that wasn't the case. She spoke very softly when she announced, "I seem to have lost my appetite, so if you don't mind, I would like to be excused from the table." Without as much as a by-your-leave, she was up and gone before anyone could say a word.

She left the house with the intention of going for a drive but realized she didn't have her keys, and was determined not to go back in the house while that man was there. She walked around the house and headed to the gazebo instead. Funny how two months ago everything in her world was perfect. Now she lived in this constant state of unrest.

She sat on a bench in the gazebo and looked at the trees. A sultry breeze swept across her face. It was mid-October in DC. And the weather hadn't yet decided what it wanted to do. The trees were still full of swaying leaves in shades of red, gold, and green. She took a deep breath, and then let it out in a forlorn sigh. She thought it kind of funny that four months ago she'd reflected on her life, and wondered why her father had never tried to set her up the way he'd done Joslyn. Now that he was trying, it was too late.

The truth was, she realized, that it didn't matter. She was in love with Jerome, and any man her father decided to bring around at this point would not do. Only Jerome could fill the hole she now carried in her chest. Her father needed to know that. She didn't know how she would tell him, but the time would come. She had no way of knowing, as she made the decision, just how soon that time would be.

It came the very next Sunday. Sasha avoided her father the entire week. She spent her time drawing up a small business proposal for a loan to open a bistro on Wisconsin Avenue, in the heart of Georgetown. She had every intention of going back after Jerome when she had her feet under herself, but she doubted her ability to win him back after the way she left that day. Nevertheless, she would try.

Using their cook as her sous chef, she prepared a special meal requested by her mother. When she was done, she took a shower. Feeling refreshed, Sasha came to the formal dining room for dinner. She was halfway into the room when she saw Malcolm already seated at the dining room table next to where she normally sat. Her eyes shot daggers at her father, knowing this was all his doing. Her anger was almost tangible as she continued her way to the table. Malcolm stood and walked to her, his unblemished amber skin made his white smile almost blinding.

His walk was polished, his look sophisticated as usual. And yet it couldn't compare to the smooth, purposeful stride of Jerome, or the barely hidden strength he carried in his straight-as-a-rod shoulders. Sasha asked, "Why are you here, Malcolm?"

Malcolm spoke. "Hello, Sasha, I've missed you terribly."

"That's funny, I've been home for eight months. I haven't heard from you once."

"I didn't think you'd want to hear from me, but if I had known you missed me, I would have called long ago."

"I didn't." She walked past him and seated herself. She could only imagine what her dad told him. It was a testament either to her father's persuasive ability, or else to Malcolm's self-inflation that he was there acting as though he'd bestowed a precious gift on her. She finished, "I still don't. Why, again, are you here?"

"Your father seems to think you've been spending your time with a rebound guy, and only because you missed me."

The anger she'd barely been trying to hold in check, showed on her face after that statement. "Really?" She sneered as she stood to leave the room, abandoning the delicious fare her mother and sister seemed suddenly consumed with. But this time her father didn't let her leave the way he had the week prior.

"Sasha! You will not leave so rudely while you have a guest here specifically to see you!"

That was the last straw. She gritted her teeth, and decided some things were going to have to change about the entire situation. All the men he'd been parading before her as though she was some mare in heat, and they the studs being overlooked for purchase, needed to end.

She'd thought if she didn't give it any encouragement that he would leave her alone and let her lick her wounds in peace, but that wasn't happening. Her dad constantly bringing by all of those eligible men, whose credentials were supposed to be better than Jerome's, wasn't going to fix anything. Her heart was broken. She had broken the heart of the best thing that had happened to her and had been regretting it every day since. No man would compare to Jerome. Not the way he held her, or touched her, not the way he looked at her, and most especially the way he loved every inch of her.

Her eyes misted thinking about him, and she decided to make certain her dad didn't do anything like this again. He needed to understand that just because he'd gotten her to leave Jerome didn't mean she'd just take up with someone else. "No, dad, *you* have a guest, so it's *your* obligation to entertain him! I won't play this game with you. You may be all powerful to stop me from seeing the man of my choice, but I'll be damned if I let you choose someone for me as if I was some Victorian miss with no thought of choosing for love!"

"You will not speak to me in my house that way, young lady!"

"That's fine with me because I would prefer not to speak with you at all! If you don't mind, I would like to be excused from the room." Without waiting for a reply, Sasha turned toward Malcolm, who was so astonished he'd forgotten to stand. Then she continued in a mocking tone directed toward him, "It has been a pleasure to see you again. Have a good life."

She swept out of the room like the pampered socialite she'd been raised to be, with all eyes on her. When Sasha was no longer in sight, all eyes turned to the professor. He cleared his throat, made a comment about the weather, and suddenly became engrossed in his meal.

∽◌◌

That evening, Professor and Mrs. Sherman stood before their separate mirrors in their spacious his and hers bathroom preparing for bed. The professor took a glance at his wife to see her rubbing cream onto her face. She was intolerably quiet, and he was sure he knew why. "Are you not speaking with me too?"

She looked at him. Since he opened the subject, she may as well go full steam ahead, "You've got yourself quite an unhappy little girl out there."

"Well, what am I supposed to do? Just let her throw her life away with a stripper?"

"And who says she would be throwing it away? Who says he isn't the best thing that could have happened to her?"

"He's a stripper, Joanne. How can that be the best thing for her?"

"What if he made her happy? I've never seen her so interested in a young man before. Not even Malcolm had her so consumed. Besides, isn't this the same boy you couldn't stop singing the praises of *before* you found out he was stripping for a living?"

"Yes, but that changes things. You know how those stripper types are, honey. They have sex with everything offering, whether they have a girlfriend or not. Do you think she would be so happy with him a year or two down the road when she's pregnant with his child, and while she sits in their crummy apartment waiting for him to come home, he's out getting some other girl at the club pregnant too?"

She poured lotion from a bottle into her hands and massaged it onto her skin, all the while looking at him contemplatively. "You know what I think?" He leaned against the wall, crossed his arms over his chest, and waited silently to hear what she would say, "I think you're judging him too harshly, mostly because you're disappointed that he isn't as squeaky clean as you first thought him to be. But I've never known you to show poor taste in judging anyone's character, and you liked him so much that you wanted to bring him home to meet the family before Sasha ever showed any interest in him."

The professor was losing his patience. She was right, and he knew it. The truth was he'd wanted Jerome for Sasha, and had been elated when she'd shown an interest in him without his even having to do anything. Which was not a surprise considering the boy's looks. A lot of other girls had been interested in him too. Once he'd decided to match Sasha and Jerome up, he'd called Sasha in France and convinced her to come home using the excuse that he'd found a great restaurant location for her to look over. He'd told her it was time to move forward with her career.

She'd agreed, and decided to maybe get her certification as a nutritionist. That would perhaps be helpful with her career as a culinary artist. She'd been home for an entire five months, and at the college for three of those months before she'd come to him asking about Jerome. He could remember how happy he'd been. Now he just felt disillusioned. He looked at his wife with a frown. "Okay, so?"

"So you're being a jerk about this, and rightly so. I mean, this is your baby girl we're talking about here. But before you condemn him completely, you should have a talk with him and find out where he's coming from."

The professor looked at his wife as though she'd grown a

second head before his eyes, "Are you saying you would be happy with your daughter dating, and falling in love with, a stripper?"

"Paul, she's already in love with him; there's no avoiding that. The question now is do you want your daughter happy with a stripper, or do you want to be happy at the expense of your daughters' happiness? Because right now she's suffering without him, and I promise you no other man will do." She rubbed her husband's cheek fondly before heading into the bedroom.

Sasha sat in her bedroom hugging her pillow and daydreaming sadly. She jumped as she heard a knock at the door. "It's open," she called.

Almost immediately the door opened, and Joslyn, entered the room walking serenely toward the bed. She placed the back of her hand on Sasha's forehead playfully. Sasha looked up with a faint smile.

"I was just making sure. What got into you talking to dad like that?"

Sasha shrugged, looking down at and playing with the pillow she'd been hugging. "After what he did, he's lucky if I ever speak to him again."

"He's got your best interest at heart. You know that."

Sasha looked at her sister discontentedly. "You're not going to start taking up for him are you? You probably wouldn't feel so generous toward him if it had been you he was trying to keep away from Ethan."

"No. I wouldn't, and, no, I'm not going to start, not seeing how miserable you are. Does he know?"

"Know what?"

"That you're in love with him."

"Does who know, Dad?"

"No silly, your guy friend."

"He probably thinks I feel nothing for him after the way I walked out after Dad's threats."

"So what now? Are you just going to give up, not even fight for him?"

Sasha shrugged miserably. "I guess so. I mean, what else can I do?"

Joslyn looked at her in disbelief.

"I'm not like you, Joslyn. I've never defied Dad on anything."

"You did tonight, and for love it's worth it. I sure wish I could have met this guy who got you to fall so hard."

She spoke softly, still looking down at the pillow. "Me too; he's so beautiful and sweet and generous."

"I don't understand why Dad doesn't like him then."

"You mean he didn't tell you? It's because Jerome's a stripper."

"Why don't we go see him? That is, if you aren't too chicken to confront your momentary lack of sense."

"No, it's over Joslyn. After the way I walked out, he probably never wants to see me again."

"There is only one way you'll ever know that." Joslyn waited for her baby sister to make a decision. When Sasha just sat looking utterly miserable, Joslyn didn't push. Instead she hugged Sasha tight. "Good night, sweetheart." She quietly withdrew, leaving Sasha to her misery.

# CHAPTER 18

After Professor Sherman concluded his lecture, the class as a whole began to leave. He watched as Jerome stood and lifted his substantial backpack onto his shoulder. He was always his favorite pupil. He shook his head as his wife's words seemed on instant replay in his mind, "Mr. Jacobs, will you stay for a few moments?"

Jerome stopped where he was. He'd been trying to get out of the class as quickly as possible. He'd carefully choreographed an avoidance waltz and been evading both of them for the past few weeks. Until now the professor seemed to like it just fine, had been dancing his own evasion dance. So what could he possibly have to say to him now? He stood still, allowing the other students to exit the class. When there was only the two of them left in the room, Jerome walked slowly toward the front where the professor stood waiting.

The professor looked at him for a long, silent moment before speaking, nodding his head as though coming to a conclusion. "Jerome, I wanted to speak with you about a private matter that has been bothering me for weeks now."

"If this is about your daughter, don't bother. I haven't seen or spoken with her since the day you called and threatened us both."

"Are you in love with my daughter?"

Jerome's jaw clenched through his struggle to hold in his anger and resentment. "If I was, I wouldn't admit it to you. Besides, what would be the point? You don't want us together, which isn't a surprise to me. She has made her choice, which doesn't surprise me overmuch either."

"Jerome, this is not the way I wanted this conversation to go."

"If this is not school related, which I see it's not, then I respectfully ask that you let me be about my way. My private life and emotions are mine alone, and I won't be sharing them for your gratification."

Jerome turned and began walking away, his long-legged stride quickly eating up the space.

The professor called out, "What would you have done? You're a stripper, for god's sake. I've spent the last twenty-five years raising Sasha so she makes the right decision when it comes to the man she would choose for herself. The right choice is all I want for her."

Jerome stopped walking and turned to look at him, his body rigid with anger over that last comment. Of all the conceited, snobbish things he'd ever heard, "To think I looked up to you as a role model, someone I thought I wanted to be like, but your small-mindedness has made me see that you're the exact opposite of everything I want to be!"

"You dance and take off your clothes for women's entertainment! On a regular basis, you likely have some strange woman's hands in your pants. Don't be upset with me because I don't want my daughter with someone like that! You made the decision; it was your choice, but—"

Jerome interrupted with an angry shout. "I had no choice! I did what I had to do to support my family! They all depended on me! On me! They needed me, and I wasn't going to let them down! I wasn't going to let myself down!"

Outside the lecture room, Dillon and Jeffery had been waiting for Jerome so they could leave together. When they heard

Jerome's voice raised in anger, they stepped closer to the door, ears tuned in.

Inside the lecture room, the discussion went on with neither of the occupants realizing they had an audience. "There had to be other options," the professor seemed to taunt.

"Maybe for you, but I had no other options. That was my option, and I took it." Jerome took a deep breath. "You know what, I don't expect you to understand," he expelled.

Professor Sherman shook his head. This talk wasn't going the way he'd planned. His goal in calling the talk had been to 'feel him out,' as his wife had suggested. He decided to change tactics. His voice when he next spoke carried less censure. "Make me understand, Jerome."

Jerome decided to give Professor Sherman a brief glimpse of his world for no other reason than to make him see that not all people could *afford* to be picky about their lifestyle. "When my dad died, I was twenty-two and had just finished premed. I was scheduled to start classes here in the fall semester. I have three younger siblings, and had $1,000 to my name. All of the responsibility for them, including my mom, fell on me, as I was the oldest child. My mom wanted me to quit school, and sure I could have; after all, I did have my bachelor's. I could have gone to work in someone's lab back home, but I was so close I couldn't quit."

Jerome stared distantly as though seeing that night and the conversation he'd had with his mother all over again. The professor sat quietly waiting for him to continue, his heart reluctantly hurting for the young man who'd had to shoulder so much responsibility.

Jerome continued. "We couldn't afford to pay my tuition, or my sister Jessica's, who'd just started her sophomore year, *and* take care of two minors. And since I wasn't born with a silver spoon in my mouth, I took a job."

Jerome put his backpack on the floor and then continued. "I

was working as a waiter, making about seven hundred per week *when* the tips were good, and staying in a crappy rat-infested off-campus apartment so I could save as much money as I could to send home to my family, which wasn't much. My mom kept telling me I could make so much more than that with my education, but I refused to quit. My rent and tuition were paid up for a few months from my dad's life insurance, so I had a little leeway. But I was slowly drowning, and couldn't figure out how to get out of my circumstances. I began to think I would eventually have to do exactly what my mom wanted me to do.

"After about six months, I met a guy who was a stripper. He introduced me to the man who owned the club he worked in. I went from seven hundred a week to fifteen hundred a week. After a few months of learning all the moves and improving on them, I was making more money in three days than I'd made in a month as a waiter. And when you have four people dependent almost entirely upon you, that take's a heavy weight off your shoulders. Again, I don't expect you to understand why I'm an exotic dancer, or why my choice was no choice at all. I have done the best I can for my family, and that's what matters to me. So with or without your approval, I have and will continue to support my family however necessary. If that disqualifies me from being good enough for your precious daughter, then so be it," he jeered. "My life is what it is, and I don't owe any apologies to anyone for doing what was needed."

Jerome looked at his watch and then said, "I really need to go. My shift starts in an hour, and I have to work tonight." He picked up his backpack and turned to walk up the aisle, but paused with the professor's next words.

"I think Sasha is in love with you. She has been miserable these last few weeks, and making my life miserable too."

Without turning around, Jerome shook his head, ignoring the way his heart sped its beat, he continued toward the exit. He wouldn't go through the pain he'd felt when she'd walked out of that door ever again, so it was best to leave things as they were. He was working on getting over her, and that was the best he could do.

Jerome left the class with his mind reeling so much that he didn't even notice that Dillon, and Jeffery was gone. The last few weeks had been difficult, with him getting drunk and then trying to soothe his pain in the arms of other women. But it wasn't the same. None of them took him there like Sasha did. Damn-it, he refused to start thinking about her again! It was over by her decree. Jerome stepped out of the college and walked right into the object of his thoughts. His heart skipped a beat when he saw the look of longing on her face, but he hardened his resolve. *She'd* broken *his* heart, so she had no right to look so heartbroken, so miserable.

Sasha was speechless. He looked cold and uninviting but just as gorgeous as ever. She found her tongue just as he moved to pass her, "Hello, Jerome, it's been a long time."

He wanted her to hurt and feel the same pain that she'd inflicted on him the night she left, when he said, "Not long enough."

A fat tear welled up and spilled down her face. *Score*, he thought to himself. *That almost made me feel better.*

"That wasn't necessary. You need not be so cruel," she spoke sadly.

"So sorry to hurt your tender feelings," he drove on mercilessly, "and so I think I have a solution to this. To keep my cruelty at bay, I think I should just remove myself from your stratosphere, and problem solved. I won't feel the urge to be cruel, and you won't have to be subjected to it."

"Jerome, can we talk, please?"

"I would really rather not," he sneered, "as I've had all the talk I want from a Sherman today. Good-bye, Sasha," he walked away without looking back. It was a good thing, because if he had, he would have seen her watching him forlornly through a torrent of tears as he moved swiftly to his motorcycle, climbed on, and sped away. If he'd seen those tears, he may have been tempted to go back and soothe them away, maybe.

Jerome didn't witness her tears, but her father did. He walked to her and pulled her into his arms in an attempt to comfort her. Sasha would have none of it. It was his fault that she was in such pain in the first place, so she definitely didn't want his comfort. She pushed away from him and ran into the building heading for the restroom. Inside she splashed water on her face to stop her eyes from swelling so badly that she couldn't see through them.

∽୧୵

Dillon and Jeffery drove toward Jeffery's room in an almost state of shock. Jeffery called Ronald and got his voice mail, "Dude, you need to call me as soon as you get this message. It's very important." He called Montgomery after he closed the line from Ronald's call and left the same message.

When they reached Jeffery's place, they went inside, and both grabbed drinks from his refrigerator. Jeffery strode across his living room, making several rounds. He was more astonished than anything, but also a little hurt that their friend didn't think he could tell them something like that. Jeffery was tall and athletic, an avid runner. He had gotten all of the guys on board with his almost daily five-mile runs. He'd won many bets at parties by crushing cans between his thighs, but he was sensible too. He wanted to hear straight from Jerome's mouth, why he didn't think he could tell them.

He stopped his pacing. His brown eyes came to settle on Dillon's green ones. Dillon asked, "Is it possible we heard wrong?"

Jeffery shook his head. His golden brown skin briefly reflected the light as he passed a lamp to sit. "I don't think so." He looked thoughtful. "You know he and Monty are the closest. Monty would know for sure."

Dillon agreed, his black hair and green eyes a startling contrast that always caught attention. His perfect tan and well-toned body did the rest. Each of the five of them in their own right could attract a respectable amount of attention from the opposite sex, but when they were all together, they were irresistible.

"Why don't we just call Jerome and ask him?" Dillon asked.

"Because if he wanted us to know, he would've said something by now. I'm gonna find out where he works."

Dillon looked unconvinced. "How?"

"I'm telling you, Monty knows."

"Well, let's go to his place."

# CHAPTER 19

The night was coming to a close at The Sinful Pleasure. Jerome was drunk again. He'd been doing fine until he'd seen her earlier, and then he couldn't stop thinking about her. All afternoon at the hospital he'd replayed the conversation over in his mind, seeing that look of devastation on her face.

So when he'd gotten off, he'd gone home and started drinking. He drank until he'd fallen asleep, and when he woke up, he drank some more. The problem was it wasn't working. He was getting drunk but couldn't stop thinking about her. He was still thinking about her when Samantha walked up to him.

"Hi, Jerome! Do you do private dances?" she asked hopefully.

"I do tonight but not here. The club is closing." He grabbed her hand. "Come with me while I get changed." He pulled her toward his dressing room. Samantha waved bye to an astonished Natalie and disappeared with Jerome.

Jerome and Samantha entered his dressing room. He closed the door behind them. He turned to lean against the wall and crooked a finger for her to come to him. Samantha was in heaven. She'd dreamed of a night like this one so many times she lost count. She moved quickly to get to him before he changed his mind.

Jerome grabbed her as soon as she was close enough to him,

pulling her forward so that her body slammed into his. He kissed her deeply while lazily exploring her body. He could hear her soft moans as he touched her expertly. He took one of her hands that clung to his shoulder and placed it on his erection, guiding her to squeeze him gently. She moaned again.

He took her hand away again, but this time when he replaced it, he put it on the inside of his pants. She rubbed her thumb across his swollen, sensitive phallus. He took a deep breath. She felt a bead of moisture on the tip of his erection and rubbed her finger across it, and could feel her body's response as her panties got wetter by the second. She desperately wanted to see if it was as beautiful as he. "May I see it?"

Jerome helped her release his penis from its binding, and she gasped. It was beautiful, thick, and long, with smooth, light veins running along the length of it. He dug his fingers into her hair, and using her hair to guide her where he wanted her, pulled her forward for a kiss. Eric burst through the door as she was living her dream with Dr. Romy.

Eric stopped short; his mouth dropped open upon seeing his brother obviously drunk again, kissing some cutie with her hands in his pants. And from the look of things, big brother was enjoying it. "I'm sorry. Maybe I should leave and come back later?"

Jerome leaned back against the wall with a half-smile of sensuality on his face. Samantha was so surprised by the interruption that she didn't seem to realize yet that she was still holding his erection.

"No, don't go yet. Samantha, you need to meet my baby brother," Jerome removed her hand from his anatomy, which caused her to blush, and then he readjusted himself to fit back into his pants. He continued with another smile that caused his dimple to flash, "Samantha, this is my baby brother, Eric. Eric, please make the acquaintance of Sammy."

Eric smiled at her; he almost felt sorry for her for the way his brother was purposely teasing her by allowing her arousal to go unfulfilled. But women talked, and in the last few weeks Jerome had taken a few offers from some lucky patrons. They liked him so much they were hoping for another chance with him, but Eric knew all he wanted was to forget Sasha. He knew also that Sammy here would not be disappointed with the night, nor would she be able to help him forget.

"I would shake your hand, but I don't really want to know my brother that intimately." To Jerome he said, "So you two just met?"

"No we work together at the hospital," Samantha answered for Jerome.

That raised red flags in Eric's head. To know his brother was to know that this was completely out of character for him. He was going to have sex with his coworker? He would never do this if he was sober and in his right mind, which he hadn't been in since Sasha left.

Eric decided to be his voice of sobriety. It was one thing to drown your sorrows in the arms of another girl. Hell, who hadn't done that? But it was another thing altogether to go against your own principles. That was like cutting off your own nose.

"Wow, Romy, you look so unsteady right now. Are you okay? Dude, are you gonna puke?" Eric rushed to him and shoved him into the bathroom in his dressing room. He closed the door and pushed Jerome to sit on the toilet, then started making gagging sounds. Jerome laughed drunkenly. Eric clapped his hands over Jerome's mouth to keep the girl from hearing it. He made another retching sound even louder than the first.

Jerome's eyes were full of laughter that was threatening to bubble over any minute. Eric shushed him and went to the door. He opened it a crack and stuck his head out. "This is just disgustingly gross. He must've had way too much to drink. You might want to catch up with your ride, and I'm gonna take him home and get him in the bed to sleep it off."

Samantha didn't want to leave, at least not without Jerome. She knew he was a bit drunk because, to her, he'd never been anything more than polite before tonight. She knew she was pretty, so that wasn't it, but he was just so damned professional all the time that she didn't know he even had a side like this. It was a side she wanted to see more of, so she said, "I'm driving, and I can give him a ride."

"Damn, girl, he's sick. Didn't you hear him? He's shooting chunks. I mean, like I know you want him bad, but so did the girl from last night too. You just happened to draw the short straw." *That's a lie, but, damn, this chick is persistent, and could she get more desperate?*

"I'm a nurse, you know, so I think I can handle a little vomit."

*Hell, I guess she could; okay so no more niceness or else this chick'll be humping him while he leans over the toilet.* "While he's all up in you? That's really gross, but seriously, why don't you come back tomorrow, 'cause tonight isn't good. I'm taking him home."

Jerome laughed this time. He just couldn't help it. Eric pressed his hand over Jerome's mouth again, and kicked him in the shin. Jerome grunted from the pain.

"In the toilet, man!" Eric said to Jerome loud enough for her to hear.

Samantha heard the grunt and leaned to the side to try and see inside the bathroom. She gave-up and left, but she wasn't happy about it.

Jerome couldn't care less, but he was very amused by, and curious of, his brother's antics. So much so he'd quietly sat in the bathroom with Eric and let him tell the most outrageous lies just to see where this was going.

"What was all of that for?" Jerome asked with an obvious slur in his words.

"Trust me, you'll thank me in the morning."

"For cock-blocking? Sammy's a cutie."

"Yeah, but she's also a coworker, and if I know nothing else about you, then I know that you wouldn't have sex with a coworker if you were in your right mind." Eric gathered up an envelope that he sat on the sink when he'd gotten Jerome into the bathroom. It was thick and filled with bills from Jerome's night of dancing, which was the reason he'd come in the first place. Then he escorted Jerome out of the building to his motorcycle and drove him home.

⸺◦◦⸺

Sasha knocked on Joslyn's door, entering with her invite. As soon as she entered her room, she climbed into her sister's bed and lay on her chest. Joslyn knew that things hadn't gone right. She'd convinced Sasha to go talk with him. "What happened?"

"I saw him today and decided to speak with him." She paused for a brief moment, then continued, "Oh, Joslyn, he was horrible to me. He insulted me and told me he'd had enough of being around a Sherman for one day, and then he just walked away. He was so hard and cold. I don't think he loves me anymore, or else he never really did."

"I'm so sorry, sweetie."

Their mother walked into the room a few moments later to see the two of them cuddled together. She asked, "Is everything okay?"

"Yes. Sasha went to talk to Jerome today. He was less than kind to her."

"Baby, what else did you expect? That he would drop to his knees and thank you for coming back after breaking his heart?"

"I didn't expect him to be so nasty. I at least thought he would be willing to speak to me, but he didn't even want to do that, just blew me off."

"You're forgetting that we're talking about a man here. If a man has nothing else, then he has his pride, and you and your father trampled all over his."

"Mom, I only did what I had to do. It's not as though I wanted to leave."

"That's not how he sees it. In fact he will never see it that way; he will only see that you chose fear over love, his love to be exact. Now I would imagine that this young man is pretty good looking if he makes as much money as you say?"

"Mom, he is utterly gorgeous—tall with beautiful skin, soft curly hair, dimples, and big white teeth."

"Yes, well, do you understand how many women he could have with those looks working in the kind of place that he works?"

"That's one of the reasons I didn't want to date him in the first place." Sasha bemoaned.

"But he showed you differently, that he could be yours only?" Sasha nodded, and Joanne continued, "He chose you out of hundreds of girls, then he fell in love with you, and you probably presented some form of stability for him that, from the way you and your dad described him, has been lacking in his life for a while now. Because he has been everyone else's rock, he has had no one to lean on until you. You offered him that stability, and then at the first sign of adversity, you slid it out from under him."

Sasha looked at her mom as though she was speaking in tongues. "What I'm trying to say is if you want him back, you're going to have to work for him. Until now he has done the work by showing you him, not his dance character, but his heart, and you turned it away. This time you will have to work for it. And he's not going to make it easy for you, because he's hurting, so he'll want you to hurt too. But if you love him as much as I think you do, then don't give up, and, whatever you do, don't let your father bully you into his choice. This is your life and happiness."

## CHAPTER 20

*J*erome awoke the next morning to a pounding headache, and his stomach threatened to release its contents with the slightest provocation. He gingerly got out of bed and headed to his shower. Why had he drunk so much yesterday? Oh, yes, the Sherman family had been determined to invade the tenuous hold he had on his well-being. He took a quick shower and got dressed for the hospital. When he walked out of his room and into the kitchen, Eric sat at the dining room table waiting for him.

"Do you have time to talk?" Eric asked.

"I have a few minutes." Jerome took a seat at the table.

"Good. I made you breakfast. So, you remember much of last night?"

His stomach recoiled at the smell of eggs and bacon, so he took a slice of toast. "Yes, I remember I was very intoxicated and doing some dumb things. I also remember you bursting through the door while I had someone's hand down my pants. It's fuzzy who and how far we went."

"Well, the *who;* was Samantha, and judging by her look of frustration when I interrupted, and you did nothing to get me to leave, her hand down your pants was as far as you got."

Jerome looked horrified when he asked, "Not my coworker Samantha?"

"Yeah, your coworker, which was why I wanted to talk to you before you left for work, just in case you weren't clear. That too is the reason I decided to play the cock-blocker. I didn't think you would've really wanted that to go all the way. So what got into you last night?"

Jerome took a sip of coffee and a nibble of dry toast. His stomach wouldn't tolerate anything else displayed on the table at the moment, and he knew Eric knew this. He would make him pay for that, but first he needed to survive his hangover. He shrugged, "I saw Sasha yesterday. She wanted to talk to me, but I'd just had a talk with her dad, and I lost it. I was out for blood and said some mean things that felt good at the time, but she got this wounded look in her eyes that I couldn't get out of my head, so I drank to forget." He sat his toast aside, looked at his watch, and stood, "I need to get going. I'll see you later."

Dillon, Jeffery, and Ronald were all on a mission. After Jeffery and Dillon overheard the argument between Jerome and Professor Sherman the day before, they'd gone to Jeffery's apartment, and tried to talk themselves out of what they thought they'd heard. They called Ronald, who'd been out with one of his girls, and hadn't gotten their message until morning.

They were now at Montgomery's place banging on the door. Montgomery opened the door semi-dressed and his usual perfectly coiffed hair was disheveled. He'd obviously been entertaining. He looked at the clock, and then back at the guys, "Seriously?"

Ronald didn't wait, but slid past Montgomery. The others filed in behind him. Ronald asked, "Remember when you told us Jerome works at a restaurant?"

Montgomery shrugged. He closed his door, and sat on the edge of an end table, "Yeah. Why?"

Jeffery asked, "Truth?"

"Truth," Montgomery lied without blinking.

"Which one?" Ronald asked.

Montgomery scratched his chest. "Where is this inquisition coming from?"

Dillon answered, "We overheard Jerome having an argument with the professor yesterday. Could've sworn he told the professor he was stripping."

"Did you ask him?" Montgomery queried.

"No, we're asking you," Jeffery stated. "Are you sure he works at a restaurant?"

Montgomery reached for his phone. "Why don't we call him and ask?"

"Because you two will just come up with another lie," Ronald opined.

Jeffery snatched the phone and moved a safe distance away. He questioned softly, "Why don't you guys just tell us? Why all the secrecy?"

Montgomery defended, "It's not my secret to tell," while watching his phone get farther away. He knew he'd never catch Jeffery, so he didn't even try.

Ronald said, "You know those hotties that hang out with the professor's daughter? Let's ask them. I bet they know."

Dillon offered, "I have Regina's number. We can call her."

Ronald looked impressed. "How'd you do that?"

The guys all exchanged knowing looks.

Dillon was browsing through his contacts, so he missed the look from the other three, "We hung out a couple of times. Here it is."

"Call her," Jeffery said.

Montgomery asked, "Why didn't you tell us?"

Before Dillon could answer, Ronald said, "You know I wanted her. I called dibs."

Dillon snorted, "Dude, you call dibs on everybody. If we waited to get a girl you didn't call dibs on, we'd all be shriveled up. Besides, she approached me." To Montgomery he said, "It was a long time ago. I just never took her number out of my phone." He pressed the send button and put the phone on speaker.

They waited for a moment. She answered the phone with a question in her voice, as though she didn't recognize the number of the caller. "Hello?"

"Hi, Regina. This is Dillon."

"Dillon who?"

"Saunders."

"Oh, Dillon *Saunders*. The Dillon who told me three years ago not to get serious with him, because he had no intention of getting serious with me, *after* I gave him the goods? That Dillon?"

Dillon looked up to see three sets of eyes burrowing into him. He shook his head. He knew this conversation would eventually happen, but it wasn't supposed to happen like this. "Regina, it wasn't the way it sounded. You're an awesome girl, and I really liked you, but I felt like you were moving too fast. I was young, and just not ready for that kind of intensity."

Regina wasn't interested in his lame excuse, she'd been crazy about him and had thought he was crazy for her, "Cancelled. What do you want?"

"You're friends with the professor's daughter aren't you?"

"Yes. Why?"

"Just wondering if you ladies ever go to the club where Jerome works?"

"Why?" She asked again with annoyance in her voice.

Dillon looked around. Ronald looked impatient as he waved his hand signaling Dillon to get to the point with the girl. Jeffery just stared in his normal inquisitive way, and Monty had moved to the far side of the room, a look of doom on his handsome face.

Dillon answered, "I'm thinking of going there tonight."

She laughed. To Dillon, that laugh was sultry, alluring, filled with promises kept. He remembered then why he'd warned her those years ago. He hadn't wanted to fall in love with her back then, but it had begun to happen, and he'd freaked out from the emotions welling inside of him. He smiled a little at her laugh, his pupils dilating unknowingly. He asked, "What's funny about that?"

"*You* are going to The Sinful Pleasure?" She laughed again, "That's live, unless of course you've found a nice man to take up with?" she asked snidely.

He laughed, "Ahhhh, I forgot how funny you are. Hey, you're right, I just wanted to hear your voice again."

"Mmm, hanging up now." She replied in a sing-song voice before she disconnected the call without saying bye.

Dillon looked around, "Did you hear that? The Sinful Pleasure."

"Ronald quipped, "So who's in the mood for a night at the strip club?"

Jeffery said, "I'm in."

Monty walked forward, stopping when he reached Ronald's side, "This is bad, Ronald. Let's not do this."

Jeffery argued, "I just want to know why he's kept it a secret."

Monty defended, "It's not like we don't all have ours." He raised his left arm in Dillon's direction, "I mean, look at Dillon. He was dating one of the hottest chicks on campus, and never said a word. Who does that?"

Ronald added, "And mistreated her. Don't you know you don't treat a Nubian queen that way?"

Dillon defended, "I didn't mistreat her, she just misunderstood my intentions ... You know what, this isn't about me, but I do agree with Monty. We do all have our secrets, and we're going to add another one." He looked at Montgomery. "Don't you say a word to him about our visit."

Monty opened his mouth to speak, but the sound they heard was that of a half-awake woman. "Monty, where are you? Come back to bed."

All eyes turned toward the sound of the voice, then to Montgomery.

Montgomery looked away from the direction of the voice and smiled. With his boyish handsomeness, he always seemed to look innocent, but they all knew he was far from it. "That's my cue. Later, fellas."

"Okay, we'll be back at seven o'clock," Ronald announced as they headed to the door.

Monty walked to the door to see the others out. He snatched his phone from Jeffery when he reached the door. He shut the door, and turned to lean on it, once again scratching his chest. "Damn it," he muttered, speed-dialing Jerome's phone. It went straight to voice mail, "Jerome, the guys overheard an argument between you and the professor. We're coming to the club tonight." He ended the call, and then went back to bed.

Jerome walked into the hospital and headed straight to his designation board to find out what doctor he was assigned to that day, and then he went to the employees' lounge. He needed another cup of coffee to get through this morning. As he was leaving the lounge, he walked almost into Samantha. "I'm glad to see you, Samantha, because we need to talk." Jerome grabbed her arm and dragged her into an empty room. "I wanted to apologize for my actions last night."

"You don't have to apologize to me, Jerome. It was everything I wanted."

Jerome ran his fingers through his hair. This was all wrong. "It shouldn't be because it wasn't me. I would never do that on general principles, but last night a lot of things were going on, and you came at a time when I just wanted to forget. Anyway, I wanted to let you know that it will never happen again."

"What if I want it to happen again?"

"Please don't. I feel guilty enough for taking advantage of you as it is. You're a great girl who deserves a man who's in love with you, not a man who is in love with someone else, and using you to try and forget her." He gave her arms a gentle squeeze, then turned and left the room, walking briskly down the hall. He had to stop thinking about Sasha and get on with his life. He just needed to figure out how.

The rest of his day was long and hectic. When he left the hospital, he had just enough time to go home, shower, and sleep for two hours before going to the club. His night became torturous when in the middle of a dance routine, Sasha and her friends waltzed in. She sat right at the front of the club holding a handful of bills and watched him with heated eyes. It drove him crazy every time he looked at her so he tried his best not to look her way. But he couldn't, and every time he did glance at her, she had a look that said, "I'm yours for the taking."

He refused to take her. Instead he took another girl to his dressing room with him. As he passed her by, he stole a quick glance at her. The pained look on her face was worse than the exchange outside of the college. He began to replay that look in his head to torture himself even more, which caused him not to be able to perform with the girl he'd brought back with him, so he sent her away and started drinking instead.

Montgomery, Dillon, Ronald, and Jeffery stood at the back of the club, having just witnessed Jerome's performance followed by him disappearing around the corner with a beautiful girl. Their faces showed differing degrees of shock. Five minutes later, Sasha and Bonnie left the club, Bonnie's arm wrapped protectively around a hysterical Sasha.

Regina walked toward the bar and paused briefly when she saw them standing there before continuing on. She ordered a six-cycle cocktail, and waited for the bartender to pass it to her before completely acknowledging their presence. She looked at Dillon, a hard glint in her eyes, "Your friend is an asshole." She looked him down, and back up. "Now I see why you guys are so chummy."

Dillon's green eyes stared into hers over the rim of his glass.

His amusement almost tangible. "Certainly you're not condemning me for my friends' actions?"

"You know what they say about birds and their feathers, right?"

"I missed you too, you sexy beast," he joked.

"Go to hell," she returned, but with seeming less resentment than she'd shown on the phone earlier. "Why are you guys lurking back here anyway?"

"The place is packed." He spoke a little louder as the MC began talking.

"You can sit at my table," she said, and walked away.

Dillon gave the others a nod to follow. As they wended their way through the crowd, quite a few of the women turned in their direction. Curiosity seeped from their pores, but was quickly overshadowed by the sound of the announcer introducing the next dancer.

The dancer came out in a cloud of green smoke as his music serenaded the audience. Although Leeza and Shelly gave the guys strange looks, neither of them said anything about their presence at the table.

Jeffery had been uncomfortable when they'd first entered the lounge. The big guy in the admittance parlor hadn't blinked twice, but he knew what kind of men usually came into a club like this. Now Jeffery watched the dancer with a critical eye. The song he danced to was kind of old, he noticed, as he listened to the verse, *"But I know she's a loser (How do you know?) Me and the crew used to do her! Poisoooooooon."* He was a good dancer, but he didn't have the technical ability Jerome had. Suddenly Jeffery was feeling kind of proud of his friend, and so many things started to make sense. For the next two dances Jeffery mentally noted everything from the dancing styles of various dancers, to the women who tossed fistfuls of dollars on the stage for the dancers. His parents were both stockbrokers, so he'd learned a lot about business.

He could see how lucrative a place like this could be. When

Jerome came back out for his final dance of the night, Jeffery had forgotten all about his initial discomfort of being inside a male strip club. He was thinking of long-term investments.

Jerome had been drinking for the past hour and a half since he'd scooted that girl out of his dressing room. He was feeling rather mellow as he made his way to the entertainment lounge to get ready for his performance. He picked up a magazine and waited for a reaction from his body. Nothing happened. He tried another but still didn't get the desired effect. He tossed the magazine in the general direction of the side table and flung himself on the couch. He tried his old trick of thinking of a moment with a hot chick ... nothing.

He wondered why he just couldn't get it up. Siren's dance was almost over, and he still wasn't ready. He closed his eyes and very carefully, as though plucking a petal from a fragile flower, conjured an image of Sasha in his head. It started at her head of thick shiny hair and traveled down her body to firm chocolate-kiss-tipped breasts, a waist span small enough for him to wrap his hands around and maintain connection between his thumb and middle fingers, down to the flare of her hips, and over to where the tops of her thighs met. He imagined her writhing in ecstasy on his bed. He groaned, and his eyes flew open. The bartender was looking at him as though he'd lost his mind.

He didn't care. It worked. Later he might reexamine this obsession he had for a woman he was supposed to hate, but for now he had a show to do. He stood, walked to the entrance, and waited for his cue. He stepped on the stage and began dancing, not caring about crowd participation. He was dancing in autopilot. Toward the end of the dance, he glanced in Sasha's direction. His heart seemed to skip a beat when he saw all four of his friends just sitting back enjoying the show as though they were at an opera. He was going to kill Monty!

As soon as his dance was over, he jumped off the stage and headed to the table. His face was contorted in a ferocious frown, and a storm brewed in his eyes. He stopped at the table. "What the hell are you guys doing here?"

Ronald looked up and joked, "Can you move that away a little?"

Jerome stepped back. "Come with me," then turned to leave. The others followed.

He grabbed a robe in the back and slid into it without skipping a beat as he proceeded to his dressing room. Once they all filed inside, he turned to repeat, "What are you doing here?" He looked directly at Montgomery, "Monty?"

"I tried to talk them out of it," Montgomery replied.

"But how do they know? Did you tell them?" Jerome asked with quiet calm.

Jeffery questioned, "Why didn't *you* tell us?" In his question was confusion, hurt. He didn't understand why Jerome felt he needed to keep this a secret.

In Jerome's inebriated and agitated state, he didn't hear confusion. He heard disgust and judgment, and he lashed out at it. "Because it's my personal life. You don't have to know everything that happens in it!"

Dillon stepped forward. "I thought we were your friends."

Ronald spoke. "We only wanted to know why this had to be such a big secret."

"How did you find out about it?" Jerome asked, still not answering their question.

Jeffery answered, "We overheard your argument with the professor yesterday."

Jerome looked at Montgomery. Montgomery nodded. Jerome said, "So you heard what's going on with his daughter and me?" Jerome asked, looking at Jeffery. At his nod, Jerome replied, "Then you know why I didn't tell you. It's the same condemnation I get every time someone finds out."

Ronald said, "But you didn't give us that choice, butthead. Just kicked us out. We had to find out from a third party, and we're supposed to be your good friends."

His anger deflating, he said, "Hell, no one knew, but Monty. Not even my family, but I'm done being ashamed of what I do. I didn't want to lose your friendship if you knew. Now I think if you really are my friends, then it shouldn't matter."

Jeffery asked, "Why did you think it would matter in the first place?"

Jerome looked at Jeffery like he'd lost his mind, "You're rich."

"Now who's condemning who?" Ronald argued.

"Look," Jerome grunted, "I've been doing this for almost four years now, and do you know how many rich people I've known, who upon finding out what I've been doing didn't shut me out?" Collectively they shook their heads. Jerome held up one finger. "Exactly one," he answered, and pointed that finger at Monty. "Not very confidence inspiring."

When he was finished working for the night, and the club had closed, he went home, showered, and fell into a deep sleep, only to awaken with sweat on his brow from the dream he'd had of her. Why couldn't he get her off of his mind? And why couldn't he just let her go?

After all, she was just a girl. He'd had girls prettier and more suited to his social status, so why was she so special? Because unlike so many others before her, he had fallen in love with her, and she was still carrying his heart with her. No matter how much he wanted to hate her, he couldn't, and he couldn't get over her either. Which left him where? It was useless to try and pursue a relationship with her if she couldn't stand up for herself.

He didn't want to be in a break up to make up relationship, but as long as she allowed everyone else to dictate their relationship to her that was exactly what they would have. So did he want to be miserable with her or miserable without her? He needed to figure this thing out before he lost his flippin' mind.

He spent the rest of that day thinking about nothing but Sasha, and he knew that no other woman would do for him, but he needed to make her understand where he stood so this would never happen again. He decided to have a talk with her. He just needed the right time and place to talk to her without her father's dominance taking over her decision.

He realized that most daddy's girls were just that because they never went against anything their fathers told them to do. Liana was exactly that way with him. Even though he wasn't her father, he was the closest thing she'd had to one for the last four years.

With his mind made up, the rest of his day went smoothly, and his performance that night was beautifully executed. He had the best sleep he'd gotten in weeks, and he woke up refreshed and ready for his day.

He completed one of the bigger exams of his schooling, which took most of the day. As he was leaving the campus, Professor Sherman stopped him in the hall. He gritted his teeth, not willing to have another verbal battle with him, so he spoke as politely as he could. "Professor, how are you today?"

"I am well, Jerome. May I have a moment of your time?"

"Is it overly important? I'm on a time constraint."

"I fear that if I do not speak with you today, then the rest of the week will pass by, and you will have very effectively ducked away from me to prevent this conversation from taking place."

Jerome's eyes widened. The professor had him pegged right. "I believe you're right, however, this will have to wait, as I don't have the time for a lengthy talk right now."

The professor smiled at his honesty, but persisted. "I will walk with you to your car, and we can talk on the way."

Jerome was not happy about his persistence, but he relented to get this *important* conversation over.

"Jerome, I like to think of myself as a fair person, as well as a great judge of character."

Jerome was not so certain about that fair part, but he kept his silence and allowed the professor to continue.

"When I first met you, I thought you would be perfect for my daughter." The professor nodded his head at the look of disbelief on Jerome's face, "It's true, but she is not someone you can just spring a man on, so I set in motion a group of events to get you two to meet without being too obvious that I wanted it to happen. You were not supposed to meet at a strip club, but that is neither here nor there. The important thing was that you two did meet, and the exact thing that I thought would happen did happen.

"I was very upset to find that you were not what I thought you were, but, Jerome, you are all and more than I ever gave you credit for. I don't say this often because I usually don't have to, but I was wrong. I apologize for breaking the two of you up."

Jerome was shocked to his core, because never in a million years would he have expected the conversation to go like that, which made him act cautiously with the situation. "Professor, why are you telling me this?"

"For some people, love comes often and leaves just as quickly, but for others love comes once, and lasts a lifetime. I have seen the change in you since Sasha left because of me—your weight loss, the tired lines on your face, and the hardness in your eyes. I am willing to bet that Sasha was your first real love, and you are having a very hard time getting over her."

Jerome would not confirm any of what he said but just continued to walk. They were coming close to his bike, and he was getting very uncomfortable with the professor's probing, but then the professor's next words made his heart leap.

"Sasha is having the same problem. She seems to be crying every time I see her. She won't go on any dates, and she yelled at me, which is something she has never done before. She has had relationships in the past but never one that she couldn't shake. Jerome, I would like to try and mend things with the two of you if it is at all possible."

"That may be too late, sir, because, you see, I've said and done some things in my anger that may have made any possibility of reconciliation with her completely out of the question."

"Why don't you come over for dinner Sunday, and we will test our theories? As I have said, I am rarely wrong."

Jerome agreed to come for dinner. The professor shook his hand, then walked away, leaving him baffled and a little dizzy. He stood beside his bike and stared as the professor walked out of sight, and then he stood a little longer feeling as though he'd just been on a roller coaster. For the life of him, he didn't think he would ever figure the professor out. One minute he was throwing out threats to the two of them and ordering them to never see one another again, and the next he was beseeching him to come over for dinner. Jerome shook his head, climbed on his bike, and drove off.

He wouldn't look a gift horse in the mouth. This just made it easier for him to make his supplications to Sasha and not have her dad's opposition, because now he was on their side. If she would have him back after what he'd done the last time he'd seen her.

He decided to wait until Sunday and not make contact with her as he'd originally intended. *The professor's right*, he thought, as he increased the speed of his bike. He had been having a very hard time getting over her, and the thought that she was suffering the same torment gave him a sordid kind of pleasure, and for the first time in weeks, he smiled genuinely.

Jerome stood in his master bathroom getting dressed for dinner with Sasha's family. The past week had been the longest week of his entire life wanting to seek Sasha out but determined to wait. She hadn't returned to the club after the last fiasco, and that wasn't lost on him.

He wore a steel blue button-down shirt with soft gray slacks and a tie that was gray with specks of blue. He looked up when he heard Eric calling him from somewhere in the condo. Shortly after calling, his head appeared in the bathroom doorway. Eric looked Jerome up and down and then stepped into the bathroom smiling in mock appraisal. He had a twinkle in his eyes, and Jerome knew instantly he was up to something.

Eric cleared his throat. "So what's the big occasion?"

Jerome looked at Eric through the mirror with a smile on his face. "Does there have to be one?"

Eric noticed that smile and was now seriously curious to know what it came from, since his brother hadn't done much of that in the last month or so. "You mean you're doing all this for me? I'm honored," Eric teased.

Jerome was exasperated with his brother's ability to never be serious, but he was in good humor mode tonight. He asked, "What do you want, Er?"

"Well, I thought I'd give you some good news, but if you're going to treat me this way, then I guess …"

Jerome interrupted him with a smile. "Out with it, Er."

Eric handed Jerome a folded piece of paper.

Jerome frowned, perplexed when he accepted it and then unfolded it to read its contents. He smiled in delight and gave a whoop of joy! He picked Eric up in a bear hug and swung him around.

Eric laughed and broke free. "Okay, it's just admittance, and there's no guarantee that I'll be good at it, or like it, or even stick with it. I'm not like you, you know. I'm not perfect," Eric admitted quietly.

Jerome patted Eric's shoulder with a somber look on his face. He hadn't realized just how much his little brother looked up to him until now, and decided to do something Sasha had mentioned to him before. "I'm proud of you, man. I'm not asking you to be like me. I'm the last person I want you to be like, and maybe this isn't for you, but then maybe it is. Either way, I respect you as the man you're becoming, and I know you'll find your right path in life."

Eric looked pleased with his brother's praise. "You're the first person I would want to be like, Romy. Don't you know that by now? I wouldn't want to be like anyone else." Eric cleared his throat in an effort to cover some of the emotion he was feeling, and then he changed the subject so they wouldn't get any mushier than they had already. "Now tell me again what you're getting all dressed up for. You have a date?"

Jerome followed his lead with a smile of understanding. "Yes."

"With whom?"

"Sasha."

"Hope you're good at dodging bullets. So are you going to skip town with her, maybe go underground?"

"Don't you ever take anything seriously?"

Eric crossed his arms over his chest and waited for an answer. "I'm going to her house for dinner."

Eric shook his head. "Some people never learn. I just hope you have your will updated because I would love to have this condo."

Jerome laughed and punched Eric in the chest. "I'd better get going, or I'll be late. Wish me luck." Jerome walked out of the room and toward the door.

Eric followed close behind. "You'll need it, or a bulletproof vest." The door closed on that last comment. Eric stood in place for a brief moment and shook his head once again. "Poor love-struck fool. May God help me if I ever fall so hard."

He walked into the kitchen and grabbed himself a bag of popcorn. He placed it in the microwave, and then he pulled a can of Pepsi from the fridge. As he waited for the popcorn, the phone rang. Taking his attention from the rotating bag, he picked up the phone to answer, "Jacob's rez."

"Hey, dude, its Poison. Let's hang out today. I can pick you up in about thirty minutes."

"Nah, I'm gonna chill today."

"Getting scared of what your big brother might say? I understand."

"Actually I'm getting scared of what you might decide to get high on next, and I don't want to be there when you overdose for good. I thought you were gonna quit that stuff anyway."

"I am. I'm just going to have one more good high."

"Yeah, famous last words. Let me know how it goes for you."

Eric hung up the phone and went back to retrieve his popcorn. He settled himself down on the comfortable sofa to indulge in a day of movies and sports.

⌒☙⌒

Jerome stood on the front porch of the Sherman household and looked around. He took a deep breath and wiped his sweaty palms on his trousers. Then, when he thought about what he'd just done, he straightened his clothes and rang the doorbell.

The professor opened the door moments later. He reached out to shake Jerome's hand. "Come in, Jerome. There are a couple of people who will be happy to see you."

Jerome caught one particular word in that sentence and repeated it. "*Will* be?"

"Sasha does not know you were expected. She is not speaking to me."

The professor led Jerome into a room where Mrs. Sherman and Joslyn sat talking. The room was spacious and airy with soft coloring meant for comfort and relaxation. He thought the women of the house probably spent a lot of time in that room.

"Joanne, dear, I have someone I would like you to meet."

Both ladies looked up in unison, and their eyes widened with identical looks of surprise. Joslyn's look showed appreciation as well.

Mrs. Sherman found her tongue and let it go free. "You are not still trying to play matchmaker are you, honey? The last time didn't go so well, and even though this boy is absolutely beautiful, the heart knows what it wants."

Joslyn laughed while Jerome cleared his throat and gave the professor a smug sideways look.

The professor frowned at his wife for her outspokenness before saying, "As I was saying, Joanne, Joslyn, I would like for you to meet Jerome Jacobs; Jerome, this is my lovely ill-mannered wife and my oldest daughter."

For the second time in minutes, the two women stared with their mouths wide open. They were beautiful women, really. The oldest daughter had features very similar to Sasha, with shoulder-length hair, exotically slanted eyes, full lush lips, and pert little nose. The difference was their skin tone. Joslyn's tone was darker by a couple of shades than Sasha's.

Mrs. Sherman was ageless. To have two daughters in their twenties, she had to be close to fifty, if not already there, but one couldn't tell just by looking at her.

Jerome smiled at the wide-open silence and the looks of utter shock on the two women's faces. "It's a pleasure to meet you both."

"Wow," was the only word that came from Joslyn's mouth as she took in the full measure of Mr. Jerome Jacobs, and she understood why her sister was having such a hard time forgetting him.

"The pleasure is all mine, Jerome, I assure you." Mrs. Sherman walked to Jerome, looped her arm through his, and turned him in the direction of the breakfast nook. As they disappeared around the corner, she could be heard saying, "I have heard so much about you."

Professor Sherman walked to Joslyn, who was still staring in the direction Jerome had just gone. "Joslyn, will you please go and let Sasha know that dinner will start shortly and that we have a guest?"

Joslyn nodded and turned to leave, pausing at the corner to take one last look at Jerome, who was sitting at the table with her mother having tea as though she was a lady and he a titled lord.

The professor stopped her before she reached the steps and said, "Joslyn, don't tell her who our guest is, okay?"

❧

Sasha sat in a chaise in her room reading. Joslyn knocked, and without waiting for a reply, gently opened the door. Sasha looked up from her book at her sister's entrance.

"Dad has requested your presence below. We have a dinner guest."

Joslyn looked like she couldn't wait to get back downstairs. Why? "Male or female?"

"Male."

"Same guy from the last time?"

"No, I don't think that guy will ever be back."

"Please tell dad I'm neither hungry nor interested."

Joslyn's eyes twinkled merrily when she said, "Too bad. This one is quite a looker, but I'm not getting caught up in your feud. If you want him to know how you feel, then you come tell him."

"He can't be better-looking than Romy, but you're right, I need to tell him in front of this guy and then maybe that will discourage his return as well. Give me a few moments to compose myself."

With that, Joslyn hurried back down the stairs. She loved her Ethan, but this Romy was pure eye candy. She almost envied Sasha.

❦

Forty-five minutes later, everyone was still waiting for Sasha to come to dinner. The professor looked at his watch for what must have been the fifteenth time, and then he stood and excused himself. He stepped out of the dining room just as Sasha was coming down the stairs, and she walked to her father, stopping before him just outside of the door.

She carried a mutinous expression on her face that showed her willingness to do battle, and the tone of her voice with the words that came next were in fact throwing down the gauntlet. "Perhaps I didn't make myself clear to you the last time you tried this, so let me try again. I'm not interested in your attempts at matchmaking, because no one that you bring here can take the place of the one I really want. So if you don't mind, I will *not* be joining you for dinner tonight!"

The professor lost all of his anger in that moment. Seeing his baby girl stand up to him made him realize all the more why he needed to fix things between them and how wrong he'd been to interfere the way that he had. So he was as patient and gentle as he knew to be with his words.

"It has always been the tradition of this family to have Sunday dinner together whenever possible, and you do need to eat. I will not push you to accept my young man, although I begin to believe even more that you two will make a great match." He grabbed her hand and placed it in his arm. "Please come eat."

Sasha, feeling humbled by the gentleness in his voice, did not protest further. The two entered the dining room together, and as they did, Jerome stood at first sight of her. When the professor left the dining room, he hadn't completely closed the door, so the occupants heard the entire conversation. Sasha looked up at Jerome when he stood, and she stopped midstride, shocked.

When she looked at her father, he smiled encouragingly, and they continued to their seats. Jerome stepped to her seat to help her with her chair, and she allowed him, at the same time breathing in deeply of the scent of him.

She watched him return to his seat and then turned to smile at her dad joyfully as Jerome reseated himself. The others watched every look and exchange in avid interest.

Jerome's eyes were warm and inviting when he spoke. "Hello, Sasha."

Sasha smiled through tear-filled eyes as she spoke to the one man that she'd ever truly loved, "Hello, Dr. Romy."

Only Sasha and Jerome knew what that meant, and Jerome smiled at Sasha intimately as the servings of food began to be passed around the table.

Everyone at the table knew what that smile meant, and the professor began thinking about how he could get Jerome off of the stage and ready for marriage.

# CHAPTER 21

*L*ater that evening, Sasha and Jerome took a walk outside. A talk to straighten out their situation was long overdue. But despite all of the problems that hadn't been worked out between them, they still walked closely together, arms touching, but neither making an attempt to grab the other's hand.

Sasha opened the conversation by saying, "I'm glad you came over, Romy. I thought you hated me."

"I did. As far as I was concerned, it was over for good."

That statement made Sasha confused. Her brows bunched together showing her bafflement, she asked, "Then what made you come over to brave the lion's den?"

"You didn't know your dad had a talk with me?"

She confirmed his query with a negative shake of her head.

"About a week ago, Professor Sherman, after ignoring me for weeks, stopped me as I was leaving the class. We had quite an explosive conversation, ending with my telling him all about how I became an exotic dancer. That was the same day that I saw you outside of the school and was quite rude to you. I'm sorry, but at the time, I was against all things Sherman.

"Then earlier this week, he stopped me again and invited me to come over for dinner. He said you were making his life a living hell, and from the sound of those words spoken outside of the dining room tonight, I'm inclined to believe him."

Sasha laughed, "I wouldn't go that far. I was just not going to tolerate his attempts to put me on rebound mode. He'd already tried three times before."

"Well, I'd already decided that this thing wasn't working. I couldn't stop thinking about you. I was mad at you for not fighting for us, but then mad at myself for not being able to let you go. So I drank to dull the pain and anger. Then I tried having sex with other women to not think about you."

"And the night I came to the club? Did you have sex with that girl?"

She was watching him like a hawk waiting to strike if his answer was not the right one. "No, I couldn't get an erection. I kept seeing that look in your eyes when I walked by with her."

Sasha looked so relieved that he knew he had to let her know right away before they went any further, so he stopped and turned to her. "That's not to say I didn't sleep with *anyone* while we were apart, because I did. I'm not proud of it, nor am I proud of my reasons for doing it."

Even though a tear slid down her check, she said, "I can't be mad at you for that, as much as hearing it hurts, because we weren't together at my decision. So how about we start from scratch, and I'll not bring up the women, if you'll completely exonerate me for walking away from you that night."

"I think I can do that." He grabbed at the line she was throwing him like a drowning man, relieved that she wouldn't hold against him those times that he'd gotten drunk and had sex with a number of girls in the club in an effort to prove to himself he was getting over her.

Sasha couldn't hold back any longer. She wrapped her arms around his waist and looked up at him, "I missed you so much. I'm just glad you decided to not stick with the thought of us being over for good and was willing to give me another chance."

"Me too, because trying to get you out of my mind was the hardest thing I think I've ever tried to do."

They met each other halfway for a steamy kiss. When they finally separated themselves, Jerome found himself in the same situation he'd been in the first day he'd met her, and that was with an erection that he could do nothing about. They walked back around to the front of the house.

Professor and Mrs. Sherman stood on the porch, his arm around his wife, and she smiled at him contentedly. "I'm so proud of you, honey. He's a really good kid. I mean, if I didn't already know, I would never think in a million years he's a stripper."

The professor frowned at his wife for the reminder. "After the talk we had, I could hardly classify him as a kid. I am perversely proud of him even though I have no right to be. Do you know that he is supporting his entire family with that money, as well as paying his way through college? I just think that is amazing. After he told me that, I have asked myself a dozen times if I did not have the privilege I did that paid my way through school, what would I have done if faced with the same circumstances?"

"And what was your answer?"

Professor and Mrs. Sherman both looked up as Jerome and Sasha came into view. The professor watched Jerome briefly before saying, "I would never have become a doctor. I would have quit at my mother's urging and gone home to find a job with the degree I had."

Mrs. Sherman kissed him quickly and then turned toward Jerome and Sasha at the sound of their approach. "How about we go inside for dessert?"

Jerome nodded his assent, but the professor detained Sasha by placing his hand on her arm. Jerome and Mrs. Sherman went inside the house to allow them privacy.

"Sasha, I just wanted to tell you how wrong I was for judging you. You are my baby girl, and I have always wanted the best for you."

"I believe he is, dad." She paused and then said, "So does this mean you're okay with him being a stripper?"

"I am still not happy about that; however, I know his motives and what is driving him, and, because I believe he will be good for you, I will turn a blind eye toward that … for now."

Sasha reached up and kissed her father on the cheek. "Thank you, Daddy."

# CHAPTER 22

$\mathcal{J}$erome entered his apartment feeling ridiculously happy. The day couldn't have gone any better if he'd designed it himself. He looked at Eric sitting on the sofa talking on the phone surrounded by the leftovers of everything he'd eaten throughout the afternoon.

He walked to the sofa and began to pick up plates, cups, and paper towels. Even the fact that his once immaculate apartment now looked like a stag house didn't upset his mood. Eric stood up and began to help him with the cleanup.

Eric spoke to the person on the phone. "I'll talk to you later, babe." Then to Jerome he said, "So how did it go? I see you made it through alive."

Jerome decided to unsettle him a bit, he owed him for the bacon and eggs. With a straight face he said, "It went great. We eloped." He innocently walked away to place the dinnerware in the kitchen.

Eric looked surprised and disbelieving at the same time, "No way. You're kidding. Well, what happened? You've got to be joking. No, you never joke about things like that. Are you serious?"

Eric's rambling had Jerome ready to burst. "Well, her dad wasn't going to just *let* us get married so ..."

"You're crazy, man. I can't believe this! Is he going to kill you when he finds out?"

"It was a joke! We had dinner, it was very nice, and then we walked and cleared the air between us. I tried to get her to come back here with me for the night, but she didn't want to give her dad an even worse impression of me than he has already after I'd done so well with the family. You know he thinks I just go to work each night and play eeny, meeny, miny, moe with girls."

"Well, you could if you wanted to." Eric passed by Jerome to place his empty cups in the sink. As he was passing back, he quipped, "You might as well marry her. You're useless to any other female at this point, poor love-struck fool that you are."

Jerome grabbed Eric and put him into a head lock in retaliation of that statement, which Eric quickly disentangled himself from. After cleaning away the dishes, they both grabbed drinks and headed to the sofa to sit.

Eric said, "It has occurred to me that we should think about getting someone to clean every once in a while."

Jerome took a swallow of his beer before replying, "This place has never needed a maid before you came to stay, so if you want one, then you need to put up the money for one."

Eric rolled his eyes. "It's not as if you can't afford it, Romy."

"That's not the point. The point is it's your mess, so you need to clean it. If you can't or won't, then *you* need to pay for someone to do it for you."

Eric shrugged in agreement. "I guess that's fair." He changed the subject, "Listen, I get to hang around the campus for a few days to kinda get the feel of the place. Do you mind if I tag along with you to class?"

"Not at all. So you paid your tuition already?"

"Just for the semester."

"That's awesome! I'm proud of you, man."

Jerome, Eric, and Jerome's buddies walked down the hall at the end of class. Eric had been hanging out with Jerome and was becoming more appreciative of his brother's hard work and effort. He looked up to him more and more.

Ronald looked at Eric and then asked him, "So, Eric, how do you like the idea of college after the last couple of days?"

Eric looked at a pretty girl passing by who paused to notice him and let him know that she'd noticed. "It looks like it comes with some nice perks."

Montgomery laughed. He'd been looking in the same direction as Eric. "That it does, my friend, and once the girls find out that you're Jerome's brother, you'll hardly ever lack for one."

Jerome, hearing this, turned to look sharply at Monty. "What's that supposed to mean, Monty? I've never encouraged any of them."

"Exactly. You have this aloof, mysterious man thing about you that drives them crazy with curiosity. I'm sure each of us could vouch for scoring a chick or two just off of some girl's curiosity about you, just ask Ronald. Eric will be in if for no other reason than that he has insider info."

Eric smiled. "I'm okay with that."

Jerome looked disgustedly at Eric, "You would be." To Ronald he said, "Did you score just because of me?"

Ronald nodded affirmatively, and Jerome opened his mouth to say something but saw Sasha and excused himself from the boys to head her way.

Sasha smiled encouragingly as he approached and reached up to hug him when he was close enough. "I've missed your hugs and kisses. Pity on you for being too busy for me this past week," she pouted.

"Yeah, tell me about it, but you know finals are coming, and I've needed all of my free time to study. Between my classes here, my rotations at the hospital, and my late-night job, I'm surprised to have any energy at all, let alone that kind." He wriggled his eyebrows suggestively.

Sasha smiled in understanding at his quip. "Why, Jerome, I think you have a split personality. I mean, one minute you're like this proper doctor, and the next you're like an exotic male dancer making these comments filled with innuendo. Who are you, a doctor or a dancer?" She asked him playfully.

"I'm a regular Dr. Jekyll and Mr. Hyde. Wonder which one I am right now? Hey, will you come to the club tonight?"

She checked her nail nonchalantly. "Can't, gotta study, finals you know."

Jerome smacked her playfully on the butt. "I start at ten tonight, but if you come early, I may give you a backstage tour."

"I've already been backstage."

"Then how about a free dance?"

"Had one, but maybe I'll give you one instead."

"Hmm, sounds interesting." He opened her shirt to peer inside. "Can I have a sneak peek?"

Sasha's friends turned the corner to meet up with her and smiled at Jerome in greeting.

Behind them, Eric stood with Jerome's college buddies, the group increasing as others filed out of the class and joined them.

Montgomery watched in awe as Jerome and Sasha exchanged a brief but passionate hug and kiss. "When did he start dating Sasha Sherman again?"

Christopher, a fellow classmate chimed in, "I tried with her once," which had everyone looking at him curiously, he shook his head regretfully. "Shot me down and never looked back. Her friends are just as haughty."

Eric laughed.

Ronald said to Eric, "No offense, but for a while I began to think Jerome was a little," he wagged his hand, "you know."

Eric laughed even harder, his beautiful white smile catching the notice of more than one passing girl. After he calmed his laughter, he said, "I assure you he isn't—just very private."

Ronald said, "Oh we get it now."

Jerome smiled at the ladies and paused, identifying the one he recognized most. "Hi, Bunny."

"You mean, Bonnie," Bonnie corrected.

Jerome looked at his watch and noted the time. He didn't have much of it left before he needed to be at the hospital. "Right."

Sasha laughed and said to Bonnie, "I know that word; he uses it often when he's stopped listening."

Jerome smiled at Sasha. "You think you know me?" He checked his watch again and said, "I'd better get going, so I'll see you later." He gave her a kiss and walked away.

Shelly watched him leave, and then turned back around to Sasha. "Girl, you're lucky I love you, 'cause if I didn't, I would hate you for that," she spoke, tilting her head in Jerome's direction.

Sasha rejoined with, "You should try his little brother. He's equally beautiful."

"Please, I do not rob cradles."

Leeza said, "I do," looking at Eric as he laughed at something Jerome's friends was saying.

The ladies all laughed as they turned to walk in the opposite direction.

Jerome walked up to the guys. "We gotta get going, Eric."

Ronald frowned. "So you weren't going to tell us you've been back with the professor's daughter?"

Jerome shrugged, "You know we've been off and on, more off than on."

"But now it's on?"

"It's on," Jerome said with a smile.

"Are you coming to the party?" Monty asked, already knowing what his answer would be.

"Sorry, man, I really have too much work to do, but when you throw yours, I'll be there, I promise."

Jerome and Eric parted from the guys and exited the college hall. They headed for Jerome's sleek motorcycle, and once they reached it, they put on their helmets. After storing their backpacks, they hopped on the bike and disappeared down the street.

# CHAPTER 23

The end of finals marked the beginning of the Christmas holiday, and Jerome took Sasha home to meet his family. Sasha and Jessica were almost inseparable by the end of the week. Jerome's mother cried tears of joy to see her son so happy, and in love. They had an early Christmas so Sasha could return to her family for their celebrations, but Jerome had to promise Liana a visit to DC before she'd let them leave.

The next three months had him preparing to graduate college, and he stayed true to his promise to bring Liana to DC. Actually, his entire family came for the graduation. It was the first time they'd seen his apartment. His mother was impressed, but didn't ask many questions. He guessed she assumed he made enough money as a Physician Assistant to be able to afford it.

He entertained his family for almost a week, spoiling his baby sister even more than she was already. During that time, he was also preparing to take his entrance exam for his residency. He was now awaiting the results.

His schedule had been hectic first with graduation, then with family, and finally with getting back to a normal routine. It was not a surprise to anyone to find Jerome asleep at his dressing table with his head lying on a textbook. Eric entered his dressing room with Sasha close behind him. Jerome had to be exhausted to be asleep at that moment, when he was supposed to be on stage in thirty minutes.

Eric held his finger to his lips requesting Sasha's silence. She complied and sat down in the chaise out of reach. Eric pulled his phone out of his pocket and set the alarm to go off in one minute, then walked quietly toward Jerome, his famous mischievous smile on his face.

Sasha smiled at that look of mischief as he carefully walked, trying not to wake him.

He sat the phone down beside Jerome's head, and the alarm went off with loud beeps. Jerome bolted up shocked.

From where she sat, Sasha laughed quietly behind her hand.

Eric laughed loudly, and then squeezed his nose shut mimicking the sound of a voice on an intercom. "Paging Dr. Romy. Dr. Romy to the emergency room, please."

Jerome picked up a bottle of water and threw it at Eric. "You are such a nitwit."

Eric sidestepped the bottle still laughing. "We're up in an hour, less if Poison doesn't make it here on time and sober."

"Poison sober? That sounds like an oxymoron."

"Well, reasonably sober."

"I thought I was doing a solo first tonight."

"You are, and that happens in thirty minutes."

Sasha laughed, causing Jerome to turn fully around. He noticed her for the first time, and he stood up smiling in welcome.

Eric gestured toward Sasha. "Brought you a gift," then he headed to the door. He stopped and laughed recalling his joke and the look on his brother's face when the alarm had gone off, "Paging Dr. Romy. That was so funny."

Jerome walked to Eric and ushered him the rest of the way out of the door. "Umm-hmm, very funny."

"I thought you'd appreciate a good joke when—"

Jerome closed the door, cutting off his words. He then turned and walked back to Sasha, who was still sitting in the same place smiling in amusement at their antics.

Eric spoke through the door, "That was so rude."

"No, that was funny." To Sasha he said, "Brothers, don't you just love them?"

"Umm-hmm," Sasha agreed as she stood and leaned in for a kiss.

The kiss turned steamy very quickly, but was disrupted by a knock at the door. Jerome took a step back, feeling pretty frustrated. His breathing was out of control as though he'd run a long distance nonstop. His body was covered in perspiration, and his erection was painful in its intensity; so he was not his most genial when he yelled, "What the hell is it!"

Siren, one of the newer dancers hired, and who'd already made it clear that he wanted Jerome's standing in the club, was on the other side of the door and called out, "Sin said to tell you that he will need you to replace one of Poison's dances ... this one."

Jerome ran his fingers through his hair in agitation, and then he looked back at Sasha, who looked as aroused as he felt and said, "I'm sorry, but I guess this will *have* to wait until later." He walked to the door and opened it a crack to say, "I'm on my way."

Closing the door, Jerome walked back to Sasha. "It's gonna be a busy night."

Sasha grabbed his throbbing erection and squeezed it lightly. He groaned. She liked that sound but needed to get him out of there before she dragged him to the chair against the wall and did some very unladylike things to him. "I guess you'll need this for your performance?"

"I guess so," Jerome replied with a sensual smile, "since I have two performances back to back."

"I'll go find a seat, but you owe me *big* time."

Jerome put on one hell of a performance, but he was only vaguely aware of the screams of excitement in the room. His mind was on Sasha and all of the things he wanted to do to her, and to some extent he acted it out on the stage.

Dancing to Robin Thicke's "*Lost without You*," his hips were in constant motion, he ran his hands slowly down his torso. When his hands reached his pelvis, he ground his erection against his hands. He brought one of his hands back to his mouth and licked his finger, and then ripped his pants off.

Through the haze of falling money, he looked at Sasha to see the hot lust in her eyes, which caused him an even harder erection. He walked to the side of the stage where she sat, and dropped to the floor. The muscles in his shoulder, back, and arms flexed and shone with perspiration as he slowly ground the floor looking directly at her.

Sasha almost forgot to breathe. The look in his eyes was mesmerizing, and she knew the promises in them would be delivered just as his body was showing her. She shifted her position in her seat while her body prepared itself.

They raced to Jerome's apartment on his motorcycle, and while Jerome drove, one of Sasha's hands slid inside of his trousers as she massaged his swollen manhood.

Jerome was threatening to explode. He had to get home as quickly as possible to avoid the disgrace of it all, but damn her hands felt good.

They burst through the door with Sasha already pulling off Jerome's shirt. Their lips never parted as he lifted her in one fluid motion and carried her to his bedroom. Settling her down on the floor beside his bed, he helped her take off her shirt.

Sasha dropped to her knees, raking her nails down his chest as she descended. She unbuckled his pants and slid down his zipper with her teeth.

Jerome watched with eyes gone cloudy. His body throbbed in anticipation of what she was going to do.

Sasha was breathing hard again, and then she did something

she'd wanted to do since the very first time she'd seen him in the club that night. She ran her tongue over the muscle forming a *V* on his pelvic bone. His hips shot forward and a moan escaped his lips.

Steadying him, she freed his penis as it pressed persistently against his pants and slid her tongue over it too. She could taste the slightly salty bead of moisture that bespoke of his arousal on her tongue, and then she slid his shaft into her mouth. His moan turned into a groan, and he began to gently rock his hips back and forward. She closed her eyes enjoying the feel of satin over steel. She reached down to stroke her swollen clitoris through her underwear, on the verge of a climax.

Jerome watched with his lip being bitten between his teeth. His groans becoming gasps of pleasure as, with her hand wrapped securely around the base of his shaft, she made love to him with her mouth. If she didn't stop soon he would release just this way, and that wouldn't be good. When she began stroking herself he lost control.

He pulled free of her adoring lips and dropped to his knees. He opened her bra and wrapped his mouth around her breast. She inhaled sharply, absorbing the pleasure, all the while he kneaded her butt cheeks.

He turned her around, gruffly telling her, "Hold on to the bed."

When she complied, he entered her in one smooth and powerful stroke. She screamed out from the pleasure and pain of it. Leaning into her, he reached around her and slid his finger into her already filled opening, creating even less space.

She gasped immediately feeling the pressure that his penis put on his finger, causing his finger to rub against her already swollen erectile tissue. His finger began to move in the limited amount of space it had, and her body went taut. He was pounding into her, and she reveled in every thrust. Finally her muscles released, and she screamed in pleasure, vaguely aware of the feeling of liquid sliding down her legs.

Jerome removed his finger and continued in measured strokes.

He could feel his release building, his muscles tightening, his shaft swelling. He leaned forward once more to whisper in her ear, "I love you, Sasha," and then he tilted back his head and groaned as hot, liquid pleasure shot from his contracting muscles. When he became aware of his surroundings, he realized that she was coming again.

When she was done, he picked her up and carried her to the bathroom. They showered, washing one another's bodies before stepping out to dry each other off, and then they climbed into the bed. Jerome held her in his arms, their voices soft as they reflected on their lives in the last eight months.

Pure bliss, was the only description Jerome could give for the month that followed He and Sasha were together as much as his work and studies would allow. Eric began his summer classes, and Jerome received results from his MCAT-2 exams. He'd passed, and was now to begin his residency, and the hospital was already ready for him. He resigned his position as Physician Assistant. One week later, he began his residency.

He entered his apartment after a long shift at the hospital and stopped, staring at Eric on the sofa with a girl on top of him, her shirt opened and her breasts spilling out.

Jerome cleared his throat, and they both looked up at the sound. He said, "You do have a room you could go to with that."

"Oh, yeah, of course, Romy."

Jerome didn't wait but headed to his own bedroom. Once inside, he stripped down to his underwear and dropped onto the bed. He immediately fell asleep.

Four hours later, he was up and ready for his night at the club. He entered the hall from his bedroom and stopped at Eric's door. He knocked on it and waited momentarily. When Eric opened the door, he was wearing a sheet around his waist, and the girl he was with was lying in the bed with a sheet covering her nudity.

Ignoring the girl, Jerome said, "It's almost nine thirty, and I'm heading in to work. Are you riding with me?"

"I can't. I gotta get her home, but I'll be in about twenty behind you."

Jerome shrugged and walked down the hall grabbing his keys on his way out of the apartment.

# CHAPTER 24

The club was in full swing by the time Eric got there. He decided to go in through the back entrance so that he could avoid running into some of the patrons still coming into the club. The only street light into the alley was broken as he walked toward the back, but the glow of street lights from the main street was light enough for him.

The closer Eric got to the door, the more he could hear the sound of a man grunting in pain interspersed with the sound of fists connecting with bones.

More out of curiosity than anything else, Eric walked closer to get a look at what poor soul was being beaten so badly, and saw two men holding Poison while one other was delivering the blows. Without hesitation, Eric rushed to his defense thinking to even the odds a little.

Eric did a pile drive into the back of the attacker (Manny) that was beating on Poison, knocking him to the ground. He kicked him in the ribs a few times and then hit him in his head with his balled fist, causing him to black out momentarily.

He turned to the man (Mac) who was still holding Poison's left arm and swung, hitting him in the jaw. The two of them began exchanging blows, which took everyone's attention away from Poison. The fighting lasted for only a couple of minutes before

Eric's fighting skills afforded him the upper hand. He grabbed Mac's neck, pushing him against the wall.

Mac looked to Rick, who stood almost stunned watching his comrade being beaten, and rasped out, "Get him off of me."

Rick released Poison and pulled out his gun.

When Poison found himself free, he ran away from the fray. Leaving Eric behind, and never looking back, he quickly entered the club.

Rick stood behind Eric, aimed his gun at his back, and fired.

Mac released a howl of pain as the bullet intended for Eric entered and exited his shoulder to lodge into the shoulder of Mac.

Eric stiffened and released the man with the sudden pain in his shoulder. He could see the blood coming from the other guy in front of him and knew he'd been shot.

While the bumbling idiot who'd shot them both realized what he had done, Eric ran toward the door of the club. While Rick made his attempt to help Mac, he fired off two more shots at Eric's departing figure. Eric fell to the ground before he reached the door. Mac stumbled to the car while Rick helped Manny up and to the car. They sped off with tires screeching.

Poison ran stumbling down the hall to Jerome's dressing room and burst inside.

Jerome was dressed in costume from the waist down and was laughing at something Sasha, who was sitting on the lounge chair, said. He looked up sharply when Poison burst through the door.

"Romy, you have to help, it's—" Poison gasped for air through his bruised lungs.

Jerome helped Poison into a chair and asked in concern, "What is it, Poison? What's happened?"

"Eric tried to help me ... in the alley ... there were three or four of them."

"And you left him?!"

Leaving Poison behind, Jerome rushed out of the room with

Sasha in tow. Red heard the commotion in his dressing room at the other end of the hall and came out to see Jerome running for the backdoor. When they passed Sin's office in such a hurry, he stepped out to see what was happening.

The excitement caused doors to open all along the corridor, and by the time they reached the exit, they had a full entourage. Jerome burst through the door and came to an almost immediate stop when he saw Eric lying on his stomach bleeding from three wounds in his back.

He kneeled down beside him and checked his pulse, finding it there but faint, and then he turned him over gently. Eric was bleeding from his shoulder, and Jerome took a moment to examine the wound. He noticed it was in perfect symmetry to have been either an entrance or exit wound from the shoulder blade.

Jerome ripped open Eric's shirt and called out to any one of the people standing around from the club, "I need clean white towels quickly!" To Sasha, he said, "Has anyone called the ambulance yet?"

Someone moved to gather the towels while someone called yes in answer to his question.

Sasha stood back with tears in her eyes, not saying a word.

Jerome whispered, "Hold on, Er, just hold on." To Sasha, he said, "Will you call my mom, please, and tell her?" His voice broke, and he cleared his throat. "Tell her that he's been shot and that, that I will call her later with an update? When you're finished, I want you to go home."

Jerome gave Sasha his phone, and she took it, scrolling through his contacts to get the number out, and then she put the phone in his pocket and walked away to call his mother.

Jerome was busy examining Eric for any other wounds and didn't notice her replacing his phone. Through all of it, Eric remained unconscious. Moments later, Red appeared with an armful of white towels, which Jerome took, and with the help of Red, lifted him and placed one between his shirt and back.

After laying him back down, he called out, "Does anyone have a belt?"

He took the first one that came into his vision and placed it over a towel that he'd put on Eric's shoulder where the exit wound was located, and then he closed the buckle as tightly as he could.

Turning him back over, he placed a towel on each of the other two wounds and applied pressure.

Red was kneeling beside him and asked solemnly, "Is he going to be okay, Romy?"

Jerome looked at Red with pain written on his face and uncertainty in his eyes, "I don't know, Red. He's losing a lot of blood."

When the paramedics arrived, two of them jumped from the ambulance and rushed toward them with their medical bags. A third medic came carrying a gurney.

Jerome expertly assisted them in getting Eric onto the gurney, all the while giving them his vital stats. "He had three gunshot wounds. Two of them are in the back and one in the shoulder; also, one in the upper chest region, possibly an entry or exit wound.

"He's lost a lot of blood, so he'll likely need a transfusion. His pulse is at about 49 and his respiratory is at 9."

One of the medics wrote down the information Jerome fired off. When Jerome was finished, the medic asked, "Can anyone identify the young man so that his family can be contacted?"

"I'm his family," Jerome said, "and I'll be coming with you."

The medic placed a detaining hand on Jerome's chest and said, "We cannot allow you to—"

Jerome removed his hand, cutting off his sentence before he could finish it. "Like hell!"

"But sir—"

Again Jerome cut him off testily. "We are wasting precious time here with this useless bickering. I'm going."

"Sir, you can follow behind, but we are not allowed to—"

Jerome began pushing the gurney to the ambulance. "You follow behind. I'll be inside that truck."

With the help of one of the other medics, they expertly maneuvered the gurney into the unit, and once they had Eric inside, Jerome climbed in behind. The medic who'd been protesting stared dumbfounded for a second while one of the others shrugged and climbed in behind him.

The arguing medic walked to the ambulatory unit and stood at the open door. "Sir, I cannot allow you to ride here. It's against company procedure, and I—"

Jerome was past anger at that point! Here his brother lay bleeding to death, and he wanted to argue about procedure. "Listen, my brother is lying here bleeding half to death while you squabble over something that's a moot point! If he dies because of this, you won't have to worry about this damn unit, or company procedures, because I will have your job and then your head! Now drive this damned ambulance!"

The gurney burst through the emergency doors of the hospital, one of the medics pushing and the other riding on the side pumping oxygen into Eric's lungs. Jerome rushed in not far behind. The admittance nurse looked up and froze in shock upon seeing Jerome, as he was still dressed the way he'd rushed from the club, which was partially.

Nancy stopped gawking, although she'd not gotten over her shock, and spoke. "Dr. Jacobs, I didn't know you were expected tonight." She cleared her throat. "Did you just come from a costume party?"

Not responding to her latter question, Jerome answered the former comment instead. "I was not, but this is my brother. It's a code blue, first priority."

Both of the paramedics that were there looked at one another in shock when they heard Nancy address him as *doctor*, in this hospital.

Nancy said, "We've been expecting him, and we were

forewarned about his condition. I didn't know we were getting your brother though."

Nancy pushed a button signaling the doctors of the emergency room. Jerome washed his hands and headed down the hall, following behind the procession. He fully intended to be in the operating room and lend a hand wherever he was needed.

When he entered the room, Eric's vital signs had worsened, and the doctors were doing an x-ray to determine the exact location of the bullets as well as to determine if there was any internal damage from them.

Jerome stood just inside of the preparation room being placed into a pristine white lab coat from one of the nurses. He'd already put on a pair of disposable scrubs, and was ready to work.

Dr. Heath walked to Jerome and placed his hand paternally on his shoulder. Jerome looked up, and when he did, Dr. Heath said, "You shouldn't be here."

"What are you talking about? This is my baby brother. Of course I'm going to be here."

"He's your baby brother, which is *exactly* why you *shouldn't* be here. Jerome, you've got too much emotion tied into this right now. These are your colleagues here. We all know how important Eric is to you, so we will treat and care for him as our own."

While they debated Jerome's presence in the OR, Eric flatlined, causing the both of them to forget the debate.

Suddenly the room was filled with ordered chaos as orders were fired off and seen to. After a few moments of CPR and getting nothing, Dr. Heath called for a heart resuscitator. With all of the proper electrodes in place, he called out, "Is everybody clear?" and he sent the shock waves through Eric's body, causing it to jump in response, but there was nothing. Again he called, "Clear," and again he got nothing.

Jerome stood with tears streaming down his face and held his breath when the doctor said, "Clear," once again, but once again there was nothing.

Jerome pushed past the other doctors gathered around to get closer to the table. "Do it again."

One of the doctors spoke what everyone else was thinking, "Jerome, I don't think it will matter. We've defibrillated three times."

*"Do it again!"* Jerome yelled, looking at Eric's still face.

"All right, everybody, charging. You're clear, I'm clear, we are all clear!" After a terse moment, there was a heartbeat. All breathed a sigh of relief.

One of the doctors said, "Let's get some blood into him and these bullets out." The x-ray showing the location of the bullets had come up on a screen on the wall.

Dr. Heath ushered Jerome out of the room and into the family waiting room. Jerome turned and said, "Please don't make me sit here and do nothing as though there were nothing I could do. I can help out in there."

"You would get in the way right now, Jerome, and we both know it." Dr. Heath made Jerome a cup of coffee and handed it to him. "Do you need to call anyone?"

Jerome seemed not to hear what the doctor said as he stared in the direction of the OR. "I feel so useless right now."

"Jerome, don't you know that if you hadn't restricted the blood flow in that alley, Eric would likely have died out there, and if you hadn't called for another shock, we would have stopped at three? You've done a great job of keeping him alive, so don't feel that way. But just let the doctors do their job, all right?"

"He's my responsibility. It's my job to keep him safe."

"I think you are being too hard on yourself, Jerome. Whether you like it or not, Eric is a grown man now, and it's his own job to keep himself safe."

Dr. Eastlin was one of the doctors in the OR when Eric flat-lined, and was the doctor to remove the bullets. He came into the waiting area to speak with Jerome. At the same time, Sasha and her father entered the waiting room as well. They all walked to Jerome at the same time. Jerome hugged and kissed Sasha in greeting, shook the professor's hand, and then shook hands with Dr. Eastlin.

He proceeded to make polite introductions when what he really wanted to know was how his brother was doing.

"I'm sure you want to know how your brother is doing, so I'll tell you he is out of OR and into ICU. He lost a lot of blood, as you know, and has to be given three units of blood. We removed the two bullets from his back, and the third one did in fact exit his chest. We don't know at this point what kind of damage the bullets have done, as one was very close to his spine, and the other seemed to miss every vital organ he has.

"Of course, you know the next twenty-four hours are crucial, but I think he's made it through the worst."

"Thank you very much, Doctor. When can I go to see him?"

"After we have him settled, but you know you can't stay."

"You kept me out of the OR, but nothing will keep me from staying with him until morning."

"Because you are who you are, I'm sure we can pull a few strings."

The doctors excused themselves to get back to work.

Professor Sherman then asked Jerome, "How are you doing?"

"Honestly, I can't believe this is happening. I've done everything I know to steer him on the right path."

"From what I've seen of him this past month, you've succeeded."

"So why are we here?" Jerome gestured around at the hospital waiting room. "What was he doing with Poison when he should have been at work?" Dismissing the questions that only Eric could answer, Jerome turned to Sasha. "Did you get in touch with my mother?"

"Yes. She wanted to take the next available flight out. I told her that you were seeing to him and that she should wait to hear from you first."

Jerome started to look for his phone but stopped himself. Remembering he'd given it to Sasha earlier, he turned to her. "Do you have my phone?"

Sasha took the phone from the pocket she'd placed it into earlier and gave it to Jerome.

"Thanks. Will you excuse me?" He spoke into his phone, "Dial home," and after a quick few seconds he said, "Mom."

"Jerome, is he dead?"

"No. He's out of surgery." He could hear her sobs of relief. "Please stop crying."

"I'm coming over, Jerome!"

"No, that won't be necessary."

"What do you mean, it won't be necessary? He needs me right now, and I need to see him."

"Mom, please calm down, or I won't be able to tell you what I know." He could hear his mom take a deep breath to collect herself. "Good. Now that we're calm, you can ask me whatever you need to ask, and I'll address it all."

"Jerome, don't handle me like I'm a crazy mother in the waiting room."

Jerome smiled. "I'm sorry, Mom. I didn't mean to handle you." The professor laughed because that was exactly what he'd just done. It was a calming technique for the distraught family members of patients.

"Please just tell me what's going on, Jerome," his mom asked almost pleadingly.

"Okay, he was shot three times in the back, and one of the bullets exited his chest, so he had two that needed to be removed. He was with Poison. You remember me telling you about him, right? He died on that table, Mom," he finished softly.

His mother's silent tears turned into a scream.

"Mom, it's okay. We brought him back. I just thought you should know."

"Jerome, I'm so scared for my baby right now."

"Sweetie, it's … everything is going to be fine."

"I thought you told me you'd gotten him to stop hanging out with that guy."

"I thought I had gotten him to leave Poison alone. I told him he was dangerous to be around but—"

"But Eric does what Eric wants to do."

"Exactly. But I think this will scare him straight, and if it doesn't, I'll be sending him someplace else for college after I put the fear of god into him."

"I still think I should be there, Jerome."

"And who will stay with Liana, or will you just pull her out of school to come here with you? I'll be here with him through the night, and I'll let you know when he wakes, and what will happen from there. Get some sleep, Mom, and if *anything* changes, I'll make certain you're the first to know."

"Anything, Jerome?"

"Anything, Mom. I promise. Okay?" Jerome hung up the phone and rejoined the professor and Sasha. The professor patted Jerome on the back reassuringly and opened his mouth to speak, but before he could say what he'd intended, Dr. Heath came into the waiting room.

He walked to Jerome. "You can come see him now."

Everyone followed the doctor to the ICU. They entered the room behind Dr. Heath. Eric lay in a bed with tubes and bandages everywhere, and Jerome walked immediately to Eric. He stood silently over him thinking about the things he could have done to keep Eric from hanging with Poison. But just as everyone kept telling him, Eric was a grown man, and there was only so much he could do.

The professor walked over to them and stood beside Jerome. He could see him arguing with himself. "He's going to be fine. I've seen people in worse condition than this survive." He pointed to the machines. "Look, his vitals are strong, he's young and healthy, and there is nothing really to stop his recovery."

"He's on life support."

"That's only standard procedure for someone who has suffered this kind of trauma, you know this. But as long as he can make it through the night, I have every confidence he will be okay."

Dr. Heath interrupted. "It's time for all guests to leave."

Jerome walked over to Sasha, who hadn't come any farther into the room than the door, and gave her a hug and kiss, and then they left.

Dr. Heath turned to Jerome. "Just let us know if you need anything."

After the doctor left the room, Jerome took a chair and tried to get comfortable. It was cold in the room with the temperature at sixty-eight, but he knew that was necessary. He tried to get some sleep but couldn't get comfortable in the cool room, so he got up and alternately paced and read, then reread, Eric's vitals on the monitor.

One of his pacing marathons was interrupted by Samantha as she came to check on Eric. After recording his stats in his chart, she turned to Jerome to say, "If you need anything, Dr. Jacobs, don't hesitate to ask. I'll be on shift until 7:00 a.m."

Jerome asked for a blanket and did finally get to sleep.

# CHAPTER 25

The next morning, the nurse on call entered Eric's room. She said to Jerome "Sir, you have a young lady in the waiting area asking for you."

Her voice woke him from an uneasy sleep. Jerome unrolled himself from the uncomfortable chair and stretched his weary muscles. He took one quick look at the still unconscious Eric before he left the room.

When Jerome entered the waiting area, he immediately saw Sasha through the throng of people. Even at eight in the morning, it was a busy place to be. He walked to her and reached down for a comforting hug and was thankful for it. He really needed that.

"How is he?" Sasha asked in concern. She cried last night for the lovable Eric, knowing how hard it would be for him to recover fully ... if he ever did.

"It was a tough night, and he had to have a second transfusion when his pressure got too low. On a good note, he was taken off of the life support and did breathe on his own, so if he continues this way, we can take him out of the ICU by the evening."

"That's great! I'm glad he's recovering at a steady rate. So tell me, how is his brother?"

Jerome smiled tiredly. "He didn't sleep much because that chair was torturous, and the room was cold."

"You do look horrible." She wrinkled her nose. "Come to think of it, you smell pretty bad too. I brought you some toiletries as well as some other clothes so you might look a little less like Dr. Romy in here, but instead of changing, why don't you go home, take a shower, and then get some sleep?"

"Because I want to see him when he wakes up."

"Go home and get some rest. I'll stay with him, and if he wakes up, I'll call you."

"You'd do that for me?"

"I'd do anything for you, Romy," she quietly admitted.

The kiss he gave her was one of love and gratitude, for her support, for her admission. "Let me get you into his room, and I'll go, but please call me the minute *anything* changes."

"I will. Just leave your phone on and close by."

∼୧∕∽

The phone would not stop ringing. It intruded into his sleep-fogged mind. He finally reached out and grabbed it, vaguely re-calling that he was expecting an important phone call but too tired to remember what it would be about. Feeling disoriented, he pressed a button without opening his eyes and groggily spoke. "Hello?"

Sasha's excited voice was on the other line. "He woke up! The doctors just headed in there!"

Those words, brought him back to reality, he sat bolt upright in bed. "I'll be there in fifteen minutes!"

"He's in room 310! They took him out of the ICU."

Jerome threw on some sweats and a T-shirt. Once his shoes were on, he headed for the door and grabbed his keys without pausing on his way out. All the way to the hospital, he couldn't stop thinking about how Eric ended up there in the first place, and he would get some answers from him as soon as the boy could talk.

It was late too. He slept long hours, which was a testament to how absolutely weary he was. He'd gotten home at ten minutes to nine that morning and immediately took a shower. When he was done he called his mom to fill her in on the latest news, which hadn't been much but had been much needed for her peace of mind. Then he ate a small breakfast, and by eleven o'clock was in the bed. He slept until the phone began to ring.

෴

He rushed through the door of the hospital holding his phone to his ear. He was giving his mother the latest news on Eric. Sasha paced back and forth in the admittance area, and rushed to him when she saw him coming. Jerome spoke to his mom. "Mom, I'll call you back in a few as soon as I have more information."

After he hung up the phone, Sasha said, "He went back to sleep." They walked swiftly toward Eric's room with Sasha leading the way. "They said that he's resting at this point as opposed to being unconscious and that he would wake up again."

"Right."

They entered Eric's room, where he lay in his hospital bed sleeping soundly, much of it coming from the drugs he received for pain. Jerome walked to the bed, grabbed Eric's hand, and sat down in a chair beside him.

"Eric, will you open your eyes for me?" After a moment, Jerome took a penlight and lifted his eyelid to take a look at his pupil.

Eric groggily spoke then. "I'm sure you shouldn't be allowed to torture patients with flashlights like this."

Jerome smiled at that bit of Eric's humor popping through. "Hey, man, it's good to see your eyes."

"You missed my eyes so much you decided to put a flashlight in them?"

"Be serious, Er. You gave us a great scare."

"How long was I out?"

"A day, and you died once, and almost a second time through the night. You had to have two blood transfusions."

"Wow!"

"What the hell were you doing with Poison anyway? I thought we agreed that you would stay away from him."

"Whoa … hold on now. I was not with Poison. I was on my way to work from taking Kelly home." Eric closed his eyes, moving slightly, and then he tensed in pain. When he reopened his eyes, he appeared more tired than he seemed moments before. "Can I have some water and a little morphine in one of those tubes?"

Jerome poured water into a glass from a pitcher beside Eric's bed. He helped Eric drink the water, and after he quenched his thirst, he cleared his throat enough to continue.

"Since I was running late, I decided to go the back way to avoid the traffic coming through the front door. When I got to the alley, I saw Poison being jumped by a few thugs, and I decided to even the odds in his favor, or at least make them a little better.

"So I charged them, and I knocked one of them unconscious and went after another. Everything after that happened so fast that I could be wrong, but as soon as they released Poison, I swear he ran. While I was fighting the second guy, the third one shot me in the back. If Poison hadn't left me stranded, he could at least have kept that bullet out of me. That'll be the last time I help him out."

Jerome couldn't believe the story Eric just told him. Okay, well, he believed it; he just couldn't believe Poison could be so stupid. Through a red haze he muttered, "After today that might never be an option … for anyone."

"You're not thinking of killing him, are you?"

"No, that would be too easy." Jerome decided to change the subject before Eric got too upset. "You need to rest and regain your strength because you have quite a bumpy road ahead of you in the way of recovery time."

"Nice try, Romy, but I'm not that tired yet. I just want you to remember that if you do something stupid, your career as a doctor will suffer."

"I wasn't planning to kill him, Er, so rest easy." He pulled his phone out of his pocket and speed-dialed their mom. "Here, talk to Mom. She's worried sick," he said as he handed the phone to Eric.

He walked to Sasha, who stood silently in the rooms' entrance.

"He's right, you know, you can't kill Poison no matter how much he may deserve it."

"I'm not planning to, honestly, but I do need to have a talk with him."

Sasha pulled her phone out and handed it to him, since Eric was still on the phone with their mom. "Here, take my phone."

"I won't need a phone, I'll be back shortly." The truth was he didn't want anyone tracking him down to try and stop him from what he was about to do to Poison. He wasn't going to kill him. That was true. But when he was done with him, the beating he'd received at the hands of those thugs would be nothing in comparison.

Sasha stood eyeing him knowingly. "Umm-hmm." She knew the reason he didn't want any phones around, and that was why he gave Eric his, and why she'd tried to give him hers. "Jerome, please tell me you'll be careful."

"I'll be careful, babe. You have nothing to worry about." He kissed her and left in a hurry before she could say another word.

# CHAPTER 26

*A*s he made the fifteen-minute drive from the hospital to the club, Jerome began to fume. *He left my brother to be shot after he helped him,* was the only thought that kept going through his mind.

He pulled up at the club on his motorcycle and parked it at the front. As he got off, he removed his helmet and tucked it under his arm continuing on into the club. He went straight to Sin's office, figuring if anyone would know where to find Poison, it would be Sin.

Sin was sitting at his desk with Poison sitting not far away. Poison's face was bruised and swollen from his beating the night before. Sin and Poison both looked up to see Jerome heading their way.

Sin called out a greeting. "Hey, Romy, how's Eric doing—"

Sin's words stopped abruptly as Jerome grabbed Poison and pulled him from his seat. Jerome hit Poison in the center of his nose, and Poison fell to the floor. Poison looked shocked that Jerome would do such a thing, as he tried to pull himself up from the floor.

Showing no mercy for Poison, Jerome kicked him in the gut as he struggled to his feet. Sin grabbed Jerome and pulled him back and away from Poison.

Jerome yelled at Poison, "I want to know who they are!"

"Who?" Poison asked wearily.

"You know exactly who, the guys who shot my brother in the back!"

"I don't know," he answered, wiping blood from his nose.

"I'm already going to beat the crap out of you for leaving Eric to be shot and nearly killed after he tried to save your miserable life, so I'm going to let you decide how many bones I break when I'm done, or you can tell me who did this and just take your ass-whipping."

Feeling disgusted, Sin released Jerome from the vice-like hold he'd had on him after hearing what Poison had done. "Is that what happened, Poison? You left him after he helped you?"

Poison spoke beseechingly, hoping Sin would be a barrier between him and Jerome. "It all happened so fast. The man let me go, and I just ran and—"

"Left him to fend for himself in a fight that wasn't even his," Jerome gritted angrily.

"I wasn't thinking. I was in pain."

"You haven't felt pain yet," he began, walking toward Poison like an animal stalking his prey. "But you will."

Poison put up his guard as best as he could. Jerome did the same, but with more grace. Jerome threw a couple of well-placed, sharp jabs and then followed with a cross jab, connecting it with Poison's jaw.

Poison staggered back slightly and then swung, but Jerome blocked the hit and counterattacked with three body blows. Poison dropped to his knees holding his already bruised body.

Sin watched the entire fight in entertained silence, never moving from the spot where he'd held Jerome. His door opened, Red and three of the other dancers came in.

Red stopped, transfixed by the battle, which really was no battle since Poison was no match for Jerome. He said to Sin, "We heard the commotion and couldn't help but wonder what was going on."

Without taking his eyes from the fight, Sin said, "Apparently Romy has a score to settle. Man, he's good." Sin spoke almost reverently.

Jerome sneered at Poison when he remained on his knees. He was trying to give up the fight. But not yet, "Get up, Poison. I'm not done with you yet."

Poison pulled himself up halfway and pile drove into Jerome, pushing him into the wall. Jerome kicked Poison with his knee, and then slammed his doubled fists into Poison's back. Once again, Poison dropped to his knees. While down, he hit Jerome in the groin.

The onlookers, which started as four and were now six, all winced in sympathetic pain as Jerome doubled over gasping for air. Poison took the opportunity to land two square punches to Jerome's face, but the third swing was once again blocked and countered by Jerome.

He grabbed Poison by the shirt and punched him three times, knocking him unconscious. Still holding his shirt, Jerome dragged Poison to the lounge chair and tossed him on it.

Sin took a seat, curious to see what Jerome would do next. The other five guys followed suit, but no one tried to stop the fight.

Jerome bent over to catch his breath from Poison's low blow. Straightening, he took a glass filled with some alcoholic beverage that Poison had at the desk and splashed it into Poison's face.

Poison jumped up with a yelp, partly from the shock of the drink in his face but mostly from the pain of the alcohol as it came into contact with his cuts. Jerome pushed him back down with his hand on his face.

Poison tried to sit back up and push Jerome's hand away, but Jerome punched him again. Poison dropped back.

"I warned you not to get my brother mixed up in your insanity. And for trying to save you, he almost lost his life. Now I want to know who did it."

"If you go after them, they'll kill us all. They aren't the kind of people you want to cross."

"So why were they beating the crap out of you in the alley? Did you cross them?"

"What happened was—"

"All I want to know, really, is who they are!"

"I can't." Poison spoke with fear in his tone.

Jerome hit Poison in the ribs. Poison screamed in pain. Sin stood to intercept. "Romy, come on now, I can't let you do this in here."

"Fine, I'll take him to the alley where everyone else beats him," Jerome shot back.

One of the guys watching sniggered at that comment.

Shocked, Sin said, "Romy, I didn't know you could be so violent."

"What man can't if given the right provocation, and that was it. Sin, nobody messes with my brother. He's lucky I'm not going to kill him." To Poison he yelled, "Talk!"

"You don't understand, Romy. These guys will kill you."

Again Jerome hit Poison in the ribs. He spoke softly and slowly. "Let me worry about my safety. Who are they, Poison? Your ribs won't hold up much longer."

Holding his badly beaten ribs, Poison spilled. "They're the hired hands of De-mon, and he's a small-time drug dealer on the rise. I get all my stuff from him."

"The stuff you were supposed to be quitting?"

"Yes."

"Where can I find this De-mon?"

"I don't know. He's slippery."

"Then how do you get your stuff?"

"I send a page. A guy responds and takes my order. They give me a spot, and I meet them to pick up. De-mon never comes."

"Do you know what he looks like?"

Poison lay where he'd been deposited on the chair without

saying a word. He was afraid of the repercussion of this "talk" because if De-mon ever found this out, he *would* kill him.

Jerome balled his fist and drew back to aim at Poison's ribs.

"Okay, wait a minute ... okay, before he got all big shot with his hired henchmen, he used to serve me himself, and he still does serve some of his regulars, from what I hear, the ones he trusts," Poison said sourly.

"But—"

Poison cut off Jerome's question before he could finish it. "I owe him too much money, so ..."

"How much?"

"Twenty thousand."

"Damned junkie, you could make that in a month and have him paid off in four, less if you budgeted, but I don't expect that from someone as irresponsible as you, so four months."

"Correction, *you* could make that in a month. I don't make the kind of money you do, Romy."

"That's because you're usually too high to stand up straight, let alone do something as complicated as dancing and taking off your clothes at the same time," Jerome insulted with loathing, then turned to look at Sin. "I'm going to need a few weeks off to get my affairs in order."

"Romy, you're my featured entertainer. You've had to be away these few days, and that's understandable, but do you know how much money I'll lose if you leave for weeks? I would need you back here before three weeks' time."

"Sin, I know how much money I've brought into this club in the past year, at least I have pretty good idea, and maybe sales will go down marginally in my absence, but when I return, I'm sure everyone will know, and the sales will go back up. You won't be any worse for wear."

"You know what your problem is? You're good, one of the best, and you know it. Go take two weeks off, but when you return, you'd better bring it."

"I'll need four weeks, Sin."

"Absolutely not!"

"Remember that thing I said I would think about and get back to you on?" When Sin nodded warily Jerome said, "Well, this is it. In lieu of a partial ownership, I'll take as much time as I need. Agreed?

"Jerome you're killing me."

"You'll lose much less money this way than you would if I started sticking my hands into your pockets. Agreed?"

"Go do whatever you need to do, but make it quick."

"You got it." To Poison he said, "Come on, you and I have work to do."

Poison looked at him warily, thinking he'd been getting that a lot this day. Poison asked, "What kind of work?"

"I'm going to pay your bill off so you can get in good with De-mon again."

"Then what?"

"Then I'll deal with the rest, but however it gets dealt with, I'll find out who shot my brother."

Jerome hauled Poison out of the chair and unceremoniously pushed him to the door.

Outside of the club, the two headed to Jerome's motorcycle. Poison eyed the bike in trepidation. After all, with all of the injuries he had, it would be easy to fall off of the damned thing.

Jerome noticed the look on Poison's face as he was handing him a helmet, and he ruthlessly said, "You'd better hold on tight and forget about your pain, because if you fall, I might leave you lying in the street to be run over."

"I don't know how I ever thought you were a good sort. You're an evil man, Romy."

"Most especially when someone endangers my family. Get on the bike."

# CHAPTER 27

*J*erome sped through town cutting expertly in and out of traffic. Poison held on tightly, afraid Jerome meant exactly what he said. After a few agonizing minutes for Poison, Jerome pulled to a stop in front of Poison's apartment. It was a neat six-story building showcasing huge balconies with large sliding glass doors.

Poison got off of the motorcycle and handed the helmet to Jerome. "So now what?"

"We'll talk inside."

Jerome got off of the motorcycle holding his helmet under his arm. He took the helmet Poison offered and placed it in a compartment under his seat and walked into Poison's apartment with him. Once they were inside, and Jerome closed the door behind them, he said, "I want you to make the call, and then tell them that you will have the money that you owe De-mon by tomorrow."

"Where am I supposed to get twenty grand from in twenty-four hours?"

"I'll take care of that. You just make the call."

Poison dialed a number to send a page and leave his code. Jerome looked on, shaking his head almost with revulsion.

"What?" Poison asked, not understanding why Jerome looked so nauseous.

"Dude, you know the number by heart? You really need to take yourself to a detox center, but since I've already preached that sermon, I'm not going to do it again."

"Please don't start in on me, Romy. Everybody can't be as perfect as you."

"I'm not perfect, far from it! I don't know why everybody keeps saying that, and I'm not asking you to be perfect. I'm saying you need to leave them drugs alone before they get you killed."

"How about we talk about something else, hmm? Like this death wish you suddenly have. What if I don't want to go through with this? If they find out you're trying to set them up? They'll kill us both ... horribly."

"I wouldn't worry about them killing you, Poison. You'll probably overdose way before they ever get the chance," Jerome said, without concern as he played with a Rubik's Cube he picked up from Poison's coffee table. "On second thought, I'm not so sure that you should have the entire twenty grand so soon. Then they *might* think you're trying to set them up and kill you anyway, so tell them you'll have five grand of the twenty, and if they ask you how you came up with it, you can tell them you borrowed it from one of your coworkers. Let them know you'll have the rest of it in the next four weeks."

While Jerome spoke, the phone began to ring. Jerome walked to stand beside Poison as he reached to answer it. "Make it good, Poison."

Poison answered the phone. "Hello."

"The voice on the other line spoke out, "You've got a lot of balls calling here to make an order."

"I'm not making an order," Poison said while holding the phone so Jerome could hear what the other person was saying.

"Then what do you want?"

"I want to pay De-mon a portion of what I owe him so maybe he won't send anybody else around my job shooting people."

There was a brief silence before the person said, "Hold on."

The next voice they heard on the line belonged to De-mon himself. "Yo, Poison, when you gon' have my money?"

"Tomorrow evening."

"You got all of it?"

"I got five grand, and I'll have the rest in the next four weeks."

"How you come up wit' that kinda money so fast, Poison?"

"I borrowed it, but I'm gonna work real hard for the next few weeks to get the rest. As soon as I get these bruises off of my body, I can get back on stage."

"Aiight, I'll call you tomorrow afternoon to let you know where you can take it. Be ready to meet within fifteen minutes of the call, and if it's all there, then you don't gotta worry 'bout me sendin' nobody out afta you. Oh, and if you try and set me up, you gon' be havin' to worry 'bout more than just getting yo ass whipped, ya heard."

"Loud and clear." He hung up the phone, then looked at Jerome. "I hope you know what you're doing."

Jerome headed to the door without addressing the statement. Instead he said, "I'll be here tomorrow at about three."

"Aren't you at least a little bit scared?" Poison asked with a tremor in his voice.

He shook his head. "Where I come from, guys like that are a dime a dozen. They left me alone, and I left them alone and kept to myself, but somehow this one ended up crossing the lines. So now they have someone in their business that it would have been better to have kept out, me."

# CHAPTER 28

*J*erome entered the hospital and headed directly for Eric's room. Sasha stopped him before he could reach the room. She looked at the bruises on his face without comment, but said instead, "Jerome, I've been waiting for you to get here."

"Why? Is Eric okay?"

"The police went in there almost a half hour ago, and they aren't letting anyone in."

Jerome checked his watch. It was almost eleven in the evening. "It's a little late for them to be here questioning him."

"Yeah, and they've been here for over an hour and a half. Eric was asleep and the doctors kept stressing how important it was for him to rest, so they made them wait until he woke up again."

❧

Eric lay slightly elevated in his bed. Standing beside him were three policemen, one uniformed and the other two in plainclothes. The uniformed officer was holding a pen and pad taking note of everything that was being said while the other two were asking the questions.

"So if you didn't know these guys," officer what's his name asked—Eric didn't bother to remember their names so they were simply numbers one, two and three to him—"What were you doing in the alley with them?"

Eric took a deep breath of impatience. "I already told you. I work at the club and was on my way in through the back entrance."

"Do you always enter through the back door?" the second officer asked.

Eric tried hard to suppress a smile. "Double pun?"

The officer looked confused, but the uniformed officer knew what he was talking about and squelched a bark of laugher.

Eric looked at the first officer incredulously after seeing the blank look on the second officer's face, then said, "Never mind. No, I don't."

"Why suddenly decide to on this particular night?" asked one.

"Because I was running late, the club was filling up, and a lot of women were coming in. I didn't want to be detained because it would have made me even later."

"So you saw a fight and decided to interrupt?"

Eric closed his eyes and wished for a blanket. His room always seemed to feel like an icebox, "One of my coworkers was getting the crap beat out of him by three guys, so I decided to even the odds and give him a hand. I mean, what else was I supposed to do, turn around and go back out to the front door? I could have just walked on by like I didn't see them, but then that's not me."

"Can you describe these men?"

"It was dark, my adrenaline was pumping … I think I would know two of them if I saw them again. Those were the two I actually fought with. The one who shot me, I couldn't say what he looked like."

"All right, great. If we have any more questions, we will be in touch."

They all filed out of Eric's room, and as they stepped out, Jerome was waiting in the hall.

Jerome said, "Can I speak with you privately?"

The police all exchanged looks before one of the officers questioned, "What is this about, sir?"

"This is about the people responsible for shooting my brother," Jerome said, turning and walking toward an office down the hall. The police all followed behind him.

Once he reached the office, he stopped a nearby nurse and said to her, "Marsha, will you make certain we're not disturbed in here?"

"Sure thing, Doctor Jacobs."

The police all exchanged another look between themselves upon hearing the form of address the nurse gave him, before they entered the room and closed the door behind them.

Without preamble, Jerome spoke. "I work in the club that my brother was shot behind. He was helping my coworker who goes by the name Poison."

Hearing this bit of information, the police all perked up. "Do you know why these guys were beating him in that alley?"

Jerome shrugged. "Drugs and money, from what I hear. They work for a small-time drug dealer on the rise. Poison owes him money."

One of the officers in plain clothes asked, "Who is this dealer?"

Jerome asked in return, "What's your name?"

"I'm Detective Spencer."

"I want you all to understand some things before we go any further. One, the only reason I'm doing what I'm doing is because those guys almost killed my brother, and I don't take too kindly to people hurting the ones I love. Two, this is a vendetta, and I don't want it to be mistaken for anything else. And three, my brother is not to be placed in the middle of this. I know more about these guys than he does, so if you need info you can come to me from now on. Whatever happened to him in that alley is all he can tell you, got it?"

They all listened in silence while Jerome gave his speech, and when he was done, the other plainclothes officer nodded his head slightly and then asked, "So what do you know?"

"You are?"

"I'm Detective Davies."

"I know this small-time dealer on the rise goes by the name of De-mon."

The name brought looks of recognition from the three.

Jerome saw the looks passed between them and said, "I see you're aware of him."

Detective Davies spoke. "We've been trying for some time now to catch him. He's not going to be as easy to fool as you think."

"That's where you're wrong. I'll catch him, and it won't take me long, but if you guys go sniffing around, and they find out, they'll start killing a lot of people."

"All the more reason why you should leave this to us."

"You obviously haven't been able to catch him thus far. He has an inside system that isn't going to allow you in. Guys like that can smell a cop a mile away. And while you ask around, they'll just tighten up and get bigger, and before you know it, they'll be too big to control." Jerome held out a hand to Davies, "I'm offering you my help in exchange for your manpower, but I need you to be invisible so I can work this out, and I'll keep you fully informed. Agreed?"

Detective Davies was interested in what this enigmatic young man had to say. After all, a doctor who stripped? A young man who looked like a Boy Scout leader, minus the bruises, knowing more about a drug dealer than he, who'd been investigating him for over a year now? He took the proffered hand, "So what's your plan?"

Jerome and Dr. Heath walked down the hall deep in discussion as the doctor tried to get Jerome to think sensibly. "I understand how you would feel about what happened to your brother, but whatever you do, you must make certain you don't do anything that would upset your life as the talented doctor I'm certain you'll become. I'll excuse you for emergency time away for the rest of the week, but next week you need to refocus yourself."

"I understand."

Jerome and Dr. Heath entered Eric's room then, and standing next to his bed was a beautiful young woman fussing over him while he soaked it all up like a ham.

Jerome joked, "Nurse Jones is going to be very jealous if she walks in here to witness this."

Dr. Heath walked to Eric and began to examine his wounds.

Eric looked at Jerome in disgruntlement. Where had he gotten those bruises? His words were a bit sharp when he spoke. "Come and get your phone, man. Where have you been?"

Jerome looked surprised that Eric had spoken to him so sharply. "I'll tell you later."

"I know you didn't go get yourself all mixed up with—"

Jerome cut him off, speaking each of his words warningly. "I said I'll … tell … you … later."

Eric looked first at Dr. Heath and then at his female friend and finally understood that this was not something his older brother wanted to discuss around them, so he tried as diplomatically as possible to change the subject. "Anika, have you met my brother, Jerome?"

"I've seen him perform, but I have never met him before."

"Well, let me have the honors. Anika, please make the acquaintance of my big brother, slash adoptive father, slash benefactor." He stopped and looked at Jerome, then said, "Have I left anything out?"

"Try disciplinarian," Jerome said with a frown.

"Yeah, let's not forget that. Anika, do you mind terribly if I have a few words with my brother?"

"Sure, sweetie."

Dr. Heath and Anika left the room. Once they were gone, Eric wasted no time. "So?"

"I had a long talk with Poison," Jerome said as he flexed his fists, which were slightly swollen.

"Did he do that to your face?"

"Yeah."

"Wow, you're slipping." Eric was shaking his head.

"Yeah, well, he did it after kicking me in the nuts, but anyway, we're going to get those guys off the streets, and the police are going to help."

"You mean the ones who were here last night?"

Jerome nodded his head while he checked his phone.

"I want you to be real careful, Romy. This isn't like you, and those guys are dangerous. I mean, look what they did to me. They obviously have no problem with killing someone."

"Don't worry, Er, I got this. Hey, you look real good, man. If you keep recovering like this, you'll be ready for rehab in no time."

"Rehab? What do you mean rehab? Never mind. Look, don't try to change the subject. This is serious stuff going on, and I'm starting to get really scared for you. For months you've told me to stay away from Poison, and I finally have a full picture of what kind of trouble he carries around with him. So now I want to warn you away from him. Romy, leave Poison alone to deal with his own demons."

Jerome looked up from his phone to see the look of concern on Eric's face. "You don't understand, Er. This isn't about Poison. Look, I have a lot of things to do, so I'll be back around later or else in the morning."

Jerome quickly exited the hospital room. Eric rolled his eyes. He knew his brother wouldn't listen, just as *he* hadn't listened to him when he'd tried to warn him. Eric felt responsible for the entire fiasco, because if he hadn't been so rebellious, thinking he could do whatever he wanted, then his brother wouldn't be trying to clean up his and Poison's mess right now and endangering himself.

Jerome, his perfect, overprotective, has to take care of everyone, older brother, was now putting himself in danger to avenge him; and Eric was worried for the first time in his life about someone other than himself. Damn.

# CHAPTER 29

*J*erome entered Poison's apartment twenty minutes before the appointed time. When he came in, he handed Poison an envelope filled with fifty crisp one hundred dollar bills.

Poison flipped through the money and whistled between his teeth. "You must make more money than even I thought, Romy."

"I don't make that much more money than you do, Poison. The difference between us is that I manage to save most of my money while the only thing you manage to do is get high with yours."

"Going for the jugular today, huh, Romy?"

"You almost got my brother killed with that punk move you pulled, and for that you're lucky you have a working jugular to go for."

"Then why are you helping me?"

"I don't know what gave you the impression that I'm helping you, but wipe such dumb thoughts from your head posthaste. Now I want you to understand something real clearly. I want these guys off the street. Dead or alive, it makes no difference to me. You know them and have direct contact with them, hence the money. Other than that, you can rot. I mean, why should I care about your life if you don't give a damn about it yourself?"

"That's not fair, Romy. I do care about myself." He squirmed.

"So much so that if you thought you could get away with it, you'd take that money and get high with it instead of paying that guy back."

Poison shook his head in the negative.

"Don't deny it, Poison. I could see it all over your face. If it wasn't the truth, you wouldn't be in debt to the tune of twenty grand. I'm going to say again what I've been saying for years, and I promise it will be the last time I repeat it. You need some help. If you don't get any, this will just be a temporary fix because you'll end up hip deep with the next dealer and the next until one of them puts you out of your misery."

The phone rang, and Poison answered it. "Hello?"

The voice on the other end of the line said, "You need to meet me at River Run. You know where it is?"

"Yes, I know where it is."

"Good. You got thirty minutes."

Poison hung up the phone.

Jerome, had been listening quietly beside Poison. He said, "My bike is parked down the street. You go on ahead. I'm sure they have someone watching you to be sure you're not trying to trick them up, so I'll leave in about five minutes when I think the coast is clear."

Poison headed to the door.

Jerome said, "From here you can get to River Run in twenty minutes easily. Take the scenic route, or else drive calmly."

Poison nodded and left the apartment, unaware that once he was gone, Jerome made a phone call to the police. "Detective Davies? He just got the call. He's meeting them at River Run in thirty minutes."

"We'll be there in twenty."

"If you must be there, please don't be conspicuous. I want him to get the money to them without any problems so he can maybe begin to regain their trust. We'll be paying them off in installments, so by the last payment, we should hopefully get some cooperation out of them."

"Consider this a stakeout. We want to gather as much information as we can to hold up in court. We'll be as inconspicuous as possible, and if De-mon hasn't put in an appearance in the next few weeks, by then we should know where to find him."

Jerome looked out of the window through a slit in the curtains and watched a car following close behind Poison. "I'd better get going. The coast should be clear."

He exited the apartment making sure to keep himself as unnoticeable as possible just in case anyone else was watching Poison's place. When he reached his motorcycle, he climbed on and sped off. He drove his motorcycle swiftly through back streets to reach a quiet residential street two blocks away from River Run.

Once he was there, he climbed off his motorcycle and began to jog the two blocks that would take him to the River Run hangout.

∽❧∽

Poison pulled up in his Lincoln Navigator and took a parking space across the street from the building he was to go into. He stepped out of his SUV and walked into the building on the corner.

Jerome was sitting across the street in a bookstore/coffee shop. He wanted to get there before Poison's arrival, and was now having a cup of coffee and holding a book, his athletic body already having recovered from the run thanks to Jeffery.

As he watched, a blue Cadillac pulled into the parking lot of a local bank, and two well-dressed gentlemen stepped out of the car, one carrying a briefcase, and entered the bank. Fifteen minutes later, Poison exited the building and walked to his car.

Three young men stepped out of the building within seconds of him and watched him as he got into his car and drove off. They signaled to someone inside of another car, and that car pulled off to follow him.

Jerome decided it was time to make his exit. As he stood to head to the cashier, he saw the two gentlemen come out of the bank, get into their car, and drive off. He purchased two books and left the shop.

Poison pulled his SUV to a stop in front of his apartment and stepped out of the vehicle. A car pulled up right behind him, and three guys — one wearing a sling and another bruised and swollen—grabbed Poison and escorted him into his apartment building. Poison recognized the men almost immediately as the three who'd beaten him in the alley of the club two nights ago. The three pushed him into his apartment and into the first seat they could reach, and then they began to look over his apartment.

Poison looked them all over purposely before he smugly asked, "Did that kid do all of that damage to you guys?"

Manny paused briefly to ask, "Did we do all that to you?"

"No. Actually his brother did. So what's this all about?"

Mac, the hothead who wore a sling, said, "Nice. If it was my brother, I'd have killed you."

Manny, the leader, responded to his question by saying, "Making sure you're not trying to set us up with the police."

"Now why do you think I would do a thing like that?"

Mac said, "Let's just say we find it a little odd that after you get yourself all beat up in an alley, two days later you come up with some money." He looked at Poison's clothes and said, "Strip."

"For you? It will be strange but whatever." He shrugged and stood as if to strip.

Manny stopped him saying, "Just take your clothes off, man."

Poison removed his clothes, leaving his underwear on, turned for their inspection, and then reseated himself as they finished their search of his place to their satisfaction.

On the way out, Rick, who'd been silent and the only one without a scratch on him, ordered menacingly, "Be in touch."

# CHAPTER 30

Sasha stood in the yard of the campus talking with her friends. She saw Bonnie look up just as the arms of a male wrapped themselves around her waist. With a smile, she leaned back and whispered, "Mmm, Connor."

All at the same time, Bonnie's eyes widened, Shelly laughed behind her hand, and Jennifer stared on as though nothing out of the ordinary had occurred.

Jerome pulled back angrily, so jealous that he didn't notice that it had been an obvious joke. "Who the hell is Connor?!"

Sasha turned abruptly, feigning surprise. "Romy!"

"Who is Connor?"

"No one."

"Please don't lie to me."

Bonnie spoke out, "We'd better get going."

Shelly wasn't quite ready to miss the fireworks. "Wait, I want to see this."

Bonnie and Jennifer both grabbed an arm and quickly left dragging an obviously interested Shelly along.

"Well?"

"Well, what? Connor is a made-up name. I knew who you were."

"Girl, don't do that to me. You had me ready to do damage to someone."

"Serves you right for ignoring me the way you have this past week and a half."

"What do you mean? I haven't been ignoring you."

"You haven't called, you haven't answered my calls, you haven't been to work, and in fact I haven't seen or heard anything from you since I left the hospital almost two weeks ago."

"I've been busy with everything," He hugged her close and kissed her neck, murmuring, "You smell so sweet."

She wanted to melt, but she couldn't let him ignore her the way he'd been lately and then just give in with a few honeyed words when he decided he was feeling horny, so she decided to play a little hard to get, and latched onto something else he'd said instead.

She pushed him back saying, "Tell me what this *everything* is you've been so busy with."

"Come to my place tonight, and I'll tell you."

"I hate when you do that," she crossed her arms.

"Do what?"

"Hand me a bone, then take it back."

"Will you come?" he asked with a knowing smile.

"If I don't, I'll never stop wondering what you're up to now."

His smile deepened, causing his dimples to appear. "See you around seven?"

Sasha smiled back teasingly as she turned and walked away, stopping long enough to say, "Wait on me."

∽◉〜

Jerome stood at the window with his hands shoved into his pockets looking out agitatedly. He checked his watch for what seemed like the hundredth time. It was eight o'clock, and she was supposed to be there by seven. Was she even coming? She never really said she was, only, what was that she said? "Wait on me."

"Damn." He went to the phone and was just dialing out when the doorbell rang. He crossed quickly to the door and took a moment to compose himself and then opened it to see Sasha standing on the other side.

She stepped past him to enter before she turned to face him. He closed the door and turned toward her. He couldn't contain his upset when he looked purposely at his watch for emphasis and then grated through clenched teeth, "You're late."

By way of a reply, Sasha opened her dress and flashed Jerome. She was completely naked beneath it. Jerome's eyes widened. He took a step forward and reached his hand out to touch her, but she stepped quickly away avoiding his touch, and then she closed her dress and walked away from him.

"Wait, what are you doing?"

"Give a bone, and take it back." She took a deep breath, and then continued, "Tell me about *everything*." She then walked to a chair across the room and sat down, waiting patiently.

He watched her from the other side of the room, his manhood throbbing in response to the all too brief glimpse of her delectable little body. With most of the blood that would normally have been nourishing his brain now nourishing other parts of his anatomy, he began to spill just about every bit of information he had, finishing with, "I've been helping the police to catch the guys responsible for putting Eric in the hospital."

Sasha was shocked and couldn't stop herself from blurting out, "Are you crazy? Those people are going to kill you?!"

Jerome spoke her name cajolingly, "Sasha."

"Romy, I want you to stop this right now!"

Then pleadingly, "Sasha."

But she was having none of it, and she interrupted him before he could talk her into it. Oh, she knew he was going to continue, but she at least had to get her point across before he *could* cajole her into acceptance.

"Romy, do you have any idea how long it has taken me to find someone like you? A long time. You're my Mr. Perfect, everything I could have ever wanted in a man. I just found you, and now that I have you, I'm not going to lose you to some … some pipe-head and his mafia crew."

Jerome smiled, tongue in cheek, and jokingly corrected, "Technically he's a functioning *drug addict*."

"This is not funny, Jerome," she responded sternly.

Jerome walked to her and pulled her from the chair for a hug. "Oh, come now, Sasha."

"Just please stop this, and let the police handle it. I'm sure they'll catch them soon."

"They've been trying to catch this guy for over a year now."

"I'm sure they'll catch them eventually," she revised.

"After how many more people are shot or killed? How many people have they killed already? Listen, I'll have them caught, and I promise I'm being careful, but I can't just let them go on hurting more people when it's in my power to stop them." He closed his eyes as a torturous thought hit him. "You've made me think of something that I hadn't thought of before, and that is … well, until they are caught, I think maybe you shouldn't be around me."

"Why? If it's safe enough for you, then it's safe enough for me."

"Sasha, I never said they were safe. If they were safe, they wouldn't need to be taken from the streets. I've arranged for Eric to be taken to a really good rehab center, where he'll be safe while getting his body in shape. I'll be going deep into this, and I could go with more peace of mind if I knew you were safe with your family and away from—"

"From you?"

"Just until this is settled."

"What if they kill you?"

"They won't. I'll be careful."

Sasha began to cry. "Jerome, please just don't—"

Jerome cut off her plea and wiped futilely at the tears streaming down her cheeks. "Sasha, this is something I have to do. Don't ask me not to." His heart began pounding painfully with her tears.

"But I really don't want you to do this."

"Please, can we not talk about this anymore? Let's spend this weekend enjoying one another, okay?"

He held her in his arms, praying he was right about this being over quickly and without any harm coming to himself or the people he loved. He was smart enough to know that even if he'd wanted to get out of it now, it was too late. He was already too deep into it and could only safely get out with De-mon and his gang locked firmly behind bars.

❧

That Sunday evening, Jerome pulled to a stop in front of the Sherman home. They stepped off the motorcycle and removed their helmets. Sasha placed hers in a slot behind the passenger seat and was pulled forward as Jerome grabbed her into an embrace, hugging her as though it would be the last time they touched. Then he kissed the top of her head.

They made love the entire weekend, and though she initially told him she wouldn't try to talk him out of this, between bouts of lovemaking she had tried anyway. But he was steadfast in his decision and wouldn't be swayed. There'd been times even when he would take her mind off of her quest by reigniting her passion and making love to her until she fell into an exhausted slumber.

Sasha's voice was filled with tears when she said to him, "Please don't keep me in the dark. Call me, and let me know you're okay."

Jerome pulled away, and his eyes were suspiciously moist when he said, "I will."

He kissed her one last time before climbing onto his motorcycle and driving away. She stood on the curb and watched in dismay as he disappeared from sight, feeling he was going to get killed, and there was nothing she could do about it.

# CHAPTER 31

Jerome sat on a park bench in conversation on his cell phone. Casey was an old friend whom he met his first year in college. They'd taken a number of classes together, he for med school and Casey for forensics. They became fast friends, and even while their courses had taken them in opposite directions, they still kept in touch. Casey was the one other of his college cronies that he'd told about his career as an exotic dancer.

"Casey, you know a lot about private investigating, right?"

Casey on the other line said, "Yes. Why do you ask?"

Jerome replied, "Because I need to have access to some bugging devices that are compact and difficult to detect."

"You want audio or visual?"

"Which is better?"

"That depends on what you're trying to accomplish. There are audio pieces that can be attached to people, and you could listen to whatever conversation is happening around the person it's attached to. Then you have visual, which would be considered surveillance. They come in many sizes from the size of a kernel of corn to an actual camera."

"Well, it won't be going on anyone, so I guess I'll go for the visual."

"Okay," Casey replied, "but these things can get very expensive."

"I think I can afford it."

"I want you to know that planting bugging devices in someone's house without authorization is against the law. Dude, I don't want you to get into trouble."

"Not to worry, Casey. It's not a house, and I happen to have a few special privileges in this particular matter. So how soon can you get them?"

"In a couple of days."

"I'll leave the choosing to your expert discretion."

"Are we going for moderately priced, or do you want the best out there?"

"The best, of course."

∿❧∽

Jerome was back working one week later. He stood behind the bar filling in for Mike the bartender while he took a break. The bar stools were filled with women, all vying for Jerome's attention. Poison was on stage finishing his number, and as the music came to a stop, Poison finished and walked off the stage to a round of applause.

Jerome handed a drink to a woman who dropped a twenty-dollar tip in the overflowing tip jar and made an offer to him that was commonplace in his world. He smiled disinterestedly and looked up to see three men walk into the club.

Jerome noticed them right away but didn't recognize any of them. Not that men never came into the club, they did upon occasion to either scope out the competition or simply to enjoy the dancers' performances, but these guys were completely out of place, which put his guard up.

They saw him, and thinking him the bartender, all three headed his way as though they'd spoken telepathically. Jerome passed a drink to another woman before addressing the three. "What can I get you, gentlemen?"

Manny asked, "Can you tell us if Poison is working today?"

"You just missed his performance, but he'll be back up in about an hour."

Mac was angry at the implication. His anger could be heard in his voice when he said, "What makes you think we want to see his performance?"

Jerome shrugged, completely unaffected by his offended tone, because he'd known what he was doing when he said it. "Could be the fact that you walked into a strip club and asked for a stripper."

Manny, 'the reasonable one,' said, "We don't want to watch him perform, but we do need to talk to him. Can you get him?"

Jerome shrugged again. "Sure ... as soon as Mike comes back to relieve me, I'll get him for you. While you wait, have a drink."

Jerome prepared drinks for the three men, and then took orders for a few more ladies while waiting for Mike to return from his break. While he was preparing the last of the drinks, Mike returned.

Mike looked at the tip jar and smiled. "Thanks, Romy, you need to do this more often."

Jerome smiled back as he passed out the drinks for the ladies. "You got it, Mike." He turned to the three men and said, "I'll go get him for you. Sit tight."

The three sat sipping their drinks as Jerome walked to the backstage area. He knocked on Poison's dressing room door and then entered. Poison was in the process of changing costumes and looked up with Jerome's entrance.

Jerome said, "There are three guys at the bar looking for you."

"Are they the ones we called to pick up the money?"

"Not sure, but I think you should come with me."

Together they walked through the backstage hall to the entertainment lounge. Jerome stopped and pulled Poison back a little at the entrance so they wouldn't be seen.

It was the same spot Jerome had stood in to watch Sasha a year ago, and here he was again doing the same thing but for not so pleasant a reason. He pointed at the three. "Those are the guys. Do you know them?"

Poison looked at the three and answered, "Those are De-mon's right-hand men slash strong arms, ergo the guys who jumped me in the alley, shot your brother, and checked me and my apartment for bugs."

"What kind of car do they drive?"

"It's usually a dark blue Ford Explorer. Why do you ask?"

Jerome stared hard at the men, trying to commit their faces to memory. "Just wanted to know. Keep them busy for about twenty minutes. Let them have a couple more drinks, then show them to your room. You can pay them there."

"How? You haven't given me the money."

"I hid the five thousand in your dressing room." Jerome turned and began to walk back down the hall.

Poison was perplexed. He couldn't understand, so he sounded very confused when he asked, "At the risk of sounding stupid, why have you hidden the money?"

Jerome wanted to laugh but refrained from doing so. Instead he answered, "Why to buy time and make it look real, of course."

"You don't think they will find it a little strange to see me searching for my own money in my own dressing room?"

"No, they'll probably just blame it on the drugs. I know I would," he said with a shrug in his voice as though he blamed everything Poison did on drugs—everything, including breathing.

He hurried down the hall. Reaching his dressing room, he rooted through his bag, pulled out a package, and opened it, taking out a wad of cash. He hadn't really left the money in Poison's dressing room because he knew if Poison had ever found it, he would have wasted no time getting high with it.

He went to his closet and pulled out a small box and tucked it under his arm. He ran down the hall to Poison's dressing room and knocked to be sure no one was there. After a few seconds he entered and crossed to Poison's dressing table. He quickly hid the money in the bottom of a drawer under a stack of paper to buy him more time. He left as quickly as he'd come.

On his way to the car he called Casey, and as soon as the phone was answered said, "Can you jimmy the locks on a Ford Explorer?"

Casey responded in an almost offended tone, "Of course I can."

"Do you happen to see three guys sitting together in the lounge?"

"Yup, sitting with Poison looking rather cozy."

"Great. Meet me in the alley."

Jerome replaced his phone and hunkered down so as not to be easily seen. He looked up at the sound of footsteps approaching. It was a woman in her late twenties. She was tall and blonde with legs that seemed to go on for miles. He stood, and she spotted him and then walked briskly to him.

Jerome said in a no-nonsense tone, "We've only got about twenty minutes. Can you do what you need to do in that amount of time?"

Casey snorted. "In twenty minutes I can have this entire parking lot bugged. Just keep an eye out."

He handed her the box and walked away to watch the alley.

After Poison bought another two rounds of drinks for the three guys, they finally asked him where the money was. His response was that it was in his dressing room.

Poison led the guys to his dressing room, and then spent ten minutes looking for the money. The three guys stood back watching him as though he was stupid, and they were used to such things from him.

Poison began to sweat. "I know I put it here somewhere."

Mac was very amused and couldn't resist saying with a snigger, "Maybe you smoked it."

"No, it's here." The knock on the door made Poison jump and turn around.

Jerome opened the door without waiting for a reply. He stuck his head inside the room to remind Poison, "You're up in ten minutes. Better get ready."

"Will you go before me? I've lost something, and I need to find it."

"Sorry, I can't. Gotta get ready myself. Besides, this is your last dance for tonight. I have two back-to-back performances."

"Romy, these guys need to get going, and what I have is for them." He gave Jerome a pleading look. "Can you help me this once?"

"Sorry." Jerome shrugged. "I'm sure they'll be willing to wait a few extra minutes for you to find whatever it is you've lost ..." Jerome was interrupted by his phone's tune letting him know he had a message. He looked down. The message read, 'All done come back and take a look.' "That's my cue. I gotta go get ready."

Jerome left closing the door behind him. He really only went there to get an idea of how much more time he had. He ran back down the hall and out of the door.

Inside of Poison's room, Mac laughed again and said, "Even your coworkers don't like you."

"He likes me. He just a little upset with me, that's all."

He located the money finally and handed the envelope to Manny, who sat down and counted the entire amount.

Jerome walked to Casey and stopped beside her as she finished reconnecting the wire. "All done. I'll tell you all about it at your place after the show. I just need to wash my hands."

The lights on the car blinked twice as she closed the door.

"You can do that in my dressing room. Come with me."

Jerome sat in a soft leather chair staring fixedly at Casey as she connected a monitor to its wire. Once she was finished, she turned the monitor on and took a seat on the edge of the desk, "Okay, so what I just set up was the surveillance equipment. It's set so that you can see and hear everything that happens in a 180-degree arc. The camera is split; one spans ninety degrees one way, and the other goes the opposite direction."

She adjusted the angle as she spoke using a little remote, and then she continued. "All of this will be recorded and automatically stored on memory chips similar to this one." She passed him a chip.

Jerome inspected the chip, which was not much bigger than a dime, before returning it to her. She continued to explain how to operate the high-tech machinery.

# CHAPTER 32

*E*ric recovered well in the hospital and was now in a rehab center. Jerome came into the center and stopped to look around for Eric. He found him sitting on an exercise machine doing arm presses while a physical therapist stood beside him giving instructions. Jerome walked to them. "Mmm, looks like fun."

Eric continued his repetitions with an occasional grimace, "If it looks like so much fun, then we should trade places."

The therapist said, "All right, give me eight more shoulder presses, and we are done for the day. Let's go, eight ... seven ..." she continued to count down to one.

Jerome responded to Eric's statement. "Now what would be the good in that?"

Eric began his reps and replied to the taunt between grunts of pain. "If you were in my place ... and I were in yours ... then maybe I could ... get you to ... stop this ... madness before you ... get yourself ... killed."

Eric finished and closed his eyes in misery. The therapist said to him, "Great job. I will see you day after tomorrow at the same time."

Eric nodded as she walked away, and then he turned to Jerome when she was gone and questioned almost desperately, "When am I getting out of here?"

Jerome smiled but didn't answer. It was his hope that all of this would be over before Eric was finished.

Sasha entered the center and stopped to sign in and get a general location on Eric. Eric looked up to speak but saw Sasha and smiled a smile of his own instead.

Jerome noticed Sasha at the same time and was surprised to see her there. "Is that Sasha?" Though he needn't have asked, the sudden rapid beat of his heart was answer enough.

"We got a little lonely, what with you pushing us out of your life and all, so she's been visiting me here."

Jerome watched as the guard pointed in their direction, and Sasha, following the direction of the guard, turned to head their way. Her steps faltered when she saw Jerome, and she began to frown, but she continued her progress.

Jerome stared at her with all of the longing he felt for her in his eyes but his voice was angry when he quietly said, "Er, you've got to be the most underhanded, despicable little—"

Jerome stopped talking abruptly when Sasha came into hearing distance and smiled a welcoming smile. Sasha ignored him completely and walked to Eric to give him a kiss on his cheek. Eric smiled smugly at Jerome's discomfort and enjoyed how put out he was with him.

"Hi, Eric, thanks for inviting me today," Sasha glanced briefly at Jerome.

At his continued stare, her cheeks grew flushed, and tiny bumps peppered her skin. She'd been shocked to see him, but Eric knew he was coming. He raised his eyebrows at Eric, knowing then that the visit was meant to be an intervention.

Sasha looked again at Eric and said almost accusingly, "I didn't know you were having other company."

Eric hadn't looked this innocent since he actually was innocent, which was clue enough for Jerome had he not already known. "Who, Romy? Oh, you just never know when he might stop by."

Jerome looked at Sasha, and again his eyes were filled with

naked emotion. God, how he'd missed her. In her pique, she'd pretend he didn't exist the entire visit. He asked her, "Why wouldn't I visit, and since when am I company?"

She stuck her nose in the air. She was put out with him for pushing her out of his life, and she was determined not to let those soul-deep eyes or the sexy little dimples sway her out of her anger. "I've never seen you here."

"Why have *you* been here so much that you would notice my absence?"

"It's because you usually are absent, and, to answer your question, you tossed your poor sick brother in a nursing home and forgot about him. The boy was lonely, and since I have so much time on my hands lately, I've been visiting. I can get credits for community service for it, too."

"Quite the little multitasker, aren't we?" He walked to her and grabbed her. She felt so good in his arms, and he asked her, "When do I get a proper greeting?" He leaned forward for a kiss.

Sasha put her hands up to stop his lips from connecting with hers, but his arms felt so good it was hard for her not to give in, but she wouldn't let him do what he wanted to do right now. In a strange way she understood and almost admired him for what he was doing for his brother and the community by trying to get this guy off the streets. At the same time she knew that if she let him, he would take her someplace, make hot passionate love to her, the kind that would curl her toes and leave them that way for a while, and then he would tell her to go and stay out of danger, ergo away from him until this all blew over. As much as she wanted him to make love to her, she didn't want him to treat her like a tool for release.

So this time when she pushed him, she pushed hard enough to gain distance from his arms. "You can have a proper greeting when I'm allowed to be your girlfriend again."

He pulled her back even closer. "That's not fair. You are my girlfriend still. You smell so good. Do you have any idea how much I've missed you and how hard it's been for me not to call you?"

"Word on the street is you've been seeing another woman, so it can't be that hard."

Eric found his first bit of entertainment from the two of them since he'd been in the rehab center, and he was enjoying it immensely. No other woman that he'd known of had *ever* pushed Romy away or made him work for it. In fact, his entire life it had been quite the contrary. They threw themselves at him in droves.

Sasha may not have known it, but that was part of the reason Jerome was so crazy about her. "I forgot how much fun it is to watch you two bicker when what you really want to do is—"

Jerome cut Eric off before he could finish his sentence and ignored him at the same time as he responded to Sasha's accusation, "I can't believe you said that. I haven't been seeing another woman."

"I can't believe you're denying it when you know I have friends that almost live at Sinful Pleasure."

Jerome was genuinely perplexed. He couldn't think of anyone who might have been mistaken for his feminine entertainment. It never occurred to him that the woman she was talking about was Casey, because the idea of a sexual relationship between Casey and himself had never entered his mind. The confusion was in his voice when he responded to her accusation. "All the more reason why I wouldn't do something that stupid, don't you think? I'm not seeing anyone else, trust me. I can't imagine what would give anyone that impression."

Sasha pulled back with a doubtful frown.

"Oh, come on," Jerome spoke with feeling, "you're not still upset with me about the decision I've made for your own safety, are you?"

"Right, for my safety you push me out of your life completely, and for Eric's safety you lock him up in this torture chamber while you go gallivanting around playing desperado."

Jerome looked to Eric to confirm Sasha's allegation. "Are you being tortured here?"

"Only with the workouts," Eric said, and then he flexed a bicep. "But I've never been in such great physical condition in my life. That Amazon has seen to it."

"Well then she's earned her pay," Jerome said unsympathetically.

Sasha finally pushed free from Jerome and backed away indignantly. Eric laughed openly, the rascally sparkle in his eyes unmistakable.

Jerome spoke innocently. "What did I say?" Jerome's phone chimed to let him know he had an urgent message, and he looked at it reading the text with a frown on his face.

"Is everything okay?" Eric asked.

"Yeah, but I've got to get going. I'm on call this weekend." Jerome patted Eric on the back and kissed Sasha on the cheek, and then he took his leave.

Sasha turned to Eric. "Did you tell him?"

"No, but he'll find out soon enough."

"You should've told him that you got your mom so worried, she made plans to have the whole family here in a couple of weeks."

"Hey, I wouldn't have gotten her all worried if I hadn't been so concerned for him myself, and if he would bother to call instead of trying to avoid her, then he would know. So you see, it really isn't my fault." Eric finished his speech with a devilish smile.

Sasha smiled at his playfulness. "You're horrible, and he's going to kill you, but I guess you'll die laughing. Come on. Let's go get lunch."

Eric smiled and stood with almost graceful ease. Sasha smiled back as they walked to the cafeteria. He was almost back to normal physical health, and they both knew that if not for Jerome, that might not have been so.

# CHAPTER 33

*J*erome sat dosing off in his study after spending an excessive amount of time going through his medical dictionary trying to find an answer to the problem of operating on a person with a blood clotting disorder. This bit of homework was given to him by one of the senior doctors on staff at the hospital. He finally came up with a solution, but had stayed awake most of the night searching for one.

The security monitor that Casey installed turned itself on every time any movement was detected in the car it had been placed into. It turned on as the three attackers got into the car.

Manny was on the phone with De-mon. "Yeah, we're on our way." He paused for a moment, long enough to hear what was being said on the other end of the line, and then said, "All right, see you in about fifteen minutes."

Mac waited until it was apparent Manny wasn't going to say anything, and then he inquired impatiently, "What'd he say?"

"Said that there's gonna be a shipment coming and that it'll be our biggest shipment yet; said that this one is gonna put us on the top."

Rick chimed in from the back seat. "Yo, man, that's what's up."

Jerome perked up instantly and leaned forward to turn up the volume. Moments later, he got his first look at De-mon as he climbed into the back seat of the SUV. He was a young man in his early to mid-thirties, of medium build. His hair had either dreds or locks, and he had a tattoo on his neck.

When he spoke, it was with a heavy street slang that to Jerome's ears sounded a bit forced. "Let's go fo' a ride, yawl." The car pulled into motion, and De-mon continued, "Yo, man, dis what's up. Yo, we got dis big shipment comin' in, yo, that's gonna put us on the map."

Mac excitedly put in, "I been waitin' for this, man!"

"Yo, but I got a lot ridin' on dis, so yawl gotta be real careful. Kay, so on Friday our shipment is comin' to the Lakeside docks at Pier 15. Got a guy who gonna hold dat crate fo' us. You gonna need a guy or two to lift that bad boy, cause it's gonna be heavy. Got a password you gonna need, and dat's 'pass the buck to Li'l Duck.' That's all you gotta say; then carry it out, and be gone. The shipment will be there 'bout 8:00 p.m., but I want yawl to wait 'til 'round midnight to pick it up, so's there ain't a lot of people hanging 'round."

Manny said, "Got it. We ready for this."

"Oh, and give Poison a call. See if he got that last five g's."

"Aiight. And what if he don't?"

"Remind him why he should."

Jerome quickly picked up his phone and called Poison.

"Hello?"

"Hey, Poison, just wanted to let you know that I'll have that last five grand for you on Friday. I should have it by about 9:00 p.m., but just to be on the safe side, if they call about it just tell them you can have it by about ten thirty."

"Okay. Hey, Romy," Poison paused for a moment and when he continued his voice was filled with appreciation, "I know you don't want to hear this from me, but thanks."

"Okay, bye." Jerome abruptly ended the phone call because it was true he really didn't want to hear it from him. He hung up the phone and immediately dialed another number. After a short two rings, the other line was answered, "Casey, are you ready?"

"I'm always ready!"

"Okay, meet me at Langley Park, and I'll tell you everything." When he hung up the phone with Casey, he called Detective Davies. He hung up the phone a few moments later feeling a bit of excitement and naively thinking the entire episode would be over within the week.

Friday, Jerome went into Sin's office early to request a few hours to put their plans in effect, he didn't, however, tell Sin what he needed the time for. "Sin, I need a few hours tonight to take care of a really important matter. I should be back by eleven or eleven thirty at the latest, and I'll close out for you."

"Romy, I can't let you continue to disappoint your followers, not to mention the fact that I'm losing business. When those ladies come here to see you especially, only to find that you're not here … well, I don't need to go into what happens next, do I?"

Jerome needed to get going and didn't have time to haggle with him, so he spoke the one thing that he knew Sin always heard, money. "I know, and I promise you that this is almost over. In a couple of weeks, Eric will be clear to return to work, and we'll put together a show stopping performance after we spend a couple of days in Vegas." Jerome paused for dramatic effect and continued, "And, Sin, you know what kind of money I usually rake in after returning from Vegas. Just think what it'll be like with the both of us. What little money you're sacrificing now will be hardly worth grieving over." As expected, it had just the effect Jerome was aiming for.

"Get out of here. I'll let your girls know to expect you here at eleven thirty and no later." As an afterthought, he asked, "Oh, what do you want me to tell your little girl if she shows up looking for you like she did a couple days ago?"

Jerome was shocked. "You mean Sasha?"

"Yes," Sin answered, eyebrows raised.

"Here?"

"Yeah, and spitting mad when you weren't, and she knew you were supposed to be."

Jerome couldn't think about that because he needed to stay focused, and he knew if he started thinking about her, he wouldn't do what was needed to be done as efficiently. "Tell her I'll be in later."

"And what about your new girl?"

"What new girl?" Jerome asked perplexed.

"The one you've been spending time locked in the private room with. Personally, I don't understand why you guys even bother with having girlfriends in this business, but especially you after the way you chased that girl until she capitulated."

"Sin, I don't have a new girl. That's just business," he defended, but it suddenly dawned on him the woman Sasha had been talking about when she asked him about the woman he'd been seeing. *Well, this won't be pretty,* he thought to himself, but pushed that thought aside as well.

"That what you want me to tell her?"

"It's the truth."

Jerome and Sin left his office to see Casey walking down the hall. With her legally blonde look, she'd gotten a lot of unsuspecting crooks to spill lots of information. She was an excellent PI who knew her craft well. When she was in speaking distance she spoke, and her voice was like warm honey. "Hey, Romy, I was just coming to look for you. Are you ready?"

"I'm ready. Is everything set to go?"

"Of course."

Sin stood watching and listening with a knowing look as though he'd just caught Jerome in a lie. When they both looked at him, he said, "It's all the truth huh, Romy?"

Jerome took a deep breath. He knew how bad this must look, but he couldn't really clear himself without telling more than

Sin needed to know. "Sin, this really isn't what it looks like," He turned to Casey. "Right, Casey?"

Casey feigned the ignorance people expected from a girl with her blonde hair and striking good looks. "What do you mean? I don't know about you, but I've been waiting for this *all* week," she purred running her hands suggestively up Jerome's chest.

Jerome looked at Casey somewhat shocked. Casey smiled provocatively, and Sin's look showed his suspicions had just been confirmed. Jerome grabbed Casey's arm and ushered her down the hall.

Sin stood watching as Jerome led the regal beauty away. He could hear Jerome mumbling something to her but couldn't quite make out exactly what. As they moved farther down the hall, he clearly heard her amused reply to whatever Jerome was fussing about, "Oh, come on, you gotta admit that was hilarious."

Sin wasn't quite sure what to make of the two of them. They'd been spending so much time together, and she was quite a beauty with her long legs, thick blonde hair, gray eyes, and smooth, tanned skin. She was no less beautiful than the one he was supposed to be in love with, but those two hadn't been seen together nearly as much as these two lately. If he was just a little younger, he'd give that boy a run for his money.

Aside from a couple of piers with the gated doors open and truck drivers unloading their goods, the docks were almost deserted at that time of night. At Pier 15, two men worked inside looking very busy moving boxes. They stopped when they saw the headlights of a dark-colored SUV coming close to their pier.

The SUV turned and backed into the loading dock at Pier 15, and inside sat four men. Three of the men stepped out of the car while the driver stayed behind the wheel.

The two dock workers stood just inside of the building, one on either side of the door, watching the occupants as they exited the vehicle. The first man, who was the taller of the two, asked, "Can I help you guys?"

To which the tallest of the three men answered, "Pass the buck to Li'l Duck."

"Yeah, man, right this way," the tall one said, gesturing inside.

The three of them followed the dock workers toward the crate. The handsome dude who spoke had green eyes and seemed the most physically fit, lifted the crate from one end. While he did that, the smallest one, who was kind of tall but reed thin and seemed way too young for that line of work, grabbed it from the other end. The workers helped them get the crate to the opening of the door, and then the third guy pitched in a hand.

The second worker nervously spoke. "It's a heavy one."

To which green eyes replied with a wicked grin, "Yeah, I know."

The three of them loaded the crate into the SUV and drove off. The occupants of the SUV sat quietly tensed while the driver sporadically looked through the side and rearview mirrors.

The man with the green eyes looked at the thin man, who was sitting beside him, and smiled before saying, "We did it!" The silence was broken, and a round of congratulations went up for a job well done.

Less than an hour later, they reached the police storage facility, where there were officers waiting to relieve the SUV of its burden. The occupants exited the vehicle, stood outside of the SUV, and watched as three officers opened the crate, marked its contents, and tagged the crate as evidence before carrying it to a unit to store.

The handsome man's green eyes came around to the driver of the vehicle, and he said to him, "Thank you, Detective Davies."

"Thank you, Jerome," Davies returned. "I don't know if we

could have pulled this off so swiftly without you and your friend here."

Casey stood back waiting patiently as the two of them spoke. When the officers returned, one gave Davies a slip. He took the paper, signed it, and returned the copy to the officer. The original would go with him to the office.

He looked back at Jerome. "Well, just in case becoming a doctor doesn't work for you, and you get tired of dancing, I think you would make a great detective."

"I don't think I could handle the intrigue."

Davies laughed and reached out to shake Jerome's hand. "It's been a pleasure working with you."

"It's not over yet. I won't be satisfied until I see this De-mon behind bars. So what do we do now?"

I'll be taking this paperwork back to my office, and I will get an arrest warrant for him."

"How long will this all take?"

"I should have it by Tuesday, and we'll go after him, but in the interim we will continue to gather information on him. The more we have, the better our case."

When Jerome and Casey drove away, Casey looked hard at Jerome for long moments, and even though he couldn't see her, he could feel her intense stare. "What is it, Casey?" he asked her softly.

"I want you to understand that this could get really ugly. The detective back there would like for you to think that it's all cut and dry but ..."

Jerome looked in Casey's direction with an unspoken question when she paused. He waited a moment, and when she said nothing, he asked, "But what?"

"But by Tuesday he could be out of the country. Once he realizes his shipment is not where it's supposed to be, he may figure out the police are on him and disappear."

"I don't think he will."

It was Casey's turn to look at Jerome questioningly. "Why is that?"

"He won't because he seemed too cocky and self-sure."

"Then that's worse, because if he doesn't run, then he'll stay and fight."

# CHAPTER 34

*P*oison sat at his dressing room table counting the money Jerome left for him to pay off the attackers. In the last six weeks, he'd given him the twenty thousand, so after the payment he was to make tonight, he would be cleared of his debt. Jerome had saved his life. He shook his head wondering aloud, "How much money does he make here anyway?"

There was a knock at the door, and Poison looked up from counting money as the three attackers entered his room without waiting for a reply.

Manny spoke the moment they entered, "We don't have a lot of time. You got it all?"

Rick was closing the door when Poison said, "Yeah, I got it," handing them the stack of bills.

Manny took the money and handed it to Mac, who counted it, folded it, and pocketed it. He nodded to his cohorts.

Manny said to Poison, "That's everything, so consider yourself paid in full. It's been fun doing business with you."

They headed to the door. As they were opening the door, Poison said somewhat sarcastically, "Do I get a receipt?"

Mac threatened, "Come by tomorrow, and we'll have one for you." They all laughed as they filed out of the dressing room.

Jerome and Casey removed their disguises before returning to the
club. Jerome was in a hurry to get changed because it was almost
eleven o'clock. He walked briskly down the hall toward his dressing room. Walking in his direction were the three attackers. They
were laughing at something as they walked away from Poison's
dressing room.

As they came closer to Jerome, he spoke politely, knowing that
what he was saying would offend them. "Gentlemen, I hope you
enjoyed the performances. Please come again soon."

Without waiting for a reply, he continued past them and
toward his dressing room. Mac turned to go after Jerome, but
Manny and Rick stopped him by pulling him back and heading
in the opposite direction.

Mac grumbled as they headed out of the club. "I'm gonna beat
the crap out of that pretty boy someday."

Jerome was still smiling at his own quip when he entered his
dressing room and walked quickly into the half bathroom, where
there was a toilet and sink. He discarded his shirt and wiped himself down, and then unbuttoned his pants to do the same.

From the dressing room, Sasha sat where she'd been sitting for
the past hour. She was waiting for him to notice her, and she was
pissed. She'd been on an emotional roller coaster ranging between
crying and cursing him out, and the evidence of her tears was still
on her face.

Jerome finished cleaning himself, reentered the dressing
room, and crossed to the closet completely missing her presence
there, but then he paused, finally sensing that he wasn't alone.
Clad in his underwear, he turned to confront the intruder and
recognized Sasha with an exhalation of breath.

"Sasha, what are you doing here by yourself?" he asked. From
the dim light spilling through the bathroom, he noticed she'd been

crying and walked over to her. "Angel, why are you crying?" he asked her gently.

He reached out to touch her face, and she smacked his hand away. Using both fists, she punched him in the chest. Jerome stumbled back in surprise.

Sasha stood up. She was mad, and she was jealous, and she didn't like feeling either. She didn't want to be the crazy girlfriend of the hot stripper, but she was being exactly that and couldn't seem to stop herself. "Who is she?"

"Who is who?" He asked, baffled.

"The woman Bonnie, Regina, Leeza, Shelly, and countless others have seen you with."

"You mean Casey?"

"Oh, Casey! So that's the woman you've been all over this place with. Funny but I thought it was too *dangerous* for your girlfriend to be seen around, or is she the reason *we* can't be seen together?" Sasha began advancing as her outburst escalated, and Jerome took a step back for every step forward she took. "Tell me, was she already in the picture, or do I at least get the privilege of saying I had you first, hmm?"

"She's not my girlfriend. She's ..." Jerome stopped talking, and his look of surprised wariness turned suddenly into a smile at her display of jealousy. "I've known her since I was nineteen. We met in college and have been *friends* since."

Feeling slightly placated, she asked, "Then why has she been spending so much time with you in those private dance rooms?"

"Because they are private." At the look of anger returning in Sasha's eyes, Jerome reiterated his statement. "What I meant to say was because no one can hear—"

His explanation was interrupted by the door opening, and in walked the unsuspecting subject of their conversation—the tall and beautiful Casey. She turned on the light and froze. Although she and Jerome had spoken of Sasha, they hadn't gone in depth about her. So Casey had no idea exactly who this girl was because she'd never seen her before.

What she did know was that Romy got hit on a really whole lot in the club, and occasionally a girl managed to slip back into the men's dressing area.

Her quick mind knew only to keep up their charade by playing the beautiful, not too smart, love-struck groupie girl caller. She affected a look of clueless surprise. "Oh, I'm sorry, Romy, I didn't know you had company. I think I'll come back later."

Jerome was looking at her as though he'd never seen her before for that performance as Casey turned to leave. He didn't see the balled fist that Sasha had aimed at his face. The power of the blow snapped his head back and Sasha turned to leave. Jerome grabbed Sasha's arm to stop her and deflected the second blow. He called out to Casey. "Casey, get back in here!"

Casey turned to see the two in what looked like a tug-of-war. Jerome was holding Sasha's hands, and she was struggling to be released. Casey came back and pushed the door closed to avoid a commotion.

Still holding Sasha's hands, Jerome said, "Casey, will you tell her who you are, please?"

❧

Poison exited his room and walked up the hall to Jerome's dressing room. He raised his hand to knock on the door, but when he heard voices raised in anger, he dropped his hand and stepped closer to the door to hear what the fuss was about.

Casey stepped to Sasha and Jerome. Sasha opened her mouth to fuss, but Casey shushed her before she could speak. Casey addressed her in no-nonsense terms. "You must be Sasha," when Sasha nodded and opened her mouth to speak, Casey shushed her again and continued, "If you love this man, if this is what your display is about, then you need to be very careful and discreet about your tantrums. We've come too close in this investigation to have it blown to pieces over some silly jealousy."

"Who said this has anything to do with jealousy?" Sasha mutinously questioned.

"Oh, so you usually punch guys in the face, like you just did Romy, for the hell of it?"

Sasha pulled free of Jerome. He released her almost reluctantly. "So then who are you?"

"I'm Casey. I'm a private investigator and Romy's *friend*, and that's all. He called me to help him with a certain matter."

"What, you mean the issue with Eric?"

Casey rolled her eyes at Jerome, "For this to be a secret, an alarming number of people know about it, but to answer your question, yes, this is about the people who shot Eric, and the people behind the people who shot Eric."

"Then why have you been spending so much time in the private rooms?"

"Because it's private. No one who might be looking would think twice about him giving me a dance. We can talk and plan and all around get things taken care of without ears and eyes."

"So there's nothing going on between you two?"

"Of course not," she snorted, "Jerome did tell you that, didn't he?"

"Well, yes, but—"

Casey interrupted Sasha's excuse in her abrupt fashion, which always seemed to take people by surprise, because it didn't match her appearance, and this time was no exception. "But you didn't believe him, so you came here and started a commotion that could get us both noticed by some people that are ruthless in their very nature and wouldn't blink an eye over blowing our brains out if they knew half of the things we've done to them."

Sasha looked sick and worried at the same time, but Casey wasn't done. She continued on relentlessly, "So if you want to see us all get out of this with all of our limbs intact, you won't make another display like this one. Especially since three of that thug's henchmen just walked down the hall twenty minutes ago."

∽◎∼

At eleven thirty the three attackers drove up to the docks to Pier 15. It was quiet as they parked beside the car containing three other guys to help them with the crate. The three guys stepped out of the car and walked to the closed door only to find it locked.

It was obvious that no one was there, but Manny separated himself and knocked on the door anyway. After waiting a few moments, he began banging. When no one answered, he walked back to the SUV and called De-mon, speaking into his cell phone. "Yeah, we're here at the docks, but no one else is."

De-mon, on the other line, spoke quietly. "Who at the gate?"

"There ain't no one at the gate. It's closed and locked."

"Then knock on it."

"I did. Nobody answered."

"Meet me at River Side. Somebody 'bout to get dealt wit'."

He hung up the phone and looked at the other two. "He's pissed, and he wants us to meet him at River Side." He spoke to the guys in the other car. "Wait here for about thirty minutes to see if anybody shows up. If they do, call us, and if they don't, meet us at River Side."

They jumped into the SUV and drove off.

Fifteen minutes later, the police showed up and locked up the men waiting in the car. Even though they couldn't charge them for drugs, and the men's story was that they'd come there just to have some drinks, they did hold them for carrying concealed weapons.

At River Side, the attackers had just gotten out of their SUV when another SUV came speeding up the street. It stopped just in front of them, and De-mon leaned out of the window. "Get in." The attackers got into the car, and it sped off with screeching tires.

# CHAPTER 35

*A*t dawn that morning, two men sat tied down to chairs, their heads covered with hoods. De-mon and his most trusted crew, which consisted of Mac, Manny, Rick, and his bodyguard, Crusher, all entered the warehouse where they brought the two men. De-mon walked to the men and pulled off their hoods one at a time.

The first glimpse the men got of their attackers let them know their lives would not be pleasant in the near future. The taller man's face immediately showed surprised fear. He greeted them with a voice that crackled with terror. "De-mon."

De-mon wasted no time in getting straight to the point. "Where's my stuff?"

"I gave it to your men."

De-mon motioned Crusher over with a tip of his head. Crusher came over and punched the bound man three times in the stomach. He coughed and gagged from the strength of the blows.

De-mon demanded, enunciating each word, "Imma try dis again. Where's my stuff?"

"I'm telling you, De-mon, I gave it to your men," he entreated.

De-mon looked back at the three. "Was it one of them?"

The man shook his head. "Nnno."

Crusher punched him again, this time in the face and head.

De-mon spoke almost in a courteous voice, "I told you what I wanted you to do. Why didn't you do dat, man?"

His voice shook, "I did exactly what you told me to do."

"Then why don't I got a shipment?"

"I don't know, De-mon."

Crusher punched him a few more times while the other man watched, flinching the entire time.

"Okay," De-mon broke into his grunts of pain. "Let's take dis from the top, yo. So my men came to get the crate and you ..."

"Was standing at the gate waiting for them when they pulled up," he gurgled.

"What were they drivin'?"

"A dark blue SUV. There was four men. Three got out, and the fourth one waited behind the wheel."

"What'd they say, man?"

"They said pass the buck to Li'l Duck, so I didn't ask no questions. I just did what you told me to do."

"What did they look like?"

"They was dressed in street clothes, and they came at about nine thirty in the evening. The one who did the talking, he was a good-looking sort, had a mustache and beard, and he had green eyes. The other two never said a word, just helped him get the crate into the SUV."

"Well, guess what? Those ain't my men!" De-mon turned and walked out of the building. The three attackers followed. Crusher stayed inside.

The four men walked until no one was within hearing distance before De-mon spoke. "Yo, man, dis ain't right."

Manny questioned, "How can somebody just walk in there and take the stuff and be gone like that?" he snapped his fingers.

"I don't know, yo, but you three are the only ones who knew the pass code. So did you talk to anybody?"

"Come on, man," Manny said. "Do I look that stupid to you? No, I didn't talk to nobody."

"No, me neither," Mac and Rick chimed in.

"I didn't think you would, yo, but I had to ask."

Manny questioned, "So what now?"

"Yo, man, I don't know. I need to think for a minute." He looked up at the three suddenly. "Yo, we was in da car when I gave y'all dat info, so if you didn' talk to nobody, and I didn', then what the hell is in dat car of yours?"

Mac asked, "What do you mean?"

"I mean we need to see dat car, but first we need to dispose of some other problems. Come on." They walked back to the building.

At dawn a code red was announced over the loudspeaker in the hospital. Dr. Heath and Jerome turned the corner of the hospital hall in a near run. Dr. Heath asked Norma, the admittance nurse, "What's the ETA on the code reds?"

Norma picked up a phone and dialed out. "What's your ETA? After a moment, she answered, "They'll be here in five minutes."

With the emergency crew standing at the ready, Dr. Heath rapidly fired off orders. "We'll need to have x-rays STAT. Also, the OR must be available for immediate surgery. Call for two emergency teams to have these guys taken care of without delay. Make certain the anesthesiologist is available along with the OR nurses. Team one take OR room 1. Team two take room 2. As soon as they get here, we're going to be busy. Let's save some lives."

Norma picked up the phone and spoke into the loudspeaker repeating everything the doctor requested. A few moments later, the doors opened to two gurneys as two teams of paramedics came rushing in. Dr. Heath and Jerome took the first team and headed them to operating room number one, while the other was taken to the second room.

The paramedic began to report. "He's been shot multiple times."

"How many times and where?" Jerome asked.

"As far as I can tell, seven times—twice in the chest, one of them very close to his heart—there is also one in the neck, which looked to have passed through without damaging any major arteries. Blood pressure is low eighty-two over fifty and dropping."

Everyone reached the OR, and the patient was stopped in front of the x-ray machine as Jerome and Dr. Heath got prepped for surgery. By the time they were ready, the patient was being rolled into the room, with the radiologist placing his x-ray sheet over a lit wall. Jerome and Dr. Heath looked to see the extent of his damages.

Dr. Heath spoke. "He's going to need a transfusion, but he's a lucky one."

"I don't think he thought so when whoever did that to him was doing it."

"Well, look at these x-rays. He definitely was lucky because I'm not certain they meant to kill him, but look at this," he pointed to the screen and each organ as he explained. "They managed to miss every vital organ he possesses. No arteries were exposed, not the lungs or any of his internal organs. Maybe they either wanted to warn him, or else someone was a very lousy shot."

"He looks to me like his shooter meant every shot he gave him."

Jerome and Dr. Heath walked over to the patient, and Jerome grabbed a tube and tilted the man's head back to get a clear view of his airway. As he started to place the tube in the man's mouth, he paused briefly, recognizing him—past all of the bruising and swelling—as the man from the docks the night before, the very same one who'd led them to the crate. "Damn!"

"What was that?" Dr. Heath asked.

"Nothing," he said as he slid the tube in the man's throat.

Around them was ordered chaos as the anesthesiologist inserted medication to numb the pain, and the nurse placed bags of blood on a hook ready to transfuse. The man's clothes were cut off completely, and the doctors assembled themselves around the patient.

A few hours later, Jerome and Dr. Heath both stepped into the hall and removed their gloves, face masks, and head gear and dropped them into a box marked 'biohazard.' Standing just across the hall, was Det. Davies.

Detective Davies walked to Jerome and Dr. Heath and shook both of their hands before questioning, "How's the patient?"

Dr. Heath nodded to Jerome to allow his answer and excused himself. Jerome answered, "It's touch and go at the moment. The next twenty-four hours will be critical for him."

"You don't think he'll wake tonight?"

Jerome ushered the detective to a quiet office before continuing. "The chances of him waking tonight are very unlikely. He's lucky to still be breathing at all. Did you find out how our other patient was doing?"

Detective Davies shook his head, "He didn't make it, and we have no idea who did this."

Jerome spoke softly. "I do."

The detective looked at him inquiringly.

Jerome answered his unspoken question. "De-mon. That guy in there is the same man that gave us the crate last night, and they shot him and left him for dead, probably because they thought he turned on them."

Detective Davies swore softly.

"I thought you guys were going to meet them at the docks."

"As it turned out, they were already gone by the time we'd gotten there, and all we got were the nobodies they left behind. We didn't tell them we wanted De-mon and his goons because we didn't want them to tip him off, so we held them on gun charges."

# CHAPTER 36

*B*etween working a thirty-six-hour on call shift, and a busy night at the club in between, Jerome hadn't been home in almost two days and he was exhausted. He dropped his bags just inside the door and then paused as the sound of the television playing registered on his tired brain.

He looked up with a bemused frown, certain he hadn't left the TV running for two days. Eric sat on the sofa, one leg resting on the coffee table, holding a remote, and watching Jerome.

When Jerome finally noticed him, Eric said, "Long night, huh? Man, but you look beat. You should go get some rest."

Jerome ran a hand tiredly over his face, not certain if he was dreaming or even ... "I'm so tired that I can barely stand, so I think I *must* be hallucinating, because you couldn't possibly be here."

Eric smiled his devilish smile. "You're right. Maybe you should go straight to bed, and when you wake up I'll probably be gone." He shrugged, adding, "Probably not, but one can always hope."

Jerome turned and walked down the hall toward his bedroom, too tired to argue with the imp sitting on his sofa.

Eric spoke under his breath. "I got your hallucination, all right."

In Jerome's bedroom, he stripped down at the door, dropping

clothes on the floor and leaving them where they fell as he stumbled to his bed. By the time he reached it, he was clad only in his sports boxers. He fell onto the bed and into an exhausted slumber.

Jerome walked out of his bedroom shoeless and shirtless, carrying an armload of clothes. He walked through the living room to the laundry closet and deposited his clothes inside the washing machine.

From across the room, Eric sat at the island in the kitchen watching and waiting for Jerome to notice him. Two cups sat in front of him. "I heard you get in the shower." He pushed one of the cups forward. "I made you some tea."

Jerome turned, not very surprised to see Eric, and walked toward the island. "I'd hoped it was a dream," he said, taking a sip of the tea. "Why aren't you at the rehab center?"

Eric took a sip as well. "I checked myself out," he answered with a shrug in his voice.

"Why Er?" Jerome asked quietly.

"Didn't need to be there anymore."

"Since when do you decide?"

"Since I'm almost twenty-two years old and therefore old enough to check myself out. Besides I've been really worried about you."

"I'm fine, so go back."

"I'm staying here, Romy," Eric insisted.

"It's more dangerous for you here now than ever, Eric, so I want you to go back … please."

"Yeah, well, I'm not going back, so stop asking."

Jerome opened his mouth to argue, but Eric held up his hand in a gesture for Jerome to be silent, a gesture he'd seen Jerome do countless times in the past. The gesture so caught Jerome off guard that he actually obeyed.

"If it's not too dangerous for you, then neither is it too dangerous for me." He looked at Jerome intently as though weighing his next words very carefully. "Why don't you just let this go, Romy? Get back to your sensible life, and let the police do their job?"

"It's not that simple anymore, Er," Jerome said, looking at his tea cup.

"I don't see why not. Just pull out and tell them to handle it from here without you. Tell them you've done all you're going to do."

"You don't understand. I can't. I'm in too deep, and the only way I can get out of this now without looking over my shoulder for the rest of my life, is for them to get caught."

Eric looked at him, measuring, and then asked quietly, "What have you done, Romy?"

"I took some things that were very important to them a few days ago. The next day we got two guys in the ER all shot up. They were the guys who'd given us the cargo. They had no clue that I wasn't who I claimed to be, but they suffered for it anyway."

Jerome looked down at the golden veins running through the granite countertop. Guilt ate at him. He muttered, "One of the guys didn't survive his wounds, the other is in a coma he may never wake from." He looked at Eric. "They're mad, Eric. It's them and me now. And I don't want you or anyone else that I love getting caught in the middle when they figure out who they're really after."

Eric listened in disbelief before exploding. "Damn, Romy, are you out of your mind? Do you have a death wish? What the hell good is that cop if he couldn't see that coming? Did you stop to think that even *if* you get this guy locked up behind bars that you may very well still end up living the rest of your life looking over your shoulder?"

"Eric, calm down. I have a plan, and I'll come out on top. I just need a little more time. Will you reconsider going back for just a couple more weeks?"

"Not a chance. I think the tables have changed between us, and I don't like it one bit. But someone has to be the sensible one here, and I guess that one is going to be me," Eric said as he paced the length of the kitchen.

Jerome watched him for a moment, thinking of how much he'd matured in the last six months. He also looked healthier than ever, and that 'Amazon,' as Eric called her, had helped him fill out beautifully. "Okay, look, if you insist on staying home, just keep a low profile until this is done with. Will you at least do that?"

"Sure, Romy," Eric said, already thinking of ways to get his brother out of the mess that he himself had started by being his most mulish self.

"Thank you," Jerome said. Turning to walk back to his bedroom, he looked back at Eric to find him watching with a thoughtful frown on his face. He looked so grown-up.

Eric watched him go, then took out his wallet and pulled out a business card. He dialed the number on the card and listened to the outgoing message, then left a message of his own. "Detective Davies, this is Eric Jacobs. I just want you to know how much danger I feel my brother is in for trying to help you out, and I want him out of this mess. So what are you going to do about it?"

Eric hung up the phone and dialed another number. He left a message, "Mom, this is Eric. I think it would be best if you guys didn't come after all, but, hey, I have a great idea. How cool would it be to pay you guys a visit instead?" Now if he could just get Jerome out of DC that would fix things. He needed to convince his brother it was time for a visit home.

# CHAPTER 37

*D*e-mon and the three attackers stood against a building in an alley in one of his turfs talking. As people passed by giving them a wide berth, it was obvious the people in the neighborhood knew them and wouldn't cross them.

Mac asked, "Tell me why we're standing out here instead of searching that car?"

"We standin' out here 'cause we know somebody got a bug planted on the car, but what we don't know is if it's in any other places too. Know what I'm sayin'? If we start lookin' 'round in dat car fo' it, then whoever watchin' us gonna know we on to them, so we gonna carry on like ain't nothing different until we catch this fool, but first I wanna have a li'l talk wit' Poison."

De-mon lit a cigarette, and blew a thick puff of smoke. "For some reason, I think he might know some stuff, yo, so tonight we gonna get our hands on a car and go have a word wit' him, aiight? And don't say nothin' in that car that'll tip our li'l voyeur off."

It was late when Poison left work. In the darkened alley, the three attackers waited in their borrowed vehicle. When Poison stepped out of the club, the attackers stepped up to him. He paused briefly as though contemplating his odds of running and getting away.

Manny spoke menacingly. "I wouldn't try it if I were you."

Rick chimed in, "Yeah, you got away from me before, but I promise you this time ..." he let the sentence hang in the air.

Poison stepped closer, ignoring the threats. "To what do I owe the pleasure of this visit, gentlemen?"

"Get in the car," Manny said.

Poison walked to the car and leaned forward to look inside. From behind him, Manny pushed him the rest of the way in.

They drove him to a remote spot that was owned by De-mon, where there was a building that barely looked like anything more than an abandoned warehouse from the outside. Fifty feet across the road sat a small building the approximate size of a large shed. Crusher and the three attackers entered the warehouse. It was large and spacious inside with various-sized boxes and crates along the walls. The wall turned in an L-shape toward the back of the warehouse, so visibility from the front was impossible. Poison had been left sitting in a chair in the middle of the room with his hands and feet tied to the chair, blindfolded and gagged. Mac walked to Poison and removed his gag and blindfold.

Poison flexed his jaw before asking, "Dude, why am I here? I paid my debt."

Standing out of sight, De-mon walked into Poison's view. He took the liberty to answer the question himself. "We got some questions I think you can answer, and if you answer them right, it'll be to your benefit."

Poison looked at De-mon much like a kid would look at his favorite idol, and cautiously asked, "What if they're wrong?"

"Then we finish what we started in the alley, 'cept this time, won't be nobody to help you." He walked to Poison. "So let's get started, huh? I had a big shipment come a few days ago, but some-body took it. Got any ideas who?"

"No."

Crusher punched Poison in the gut.

"You sure? 'Cause I can do dis all day."

"I don't know anything about it, D, honestly."

Crusher punched him again, this time in the ribs. Poison bent forward as far as his bonds would allow, grunting in pain.

De-mon continued. His voice sounded as though he was having tea and scones. "Now why don't I believe you, Poison?"

"I don't know why you think I'd know anything about it," Poison said on a gasp.

"You wanna know why?"

Poison nodded his head, hardly able to speak.

"'Cause ever since my men met with you in that alley, you been havin' this money to pay in large amounts. Money you ain't never had before, plus extra to get high wit', but that ain't all, Poison. Too much crazy stuff been goin' on, and I think it was you."

"It could just be coincidence. You can't honestly believe I would, or even could, take your shipment, do you?"

"First of all, I don't believe in coincidence, and second, I don't think you smart enough to walk away wit' a shipment like that right under my nose. Who'd you get the money from?"

"From my coworker."

"What's his name?"

Poison paused, thinking of the beating he'd gotten from Romy after Eric had been hospitalized. He still had nightmares over that beating, and he certainly didn't want another. In fact, Romy said he would kill him the next time, and he believed him. "I can't say."

Crusher hit Poison in the face, opening a cut above his brow.

Poison cried out in pain. "He made me promise, or else he would beat the crap out of me."

Crusher hit Poison a few more times, causing him to cry out again.

De-mon sniggered, saying, "'Pears to me that's exactly what hapnin' anyways. You know why we call him Crusher?"

Poison shrugged. "Then I think I'll save myself two and just take this one. My coworker hits really hard."

Crusher spent the next few minutes beating Poison soundly. De-mon stopped him and then devoted a few moments beating him too. Mac grunted in approval. De-mon pulled out his gun, holding it casually yet threateningly in his hand.

"Only problem wit' that is," De-mon responded to Poison's earlier comment as though no time had lapsed, "you might not survive this if I don't start getting some answers. You don't really got no options here, Poison, so spill."

Poison sighed, "His name is Jerome."

"Why'd he give you the money?"

"He wanted to find out who shot his little brother."

"So what I got to do wit' that?"

"It was one of your guys who did it."

De-mon asked curiously, "So what happens once he find who he's lookin' for?"

Poison shrugged and then winced. "I don't know."

De-mon cocked his pistol.

"Wait, okay, I'll tell you all I know but ..."

"But what?"

"What will you do to him?"

"Nothin' if he don't got nothing to do wit' my shipment that pulled a Whoodini."

"So what's in it for me?"

"You get to live, fool."

Poison's lips tightened.

"Okay, wait, what you want?"

"The twenty thousand back."

De-mon raised his gun at Poison. "Man, I ought to shoot you in the head just for that."

"Hold on, D. Look, I think I just may have some info that would be very helpful to you."

De-mon lowered the gun. "Tell you what, you make it worth my while, and I'll give you back two thousand."

Poison scoffed. Crusher and the three attackers all looked at De-mon as though he'd lost his mind.

De-mon continued, "And one thousand dollars' worth of smack, your pick."

Poison needed no further urging. "Okay, so Jerome works with me at the club as a dancer. He goes by the name of Romy."

The nickname caught the attackers' attention when they heard it.

Poison saw their recognition and told them, "It was his brother you guys shot behind the club, and ever since he's been lobbying for your heads on a silver platter."

Manny spoke out. "We been to that club and seen him on numerous occasions. If he wanted us, why didn't he get us then?"

"Because you're not the main person he wanted. He wanted the person you represent," Poison looked at De-mon pointedly.

De-mon spoke in a bored tone. "Get to the part that'll be worth my time."

"All of this is. You don't know, but Romy makes one powerful enemy."

He sneered, "Maybe to you, but I ain't too concerned 'bout what some stripper wants to do to me. Just get to the helpful part."

Poison shook his head and sighed as if talking to a brick wall. If De-mon didn't take Romy seriously, then that was on him, but he himself would rather be far away from the whole town when Romy found out what he'd done. "Romy has this girlfriend, and she's a pretty little thing. Everybody thought he was falling for her, but then he stopped seeing her and stopped her from coming to the club. So the next thing you know, he has this long-legged hottie hanging around."

He looked up at De-mon meaningfully. "Right after you shot his brother. Anyway, last Friday, Romy doesn't come to work until late, and when he did his girlfriend put up a massive fuss because his new girl was there. I just happened to be passing his door when I heard them talking about what was probably your shipment. They said they had taken something from a very bad person and that his goons had just left twenty minutes before."

Poison turned to give the three attackers the same pointed look he'd given De-mon. He continued to tell them everything he'd heard that night he'd eavesdropped outside of Romy's door.

Reluctantly De-mon began thinking this guy might be a bigger threat than he'd given him credit for. Maybe Poison was right to be wary of him, which was all the more reason he needed to be disposed of.

Jerome sat in his study staring blankly at no particular thing as he tried to think of the easiest way to get out of his situation. Eric was right. This had gone too far, and he knew that, but there was no other way out of it. He needed to get these guys off the street and firmly behind bars in order to return his life back to normalcy.

Suddenly the monitor began to show activity. It had been rather quiet in the last few days since he'd taken that shipment of theirs.

The three attackers and De-mon entered the car and were up to no good. Mac asked De-mon, "Where are we going?"

"We goin' to River Run, yo, I got a package to pick up. It'll hold us up from the one we lost. It ain't as big, but should help us level off some of our lost. We gonna take it back to the compound ourselves so nothing gets gone. You gotta hurry up, though, 'cause they only gonna wait twenty minutes."

Jerome sprang into action, reaching for his phone. He called Detective Davies and got his voice mail, "Damn, Detective Davies, they're on their way to River Run, but I only have twenty minutes to follow them! They're picking up a package and taking it to their compound. I don't want to miss this opportunity to see where it is!"

Jerome entered the living room where Eric sat on the sofa. He looked up at Jerome as he hastened to get to the door. "What, are you on call or something?"

Jerome was preoccupied getting his things and didn't think about the question before answering, "No, why do you ask?"

"You're in an awful big hurry." It dawned on Eric why, and he jumped up. "I'm coming with you."

"No!"

"You can't stop me!"

"You're not coming, and that's final! Now stay here!" Jerome left on that order.

Eric jumped up and raced to the study. He went to the monitor and grabbed the remote to rewind and watch the scene in playback mode, cursing to himself. He called Detective Davies, threw on some clothes and headed out the door.

# CHAPTER 38

Jerome was pushed into the abandoned-looking warehouse. His hands were tied behind his back, and his clothes were damp in areas. Streaks of dirt covered the knees of his pants and shoes. His face throbbed, and a trail of blood ran down his temple from somewhere in his scalp. Sitting in the middle of the room was a man whose face was covered, but he had an instant feeling of familiarity with the man.

Jerome, however, didn't have much time to ponder why the man sat there with his hands tied behind his back and his legs tied to the chair. When Mac and Manny roughly pushed him against a wall, a new battle similar to the one that brought him there started. Jerome lashed out in defense, kicking a roundhouse that caught Mac, who was the closest to that side of him, in the chest.

The two of them set upon him. They'd already been soundly thrashed, and if not for the fact that Jerome was the only person who knew where the crate was, Rick would have shot him just as he had his brother. The brother was nothing compared to the way this man fought, besting the three of them until being hit over the head with the gun.

They quickly tied his hands and feet to the wall, and left the warehouse to doctor their bruised and bloody bodies. Once he'd been properly bound, De-mon approached him. He looked

Jerome over assessing, and after seeing three out of four of his most powerful, bloodthirsty men sporting multiple bruises from this one man, he had to acknowledge him as a worthy adversary.

When he spoke, there was much less of the street slang in his voice than anyone had heard before. Somehow he knew this man would respond better to intelligence. "You want to tell me where you put my shipment?"

Jerome looked at the figure sitting bound and then back at De-mon. "I'm not sure I know what you're talking about."

So much for responding to intelligence. "You gonna stand here and lie to my face when we both know you know exactly what I'm talking about?"

"Who are you, anyway?" Jerome asked rudely, letting him know he wasn't important to him.

"I'm the man you been stalkin'. Anything about that coming back to you?"

Jerome slowly shook his head, and De-mon punched him a few times in the face and stomach. Jerome stiffened from the pain but made no sound.

"You know I would believe your li'l innocent act if our stooge here hadn't ratted you out already." He walked to Poison. "But guess what?" He pulled the hood off of his head and said, "Your secret *is* out."

Jerome's anger showed in the brief tensing of his body as the reason for the familiarity of that hooded person was finally revealed. De-mon untied Poison's right wrist and made a show of counting out a large amount of money and gave it to him. He then pulled the gag free from his mouth.

Poison glanced briefly at Jerome but was afraid to look again because he could see the anger simmering behind his clear brown eyes.

"When I get out of this, I'll kill you with my bare hands," Jerome gritted to Poison menacingly between clinched teeth.

"You not getting out of nothing if I don't get my stuff back," De-mon threatened.

"Am I supposed to be so stupid to believe you would let me go if you did get it back?"

"You'll give it back, or pay the consequences."

"I don't have it to give back."

"Then you owe me 5 mil 'G.' How you wanna pay for that?"

"Hard labor?" Jerome said half-jokingly.

"Yo, Crusher," De-mon yelled out.

Crusher walked in from just outside of the door and began to beat Jerome. He could no longer resist the grunts of pain as the beating from this man much larger than De-mon and all of his goons became more severe. De-mon walked back to Poison and gave him five baggies, all containing drugs of varying color and strength.

Poison asked De-mon, "You aren't going to kill him, are you?"

"Now what would be the good in 'dat huh? If I did, I'd never get my stuff back. The fact that he's the only person in this room 'dat knows where it is, is what keeping him alive, and he knows it. But you shouldn't be so worried 'bout him being kept alive, 'cause if he lives, I believe he will kill you. Jus' like he said."

De-mon walked away and called for Crusher to quit. Crusher walked away only after Jerome passed out from the pain of constant blows. With his arm free, Poison wasted no time diving into the drugs.

Detective Davies responded quickly to Eric's frantic call and picked him up, and then drove with him to River Run, but they were too late. They'd gotten there within forty-five minutes of the time the thugs were set to get their shipment, which was twenty-five minutes past the time allotted.

That had been thirty minutes ago, and since then, Eric and Detective Davies sat waiting and hoping someone would come back there that they could follow. They had nothing otherwise. Eric sat looking angrily out of the passenger window.

Detective Davies hadn't taken his eyes off of the street when he said, "I don't think we're going to see him here."

"Gee, you think? Hey, here's a thought; maybe they caught him spying on them. Maybe you should go straight to their compound."

"If I knew where that was, do you think I'd be sitting here?"

Eric looked at the detective in astonishment. "You don't even know? You've been watching this guy for two months, and you don't know? If anything happens to my brother, I'll make sure you never work this crappy excuse for a job ever again."

"Calm down, kid. We'll find your brother."

"How are we going to do that sitting here?" Eric decided to call Casey. He was certain she'd be more useful. When she answered her phone he said, "They got him!"

Casey said, "What kind of phone does he have?"

"What kind of question is that?"

"Just answer the question."

"He has an iPhone eight."

Detective Davies said, "That phone has a tracking system in it."

Casey said, "I'm logging into your phone carriers account!" After a terse few minutes she ordered, "One of you call him now."

Detective Davies picked up his phone and dialed Jerome's number.

Jerome's phone rang in his pocket, the vibration waking him. He opened his eyes and looked around. Poison sat in the same place he'd been in earlier. How long ago that was, he had no clue. Poison appeared to be in a drug-induced stupor.

Jerome twisted his wrists to see if he could maneuver his hands free, but gave up after a few moments of getting nowhere. His only prize for his effort was chafed wrists. "Poison, are you really going to sit there and watch while they kill me?" Poison looked up at him through eyes slightly off focus. "Please help me loose."

"Why, so you can kill me?"

Jerome's level of tolerance for Poison was officially at its peak. He lashed out the only way he could just then, verbally. "You're an idiot if you think they have any intentions of letting you go when this is all over! You're just as dead as me right now if we don't get out of this, because you know entirely too much for them to let you just walk away!"

De-mon walked back inside the warehouse followed by the three attackers pulling along a struggling Sasha. Jerome's heart leaped into his throat, and he began to strain against his restraints while helplessly watching them as they tied her to the wall less than twenty feet away. Crusher stood just inside the doorway waiting patiently.

Sasha looked directly at Jerome, and he could see the raw fear in her eyes. He spoke the only word he could get past the lump in his throat, "Please."

De-mon pounced. "Are you ready to talk?"

Jerome looked at Sasha.

She stared at him horrified. His shirt was all but ripped off, and bruises covered his face and torso. A trickle of dried blood was on his neck and shoulder that had come from somewhere on his head. He was tied so that there was no give in his arms. He couldn't even bend his elbows a little.

His muscles strained, and she knew they must hurt from that never-ending position. His phone rang, and De-mon walked to him and pulled the phone out of his pocket. It stopped ringing as the touch screen was released. He dropped the phone on the floor and smashed it under his foot.

He waited a moment for Jerome to speak, and when nothing else came out of his mouth, he said to Crusher, "Try not to break any bones."

Crusher walked to Sasha, and she squirmed, then shrank back

against the wall in terror. She looked at Jerome, pleading. "Romy, help me," she gasped as Crusher ripped her shirt open.

He pulled a Taser out of his pocket, and her eyes widened as he turned it on, then off. The crackle sound reminiscent of a bug that has strayed too close to a bug zapper. He taunted her with the gun, running it down her chest and then back up before asking, "Bet you've never been stunned before, have you?" He stood back and aimed the gun, preparing to fire it.

When Sasha screamed, Jerome called out in defeat, "Please stop. I'll tell you whatever you want to know!"

De-mon asked, "Where's my stash?"

"At the cove. It's the only place I knew safe to take it."

De-mon and his cohorts all left in a hurry. Poison appeared to be asleep, while Jerome's head hung listlessly.

Jerome lifted his head when he heard their car speed off, and he called out, "Poison, wake up, man. We don't have much time."

Poison opened his eyes groggily and closed them again.

"Damn, my ties are too tight," Jerome said in agitation.

Sasha spoke shakily, "Mine aren't."

Jerome perked up a little bit. "Can you break free?"

"I'm working on it." She winced as she finally slipped her hand free, and then worked out the knots on her other hand. After she freed herself, she ran to Jerome and kissed him frantically, reassuring herself that he was okay. And then she began working on his ties.

While she struggled with the impossibly tight knots, Jerome asked her apologetically, "How did they get you?"

"I went to the club," she answered without looking up. "I thought I'd get there early to talk to you, and then stay late to hang out with you after work." She paused as she finished one hand and started on the other. Her hands were visibly shaking, but she continued with the ties. "They got me out of my car ... I don't even know how they knew me." She finished and dropped to her knees to begin working on his feet.

"His goons have been at the club a few times. Besides that, Poison ratted me out for some drugs. Now do you see why I didn't want you around me?"

She nodded, and then asked him in turn, "How did they get you?"

"They set a trap, and I fell right into it. They were waiting for me when I got to River Run and pounced on me. The next thing I know I was waking up being dragged here."

She finished with the ties and stepped back. He closed his eyes, rubbing his wrist, which were red and raw, and then he took a few deep breaths and stepped cautiously away from the wall. His ribs were fractured, and he knew it.

"Help me find something we can use as weapons; there're about ten of them if my count was accurate. He only took his favored three with him, I'm sure, and maybe that ox of his to help carry the load. I know they're all armed, so our best defense is to catch them by surprise and try to pluck them off one by one."

Together they walked through the spacious warehouse looking around, and then finally went to some boxes and crates along the wall of the back of the warehouse. After opening a few boxes, he found one filled with an assortment of weaponry. Not knowing much about guns, he passed over them and took out a couple of knives and sticks large and small.

Sasha noticed he hadn't taken a gun and said, "What, no gun?"

"Can't shoot one. Can you?"

"No, but what are you going to do with this stuff?" she asked, pointing to the sticks and knives.

"Try and get us out of here. I'm going to take out as many of them as I can before De-mon returns, but when they do return, I want you to hide. No matter what happens, don't come out before help arrives." As an afterthought he asked, "Do you have your cell phone?"

"No, it's in my purse. What kind of help are we expecting? And if we have some, then what's taking them so long?"

"I left Detective Davies a message before I came out after these guys. I think he's smart enough to find me here."

"You mean he doesn't even know where we are?"

Jerome shook his head. "Come on. Let's go."

"What about him?" she asked, gesturing toward Poison.

"Let him rot," Jerome said heading to an unopened box to rummage inside. He inspected the weaponry piece by piece.

"That does not sound like something someone under the Hippocratic Oath should be saying." She walked to Poison and untied his feet.

He looked at her, slightly impressed by her misplaced compassion, and then burst her bubble. "He's just as responsible for us being here as they are for bringing us here." He stopped what he was doing for a split second, looking appalled. "Please don't tell me after I crack a few skulls that I should turn around and stitch them up."

She smiled at his dry humor. Even at a time like this, it softened the mood a little, because she'd never been so frightened in her entire life. "Oh, ha-ha, he's got jokes."

Jerome finished what he was doing at the weaponry and walked to where Sasha stood beside Poison, and with the big stick he held, he tapped Poison on the shoulder. "Come on, Poison, it's every man for himself."

Poison didn't respond, and Sasha asked in concern, "Is he okay?"

"I think the fool has overdosed again," Jerome said in disgust. He leaned forward to check his vitals and said, "His heart rate is choppy, and his breathing is slow. He probably won't last out the night if he doesn't get medical attention soon."

"What has he taken?" Sasha asked tearfully.

Jerome looked at Sasha, thinking for one split second how peculiar she was, and then shook his head before answering, "I don't know, but it was a cocktail of stuff." He picked up a handful of the colorful little bags De-mon had given him. "Anyway we can't worry ourselves about him right now. We've got to get ourselves out of this mess, and if he's still alive at the end of this, then maybe we can get him some help."

He gave Sasha a reassuring kiss and said, "Now I'm going to drag whoever is at the outside of that door in here and take him out. You stand on the other side of it." He pointed to a spot behind the wooden door, "And if someone else passes through, you hit him as hard as you can and try to knock him out. Got it?"

"I don't know if I can just hit someone like that, Romy," Sasha fretted.

"It's either them or us, Sasha. Just think about what that guy with the stun gun would have done to you." When he saw the fear return to her eyes, Jerome nodded. "Exactly, these guys are no different. They all work for the same man. Let's do this, okay?"

She nodded, and they took their places. Jerome motioned for Sasha to be as quiet as possible. He peeked through the door, and then quickly pulled it open, slamming the stick down on the man's head before he could react.

He slithered to the ground soundlessly, and Jerome pulled him inside. The two of them hog-tied the man and dragged him to the back of the warehouse where he couldn't easily be seen.

He came back to Sasha and picked his stick up from the floor. He held the stick in his right hand, favoring his ribs with his left arm as he walked to the door to peep outside.

Across the road, two men stepped out of the shed-like building smoking cigarettes and talking. Jerome watched them through a small crack in the door for a moment before stepping back and whispering to Sasha, "In a minute, I want you to scream as loud and hysterically as you can. Two men are out there, and when they come running, as soon as they cross the threshold, I'll take the first one in. Waste no time bashing the second over the head. Got it?"

She nodded nervously, and they took their places. Jerome motioned to Sasha to scream. She had no trouble sounding hysterical with the way she felt. Within seconds, the two men entered the warehouse with their guns drawn.

Jerome's and Sasha's sticks came crashing down almost simultaneously. Jerome's target fell instantly. Sasha's target was dazed but didn't fall. Instead he turned to her aiming his gun. Jerome brought his stick crashing down on the man's hand.

He dropped his gun with a howl of pain, the sound of it almost drowning out the sound of his bones shattering. His scream of pain was cut off almost instantly when Jerome brought the stick back up to connect with his chin. He hit the floor with a loud thud. Jerome grabbed more of the rope to tie them with.

Sasha stepped behind the door to retrieve the rope they'd used on her. Jerome was preoccupied tying the two men down and didn't hear when another man entered, his focus solely on Jerome as he rushed over and wrapped his arm around Jerome's throat. Jerome grabbed the man's arm to relieve the pressure on his neck and try and break his hold. When that didn't work, Jerome closed one hand over the other making a double fist and swung them up and over his head, connecting his fists with the man's head.

At the same time, Sasha brought her stick down on the back of the man's neck, knocking him out cold. She dropped to her knees. "Did I kill him?"

Jerome collapsed in a fit of coughing as he struggled to get air into his starving lungs. After a little while, he rubbed his aching neck and answered her question in a rasping voice. "I hope so. Where did he come from anyway?"

He got up and closed the door, then walked back to the three men. Sasha threw him the rope she'd been after originally, and he used it to tie the last two men together before pulling them all to the back to join the other one.

It was getting darker outside, and Jerome knew those goons would be coming back soon. He'd lied about where the shipment was to get that dude's hands off of Sasha and buy them some time.

"I need to go check this place out. Stay here, and if anyone comes in, you brain him."

He exited the warehouse crouching low and staying close to the wall. He circled around the warehouse, finding no one, and then went to the building across the road. It was small and dark inside with a sturdy desk and chair. The desk had a computer on it that he was sure was workable. He tried getting into one of the user accounts. They were all locked. He knew if he had time he could find a way in but feared leaving Sasha alone for too long in case those guys returned.

He kept thinking about the look on her face when that ox ripped her shirt open and threatened to stun her. The fear in her eyes and the way she'd looked at him as though she knew he would save her had broken his heart. Even more heartbreaking was the fact that he couldn't, but neither could he watch them torture her.

They were going to be murderous when they found out there was no crate at the cove, and he needed to be able to defend them against those five. Remembering that look in her eyes was giving him the strength to fight this thing through, even through all of the pain he felt.

# CHAPTER 39

*A*s the car speed through the night, Eric sat brooding as he stared out of the window. Following behind them, was a cavalcade of cars. His fear for his brother grew steadily until it left an acrid taste in his mouth. His thoughts deep in his concern for Jerome, he hadn't spoken a word in over an hour, not since the call they made to Jerome's phone picked up, and then suddenly went dead.

His brother could be too, just lying in a ditch in the middle of nowhere. How would he tell his mom? That knowledge would surely kill her.

Detective Davies looked at the handsome young man. He knew he was worried about his brother, but Detective Davies knew Jerome was smart and cunning. It would take a lot to bring that boy down. "Are you all right, Eric?"

"My brother could be dead by now. How did you make it to become a detective? You've got to be the slowest cop I've ever had the displeasure of knowing," Eric answered sullenly.

Detective Davies's jaw tightened. "I know you're worried about your brother, so I won't take offense. I needed to be certain to cross my T's and dot my I's. In other words, I needed to get backup, and an arrest warrant, or else everything that we've worked for might fall apart."

"That's BS, and you know it! You and I both know if one of your comrades had been taken captive by that maniac, you would have flown to his rescue, warrant or not! I mean, who needs a warrant when a man has been kidnapped?"

Jerome returned from the shed disappointed. His scout of the area turned up nothing tangible they could use to get out of there. On the good side, there wasn't anyone else on the compound. Together he and Sasha dismantled the guards De-mon left behind. Now they stood again over the box of weapons. He picked up two more small-sized sticks and placed them into his waistband. He then grabbed an automatic, and examining it, pressed a couple of buttons; the bottom slid out, and he looked at the clip. It was loaded, so he replaced it and took the safety off, then handed it to Sasha. She looked at it in obvious consternation.

He answered the question she couldn't seem to get past a throat that felt clogged with cotton. "When they return, I don't want you in here. That shed across the way is empty, and it has many nooks you can hide in, so I want you to go inside it and hide. Sasha, I realized these guys are maybe a little too strong for you to stand toe to toe against even with a stick. Your best defense if I can't be near is for you to not let them get close enough to you, so if someone comes through that door that does not announce himself as friend, you're to shoot first and ask questions later."

"But I don't know how …"

"Hold it firmly with both hands, aim, and squeeze. That's all I know to tell you."

"That's it?" she asked in a panic.

"Police are taught to aim for the large area of the body," he said gently, slowly rubbing her arms up and down. "And, whatever you do, don't drop that gun and don't stop shooting until they're no longer standing."

Sasha hugged Jerome tightly. Tearfully she admonished, "Please be careful."

He grunted a little, willing to endure the pain to his battered body for that hug. He nodded and ushered her outside into the night and across the road to the shack. When he returned, he found a place toward the back of the warehouse where he would not easily be detected and waited.

While Sasha hid in the shed, she noticed the computer and tried logging in. When she couldn't get past any passwords, she shut down the computer. She restarted it in safe mode and changed the log-in credentials. When she restarted the computer, she sent out an emergency request to the police giving the best description she could as to their location, cautioning them not to try and respond to her from where she was. Then she hid because she didn't want the scary men to return and find her standing before the computer.

Within twenty minutes, De-mon, Crusher, Manny, Mac, and Rick reentered the warehouse. De-mon held his pistol aimed where he expected to find Jerome. They all came to an immediate standstill when the only person still where he'd been left was Poison.

De-mon cursed. "Son of a ... we gonna find them, and when we do, kill the girl, but save Romy fo' me. Rick, you stay here and wait fo' us. Keep a lookout fo' Sam, Wallace, and Derec. Maybe they went after them when they got away. Crusher and Mac, we gonna drive toward the woods and see if we can find them before they get too far. Manny, you check the shed."

Everyone sprang into action. As tires screeched, and the sound of the car quickly faded, Jerome stood quietly listening to everything from his position in the back of the warehouse. After the car was gone, Rick walked toward the back of the warehouse and paused as he saw the tied feet of one of the men.

He ran to untie him, but a clothesline from Jerome stopped him before he ever reached the man. The muscled arm nearly crushed Rick's windpipe as the force of the blow knocked him on his back and robbed him of precious oxygen. Jerome stepped into Rick's view as he struggled simultaneously to breathe and get up. Jerome hit him on the side of his head, making quick work of rendering him unconscious.

After he shoved the man's socks into his mouth to use as a gag, Jerome tied knots around Rick's ankles and wrists. He jumped when, from outside of the warehouse, five shots were released in rapid succession. His heart lurched sickeningly in his chest, and he bounded up, sprinting out of the warehouse, his only thought for Sasha. He ran low crossing the road to see a body lying on his back in the darkness just outside of the shed.

"Sasha, are you all right?" he asked her softly.

In a barely audible whisper, she answered, "I'm okay."

He dropped to his knees and removed the man's weapons. "I'll be right back."

Jerome dragged the attacker across the road and behind the warehouse, knowing it was likely where he would die, and surprising himself that he didn't care overmuch. Knowing this could be the man who shot Eric, and that he wouldn't have hesitated to kill Sasha, made him unwilling to feel the slightest remorse.

He looked up and could see headlights drawing near. He rushed back to the shed. "Somebody's coming; keep the loaded gun close and stay low. I'll be behind the shed."

He ducked behind the shed, and a few moments later, the car came to a screeching stop. The three occupants exited the vehicle. Crusher headed straight for the warehouse.

De-mon called out, "Crusher, you see if Rick in there. Mac, wait here."

De-mon entered the shed. Jerome walked stealthily around the shed and wrapped one arm around Mac's neck, his other hand covering his mouth, and dragged him behind the shed, hitting him solidly, and then once again for good measure.

Sasha held the gun toward the shadow, her finger pressing the trigger. The sound of shuffling feet detoured his direction from the light switch to the door.

A fight ensued between Romy and De-mon. De-mon swung for Jerome's face. Jerome easily deflected the blow and countered with two hard right-hand jabs. De-mon swung a combo aiming for Jerome's ribs and connected.

The pain of De-mon's fist connecting with his already fractured ribs knocked the breath out of Jerome and dropped him to his knees. De-mon kicked Jerome in the chest, then aimed to kick him a second time. But Jerome threw an uppercut to De-mon's groin, doubling him over in pain. Jerome hit him in the face and regained his feet. De-mon quickly gained his footing, but his grimace showed Jerome their last collision left a little damage. Not enough damage to stop De-mon from assuming the position of offense by charging at Jerome in an attempt to take him off his feet.

Ignoring the stabbing pain in his sides, Jerome dropped to his haunches, stuck his right leg out, and rotated 360 degrees. The action swept De-mon off his feet and knocked the wind out of him as he hit the hard-packed earth. Jerome rapidly drew in the same leg, and then kicked out to make contact with De-mon's ribs as he landed on the ground. Jerome once again drew his leg in, and rose as gracefully as his abused body would allow.

De-mon stood, though not as quickly as before, and prepared to fight. He'd been so angry to be bested by the dancer, that all he wanted was to beat him soundly to work off his fury. Then he could focus on what was important, his crate worth $30 million. He'd borrowed half the money to pay for it, and invested most of his own earnings. The crate would pay his sponsor back plus an additional $3 million, and leave him in position the next time to double the worth of the crate.

This was what he'd worked almost ten years for, but this Romy had screwed up everything. Worst was he hadn't been able to punch his anger out on the guy, because he was an excellent fighter. And suddenly, the warning Poison had given him rang true. He couldn't beat Romy.

After Jerome dodged numerous attempts from De-mon, and

countered them with painfully well-laid blows, De-mon pulled out his gun. He knew he couldn't beat Jerome, and his energy was draining from him like water from a dripping faucet.

Seeing the gun, Jerome pulled out the two smaller-sized sticks he'd stuck into his waistband. With sharp, quick twists of his wrists, he hit the hand that held the gun, knocking it out of De-mon's hand. It landed a few feet from them and fired harmlessly as it touched the ground. Jerome began swinging the two sticks in rapid succession. He hit him in the arm, stomach, and chest, then face.

Seconds after the gun sounded, Crusher came running out of the warehouse. Unaware of Crusher's presence, Jerome and De-mon continued to battle, with De-mon losing the battle. Behind them, Crusher raised his gun and fired, hitting Jerome in the shoulder.

Jerome yelled in pain, grabbed De-mon, and turned 180 degrees, placing De-mon as both shield and target.

Crusher rushed toward the two men, passing the shed as he went. Sasha stepped from the doorway as Crusher passed by, pointed the gun held tightly between her hands at Crusher, and held down the trigger, her arms jerking with each release of the gun. Crusher never made it to the combatants. Sasha dropped to her knees.

Coming upon them was a line of at least fifteen cars. Jerome held pressure on De-mon's neck. The last thing he saw before he passed out, was his body guard hit the ground.

Sasha stood and ran to Jerome when she saw all of the cars coming. "We have to get out of here," she pleaded frantically.

His strength draining along with his blood, Jerome could do no more. He fell to his knees and struggled to get up. With Sasha's help he stood, and took three steps before his knees buckled under him. She wrapped his arm over her shoulder, and laboriously they made their way toward the car the attackers jumped out of when they'd returned.

Jerome, bleeding and weak, fell once again to his knees. He made a valiant attempt to regain his footing, but his legs felt like jelly.

Sasha wanted to drag him to the car, and would have. But it was too late, as the group of cars she'd seen in the distance got to them before they could get to the car. She looked up, determined to protect him with her last breath if necessary, when she realized that the cars, as they came to screeching stops followed by wagons and paramedics, were police cars.

Jerome collapsed fully then, unable to fight the oblivion that had been threatening to overtake him since he'd been shot. Sobbing, Sasha dropped down and grabbed Jerome's head, cradling it in her lap.

Rick came stumbling out of the warehouse disoriented, having been untied by Crusher before he responded to the gunshot.

A police officer yelled, "Don't move!" Other officers ran inside the warehouse, and still others into the shed.

Casey jumped out of her car and ran to Sasha as Eric and Detective Davies rushed to their side. Detective Davies yelled, "Get me a medic over here now!"

A paramedic rushed to examine Jerome, followed closely by another medic carrying a stretcher. Sasha sat weeping softly. The medics placed Jerome on a gurney and took him to a waiting ambulance. Following close behind were Sasha, Eric and Casey. Eric's arm was wrapped consolingly around Sasha.

Around them, men were being carried away, some in cuffs and others on gurneys.

A total of three fatalities occurred that night—Manny, who'd been shot by Sasha in self-defense; Crusher, who'd been shot also by Sasha in defense of Jerome; and Poison, who'd overdosed on the uncut drugs given to him by De-mon.

# CHAPTER 40

*T*wo days later, Jerome lay in an upright position in his hospital bed, his torso covered in bandages. Sasha sat by his bedside, where she'd primarily been since the paramedics wheeled him in. He'd been unconscious until the morning. His mother arrived the morning before—Eric's concerns had frightened her. She'd come to the hospital straight from the airport to assure herself that her oldest child wouldn't die. She cried the entire time Dr. Heath had spoken to her, her beautiful face hidden behind the tissue.

Sin came into the room and sat down beside the bed. He looked at Sasha and asked her, "Does he know?"

"Know what?" Jerome asked in a cracked voice.

"That Poison's dead from an overdose." Jerome moved a little. He winced, but Sin couldn't tell if he winced from pain, or the news of Poison's death.

"Not surprising." Jerome said after a long pause.

Eric entered the room, followed by his mother and sisters. His mother quickly closed the space between them. With tears running down her face, she hugged him tightly. Jerome winced, returning his mother's hug, and looked over her shoulder accusingly at Eric.

Eric stood close by the door looking on innocently, but

mischief shone in his eyes. Jerome shook his head. *Some things will never change*, he thought.

His mother looked around at the occupants of the room. "If you will all excuse us?" Everyone, including Eric, turned to leave. She stopped him, "Not you, Eric."

Eric slowly headed to the bed while his mother stood quietly waiting for the room to clear. The look Sin turned back on her before he shut the door behind him didn't escape Jerome's notice. He quickly looked at his mother to gauge her reaction, but her frowning attention seemed for Eric only, at the moment. Then she turned to Jerome. "Would you like to explain to me why I just found out that you've been a male stripper this entire time?"

"Because telling you would've resulted in my death?" he half seriously joked.

"Not funny," she gritted, "and then you get your brother caught up with it."

He closed his eyes. "Not true."

"Not true what?"

"That I've been doing this the entire time. I spent the first year doing a slew of other things. Also not true, that I got Eric involved. He went behind my back and got himself hired. I did everything I could to stop it."

"Why, Jerome?"

"Because I didn't want him doing—"

"Why this?" she interrupted.

"The money." He opened his eyes to look at her. "I tried everything else, but this was what paid the bills ... all of the bills. I didn't like it, but ..."

"You're making excuses."

"And you're being small-minded." At her look of shock, he apologized. "I'm sorry. I did what I had to do; I'd do it over and again."

"Unacceptable! There's many things you could've done!"

"Name one!"

Eric spoke up. "Mom, stop!"

She looked at him incredulously. "You'll not speak to me that way!"

"I'm sorry, but you know something I've realized? How unfair this has all been for Romy. He didn't complain when he was struggling trying to take care of a family he didn't create. He was no more than nine years older than the youngest of us, and had to become a sudden father. Had to take care of you, us, the mortgage, the bills, and college. And I gotta tell you, I wouldn't have been able to do it."

Jerome cut Eric off, "That's enough."

Eric wouldn't be deterred. He'd taken a lot of things for granted before moving in with Jerome, but after almost a year living with him, Eric would never see his brother the same. To him, he was a hero, "No. It took me being here with you to see what you've sacrificed for us." He looked at their mother. "While we all sat home grieving, and you made your way back into the workforce, he had to figure out how to take care of us. He never had a chance to hurt, or miss dad. He was the same age then that I am now. Would you have demanded that of me?"

At her silence, Eric shook his head and left. Sin entered on the heels of Eric's departure. "I heard you guys in here, and I just wanted to say, you've raised a great young man here. If I ever had children, I'd want them to be just like him."

"Her face still held a frown, albeit less severe, for Sin. Her words, however, were scathing when she said, "So you'd hire your son to work in your club as a stripper?"

Sin smiled a dazzling smile meant to disarm. "As a stripper? No. But an exotic dancer? Absolutely. I run a classy joint."

"Sounds like an oxymoron."

"I invite you to come and view for yourself." He glanced at the frown on Jerome's face and amended, "When neither of your boys are there, of course."

She turned to look at Jerome. All of the words spoken over the last couple of days ran on instant replay in her head. She had a lot to think about.

∽⦿⁓

Jerome's world was returned to normal, with one exception, he currently held a twenty-five percent share of Sinful Pleasure. He spent more time in the back offices than on stage lately, because Sin had taken a liking to his mother and often flew to Connecticut for weekend visits to her. The altercation they had in the hospital hadn't been spoken of again. Jerome assumed it meant either a truce, or Sin had changed her mind. *His* mind shied away from that train of thought. It made him gag to think about.

Jerome made his way to the courthouse. The trial for De-mon was coming to an end, six months after the kidnapping. He faced a long list of criminal charges that would keep him locked behind bars for the rest of his life if found guilty. Mac and Rick received the opportunity to plead to lesser charges in exchange for turning state's evidence against De-mon.

He entered the courthouse and went to the room where the session was being held for De-mon's crimes. The jury found him guilty on all counts—drug trafficking, five counts kidnapping, two counts murder, and three counts attempted murder. He was sentenced to two life sentences.

# CHAPTER 41

*J*erome and Sasha entered the Sherman family's formal dining room hand in hand for Sunday dinner. Everyone else waited for them before they began the meal.

Sasha said, "Everybody we have an announcement to make. Jerome has asked me to marry him, and I've graciously accepted!" She bubbled with excitement.

Her mom and sister jumped out of their seats with squeals of joy, and she momentarily disappeared behind the hugs and kisses.

Professor Sherman walked to Jerome smiling broadly. He shook his hand, "I always knew you'd be perfect for my daughter," he had from the moment he'd met Jerome and decided it was time for Sasha to come home from France.

Jerome smiled, thinking there definitely had been a time when the professor hadn't been so sure. That didn't matter now. He had the love of his life, the woman he was certain he'd loved from the moment he laid eyes on her, and *that* was all that mattered.

∽❦∽

One year later, Jerome stood erect on the podium of the beautifully decorated country club where Sasha's father was a member. He resembled a model for weddings in his custom black tuxedo with a silver cummerbund. His lapel held a teal-colored rose to match the wedding colors.

The moment Jerome had been waiting for came as Professor Sherman escorted Sasha down the aisle. A hush fell on the crowd of four hundred guests. The gown appeared to be satin and was fitted to show the narrowness of her waist. A sheer fabric banner with designs of flowers, holding tiny silver beads in the middle of each flower, crossed her heart. It continued down to a *v* just below her breast. That same design showed in the sheer fabric over satin on the bodice of the gown as it wrapped around her waist to her hip and then sporadically as it flared to the floor. Sasha wore a tiara on her head, and her hair was swept up on the sides and back of her head, then was held in place by teal and silver flowers as the rest of her hair cascaded in soft curls.

Jerome had to remind himself to breathe when he began to feel lightheaded. The minister asked who was giving her away, and her father answered that he would. After her father kissed her cheek and placed her hand in his, Jerome smiled.

When Sasha looked up at Jerome, it was to see all the love, devotion, and promise he felt for her shining in his eyes. The minister asked them to love, honor, and cherish one another, forsaking all others until parted by death, and they both agreed, and then it was time for them to recite the vows they'd written.

They turned, grasped each other's hands, and Sasha began, "Jerome, I feel as though you were created in the heavens especially for me. If anyone had ever asked me to describe all of the things that would create my perfect man, my description would have been of you. I thank God for the night my friends took me to Sinful Pleasure, because that was where I met my destiny. I will spend the rest of my life trying to make you as happy as you make me. I love you here, now, and forever."

It was Jerome's turn, and he took a swallow to clear his throat from the obstruction that formed there as Sasha spoke her vows. When he spoke, his voice was soft and clear. "I love you. I think

I've loved you from the moment I first laid eyes on you. I couldn't think or sleep, all I saw was you. You are everything to me, and my only wish." He paused, their eyes melded, and then he continued, "My only wish in this world, is to make you deliriously happy."

Sasha smiled as a tear slid down her face. She remembered telling him that he might just be able to make her deliriously happy.

He finished, "Before you, my life was incomplete; you came and changed it all for me. I feel I started living the day you walked into Sinful Pleasure. You are my light, my love, and my … everything. I love you, Sasha, here, now, and for always."

The minister proudly smiled and said, "By the power vested in me by the District of Columbia, I now pronounce you man and wife. You may kiss your bride."

Jerome needed no further urging, but leaned forward and claimed Sasha's lips in a demanding kiss that left them both breathless.

The minister said, "Ladies and gentlemen, I now present to you Mr. and Mrs. Jerome Jacobs."

The club erupted in a loud burst of applause, and when they stepped down from the podium, they were inundated with well-wishers. Jerome's mom couldn't stop crying as she hugged her firstborn tight.

She whispered in his ear, "You're the best son a mother could ask for. You've sacrificed your youth for us, and I'm in awe of the man you've become. I love you." She turned to Sasha and hugged her just as tightly. She whispered into Sasha's ear two words, "Thank you."

∞⊘∾

The reception was over. It had been a wonderful affair with laughter and dancing. Jerome endured some good-natured ribbing from his college buddies, who'd learned the truth about why he'd always been in such a hurry, through subterfuge. And to think they'd wondered upon occasion if he wasn't interested in women. It was now evident to them why he never wanted to go to any parties. Jerome carried Sasha over the threshold and sat her in a lounge chair, admonishing her, "Don't move a muscle." He disappeared down the hall and into his room. When he finally came out of the room, he was dressed in one of his costumes.

Jerome picked up a remote and turned on the CD player. The song *Sex Therapy* began to play, and Jerome's hips began to move.

Sasha sat spellbound watching her beautiful man dance just for her. She may not have initially wanted his attention because he was a stripper, but she was certainly glad now he'd given it. The same experience that made her shy away from him that first night was what she never seemed to tire of—watching him dance, or enjoying the fruits of his labor. Jerome took off everything but his sexy underwear, which was a replica of the tuxedo he'd worn for their wedding, and her fingers itched to touch it.

He was just about to take it off when Sasha stopped him, "No, let me do it."

His face showed pleasure and surprise at the same time, she would never tire of that expression. Sasha grabbed the bulge in the mini-tux and gently teased the sacks. She slid off of the chair onto her knees and kissed the inside of his thigh. Sliding his underwear off, she wrapped her right hand around the base of his erection, wrapped her left around his scrotum, and proceeded to suck between the two. He closed his eyes in ecstasy but they popped back open, unable to resist watching her as she grazed her teeth across his already swollen manhood. He reached down and grabbed her arms to pull her up. He wanted her clothes off fast before he lost control and disgraced himself on his wedding night.

He undressed her like a present until she wore only her underwear. Then he removed her bra. He turned her around and pressed his erection against her behind. He loved the feel of her soft bottom and decided she should know. His husky voice was filled with want when he whispered against her ear, "I love your soft little ass, and the way it feels pressed against me right now."

Sasha shivered from the timbre of his voice, then she turned her head to the side to kiss his lips, and while they kissed she slowly ground her hips against his erection.

He groaned into her mouth as the friction created an even deeper pleasure for him, and he slid his hands down her torso, stopping to caress her breasts and then circle her areolas, before moving down to her navel to circle and briefly dip a finger into her belly button. Finally he stopped at the juncture of her thighs; all the while he whispered words of love and devotion between kisses.

His words were almost as arousing as his fingers, and she moaned softly as her body reacted to his every word and touch. He squeezed her engorged clitoris between his thumb and forefinger, then slid his fingers back and forth as though he was jerking her off. Her hips bucked, stroking his fingers. When his fingers finally entered her, her body began to convulse uncontrollably, her deep moans filled with ecstasy.

Jerome watched as his wife seemed to experience a mind shattering orgasm. And it made him crazy with need. Without removing his finger, he slid her panties down with his free hand and entered her from behind, replacing his finger.

He closed his eyes for a moment just to intensify his pleasure. It was then that he felt her convulsions strengthen around him. He lost all control at that moment, and bent her over the lounge chair, sinking deeper inside of her. He stared transfixed at her bottom and the soft jiggle it made every time he entered her. He was on cloud nine.

Sasha's walls tightened again, and she could feel herself building again as Jerome's breathing became erratic, and his long measured strokes became a gentle pounding. She screamed her climax, and a minute later Jerome leaned forward and called her name as he found his own release.

He picked her up and carried her to their bedroom, heading

straight to the shower, where he proceeded to wash her from head to toe and then himself. Finished, he dried them off and carried her to their bed, where he made slow, passionate love to her.

When they were done, they fell asleep in each other's arms. Jerome's last thought before drifting off to sleep as he looked at Sasha was that he was now living in his own perfect world.

# EPILOGUE

*O*ne year later.

An hour before the club was set to open for the night, a beautiful woman in a slinky white dress, walked into Sinful Pleasure, and it was obvious she was she was on a mission. A couple of the guys working looked up when she passed by, but no one tried to stop her as she walked with a purpose through the entrance of the entertainers' lobby. She entered the back hall and headed toward the owner's office area.

Jerome sat in his office going over paperwork. He was now a partner with Sin, and together they'd opened a second club in California. Jeffery wanted to join in their investment, so in the next six months, a third club was slated to open in Las Vegas. Jerome was chomping at the bit to get this night over so he could get home to Sasha. He'd rushed back from California from the opening of their second club because their first anniversary was in two days, and he refused to miss it. As it was he hadn't seen his wife in a month, and he missed her terribly.

So it was upsetting for him that no sooner than he'd landed in DC, his phone began ringing off of the hook. Two of the featured dancers had gone out to dinner the night before and ended up with food poisoning. The backup dancers that would normally be on standby were in California spotlighting for the new club, so Dr. Romy now had to perform in their stead.

It was a rare occasion in the last six months to see Jerome on stage and Eric's hilarity at Jerome's lack of enthusiasm over the realization that he would be dancing instead of going straight home, had Jerome retaliating by adding two dances to Eric's night. Eric knew how much Jerome wanted to get to his wife and divest her of her clothes wherever she stood. Even if that happened to be in her restaurant, a five-star affair that catered to DC's elite. She'd already been awarded for her healthy options menu, as well as nominated for best new restaurateur of the year.

Jerome felt marginally better when Eric left the office grumbling and in much less of a good mood. Jerome then called Sasha to let her know he was back but wouldn't be able to get home before three that morning because of the chaos happening at the club. He'd also told her to be prepared when he got home.

He spent the next hour clearing away the mountain of paperwork on his desk. He needed to start getting ready for the evening. There was a knock on his office door, and he said, "Come in." When the door opened, the beautiful woman entered. She closed the door behind her, and Jerome stood and stared. It had been a moment since he'd seen anyone so finely made.

He caught himself; stopping thoughts like that was paramount in keeping him out of trouble, especially before the club was even open for business. But he was only a man, it had been a month since he'd been with his wife, and this woman was tantalizing to his senses.

When she spoke, her warm, husky voice sent a shiver down his spine. "You're Dr. Romy?"

"Yes. How can I help you?" he answered with the first smile he'd displayed since leaving California.

"I was really hoping you would give me a private dance; money is no problem to me, so I can pay you anything you like."

"Well, I usually don't do private dances."

"But you see," she purred, "I've heard of what a wonderful dancer you are, and I would like to see for myself."

"I think, for you, I can make an exception. In fact, for you, I may be willing to do anything," he replied seductively.

"Anything?" she inquired smiling as he took her hand and led her to a set of chairs, and then walked away.

Jerome was feeling naughty. He knew he should've been getting ready for the night's entertainment, but this was an opportunity too good to pass up. He pushed a couple of buttons on a remote, and soft music immediately began to play. He turned back around smiling his sexy smile at her. He began to dance, and then answered her question. "Yes, anything for my wife. Does that make you happy?"

She smiled, "Deliriously."

Yashalina Blair was born and raised in the District of Columbia. She has been a senior cosmetologist for twenty-one years and is currently studying IT. She wrote her first book in 2009. She currently lives with her husband and their two children in Maryland.

Printed in the United States
By Bookmasters

Couples Tower Isle                    Catamaran Cruise
   - 24-hr Gourmet Dining
   - unlimited premium drinks               226
   - Golf + Tennis (clubs + carts not included)   rooms
   - unlimited H₂O sports         6 rest     5 Bars

* San Souci -
       + = Less Rooms but more bars + rest.
          no catamaran cruise
150 rooms        5 rest. 7 bars

# Travel Agency Niche - Possibilities

- Family & Friends / Group Travel
- Romantic Trips for couples
- Adventurous Solo Traveler
- Foodie Traveler
- Girls Travel
- African- ~~American~~ History Travel
  Diaspora

"If I could give you one thing in life, I would give you the ability to see yourself through my eyes. Only then would you realize how special you are to me."
                                        — Unknown